CROSS ROADS

By

Drew O'Brien

1

For my husband, Scott, and all the other brave people who find
their way in the dark

CROSS ROADS

1.

Cardinal Bonfiglio struggled to speak. His breath left him despite the reassuring plastic tubes that kept oxygen flowing into his nostrils. The oxygen tank sat firmly attached to the wheelchair he had long ago nicknamed his guardian angel Gabriel. He slammed his hand down on the armrest of the wheelchair, his Sicilian ire rising in his chest. Cardinal Adamanto reached over and patted his hand to soothe him. Bonfiglio's black-brown eyes softened with appreciation.

"Damn cigarettes," Bonfiglio whispered.

"I understand your impatience, your eminence," Adamanto said.

He folded a linen cloth stained from centuries of use and wrapped it around a human finger bone. He gingerly picked up the relic with his gloved hands and placed it inside a green velvet pouch. He crossed himself and placed the relic inside a reliquary that resembled a gilded birdcage. He slid the reliquary back into a niche in a blonde marble wall and closed a small wrought iron gate and locked it. Above the niche, bronze, medieval letters read: 'San Tomasso Doubter'. Adamanto crossed himself as Bonfiglio made the sign of the cross with his thumb on his chin.

"Except for the relics of the cross," Bonfiglio whispered, "That is the most sacred of all saint relics. He touched our Lord with that finger."

Adamanto picked up a clipboard and iPad. He made a checkmark on the page of the clipboard and then added a note into his iPad.

"Cardinal, you have my word on my heart that I will perform the tasks and duties of this office on your behalf with utmost care," Adamanto said.

Bonfiglio rolled his chair to the ledge of a narrow, stained-glass window that reflected a rainbow on the marble casement and across his white shock of hair. He wheezed and drew a labored, shallow breath.

"You speak as if I am going on a vacation to Capri. It's very kind. I am never going to leave the Vatican."

"Cardinal, my words have somehow upset you," Adamanto said.

"No, no. I *will* be with the Lord soon."

"I am relieved that you have such peace," Adamanto said.

Bonfiglio shrugged and raised his hands upward in a gesture of surrender. He turned his attention to the window.

"I have always loved this window and the play of sunlight," Bonfiglio said.

"Cardinal Bonfiglio, you said there was one other relic that was significant. Did you want to discuss that today?"

Bonfiglio rotated his chair slowly toward Adamanto. He tapped the back of the chair with his right hand. Exhausted by the effort, his hand fell limply back onto his lap.

"If you will take over pushing for awhile, I will explain the Flynn cross and who will be coming for it tomorrow. Please, let's walk outdoors through the cloister."

The following day, Cardinal Adamanto turned the key in the ancient door making the lock tumblers echo. Tarnished silver letters above the door read: 'Locus Reliquiarium.' Cardinal Bonfiglio sat in his wheelchair next to him. He nodded toward the two Swiss guards in their orange and indigo-striped uniforms. They nodded back. Adamanto pushed Bonfiglio's wheelchair through the open door. One of the guards reached over and closed the door hard behind them. The cardinals walked past ornate cabinets and bureaus. Adamanto's black robe made him into a silhouette against the blonde marble walls brightened by slivers of afternoon sunlight. The grand room was silent except for the click of his heels and the squeak of the wheelchair's axle as it rolled along against the stone floor. Shelves held ornate gold and silver boxes and miniatures of cathedrals. Bonfiglio suddenly slammed his hand down on the arm of the wheelchair.

"Stop here," he wheezed. "This is the Blessed Terrence Flynn reliquary."

They paused at a simple wooden cabinet with iron hinges that sat on its own marble shelf. Adamanto opened the door. Inside, he saw a small wooden box, half the size of a one-pound carton of butter, its lid inlaid with four faded tiles. He removed it and held it up to Bonfiglio.

"Yes, yes. That is it. Bring it along."

Adamanto tucked the box into the pocket under his cassock. They made their way back to the entrance. Adamanto nodded toward the guards as they passed through the door and continued down a corridor. Just down a side hall, they entered a chamber. The door of the chamber read in gold lettering: 'Congregatio de Causus Sanctorum' and below that 'Cardinal Adamanto'

Inside the chamber, a large oak desk sat surrounded by walls of mahogany shelves. Books, papers, and binders flowed from the shelves and down across the top of the desk. Adamanto wheeled Bonfiglio to the right side of the desk, and then took the tufted, leather chair behind it. Adamanto's thick jowls pushed into the collar of his uniform. Adamanto placed the small box on the desk and folded his chubby hands.

"Cardinal Adamanto, please say hello to Antony Palermo."

Across from them sat a man in sunglasses with slicked-back hair that resembled black satin. He tapped the arm of his chair nervously.

Why so anxious, my son?" Adamanto asked.

Antony stood and removed his sunglasses. His eyes regarded Adamanto suspiciously. Adamanto, taken aback by Antony's expression, simply nodded.

Antony sat and adjusted his cream-colored shirt cuff. Adamanto admired the peridot cufflink that so nicely complemented Antony's burnt orange, wool suit. Antony reached down and placed an attaché case onto the Cardinal's desk. He clicked it open. Adamanto's amber eyes widened.

"Yes, your eminence. That is ninety-three thousand Euros. That's what they sent me with and they said you'd know what they want."

Adamanto regarded the money for a moment. He closed the attaché case and looked over toward Bonfiglio.

"I don't understand," Adamanto said. "You only told me about the history of the cross yesterday in the cloister. And that the cross was needed for a festival. Nothing about this."

Bonfiglio nodded and took a deep breath. "So I committed the sin of omission. It's not the worst thing I'll be judged for."

He gestured for Adamanto to open the attaché case once again. His eyes scanned the bills.

"It is for the children of South America," Bonfiglio said. His craggy, pained face seemed to resist his effort to smile. But he was able to offer the slightest grin.

"We do the Lord's work. In return, the nice people borrow this for two weeks."

Bonfiglio reached for the small box containing the cross. He nudged it toward the man.

Antony reached for it and opened it. His eyebrows knitted as he replaced his sunglasses.

"All that for this little cross? And it's silver, not even gold. My brother must know what he's doing."

"You see the inscription on the underside of the lid?" Bonfiglio struggled with his breath.

"Yeah. So what?"

"The Arabic translates to 'He who betrays shall be revealed.' This cross is believed to have come from the silver of Judas. It is imbued with holy power."

Antony closed the lid. He ran his fingertip over the four tiles that were now faded and cracked from the centuries. He checked his fingertip for dust, rubbed it with his thumb, and then slid the box into his pocket. He stood.

"As usual, the cross must be returned in two weeks," Cardinal Bonfiglio said. "I pray that the cross is only used for good."

Antony shrugged. "The Feast of St. Rosalia is next week."

Cardinal Bonfiglio smiled. Cardinal Adamanto glanced between Bonfiglio and Antony. Still confused about the money, Cardinal Adamanto stood. He held his right hand out to Antony. Antony leaned over and kissed the ring on his finger. When Antony left, Bonfiglio closed the attaché case.

"Ring for a guard, my son," he said.

The Il Capo Market in Palermo burst to life with the coming of dawn. Voices yelled, parasols of red, blue, and gold snapped open like blossoming flowers while grocers hustled their crates of oranges, peppers, geraniums, and everything in between. Corrugated metal doors shrieked open at the higher-end stalls. At Pablo Pesce Market, Pablo the fishmonger stretched one more time before he walked into the rear of his stall to the ice machine. As he filled a bin to bring out to his tray of monkfish, he noticed something odd about the fish waste barrel: two human legs protruded from it.

Pablo dropped the ice bin and the cubes rattled across the brick floor. In shock, he crossed himself and walked slowly up to the barrel. He could now see the shoes and hairy calves of a man. The dead man's pant legs had collapsed like unstaked tents to his knees. Somewhere deep in the fish guts and rotting juices were his head and shoulders and the thought of it gave Pablo a chill. He ran to the front of the market and screamed for the police.

"There were also two in the Oreto. It's the purge season, yep," a policeman said a few minutes later as he examined the body that now lay on the street in front of the fish market. A crowd of vendors stood around talking in hushed tones. A female tourist in a wide hat, floral scarf and sunglasses looked at the policeman.

"Purge season?" she asked.

"Sh, sh, shhh!!!" several of the women in the crowd of vendors said.

"Let's just say the Family finds out if you have double-crossed them and then they 'purge' you. Got it?" the policeman said. The tourist inhaled sharply and nodded. Another policeman joined the group.

"Got another over at San Cataldo. In the dumpster."

The policemen looked at each other as they held up fingers.

"Four!" they said in unison.

"A busy season this time," Pablo said. He dabbed at his face with a handkerchief. The cloudless morning was beginning to warm up. Somewhere off on Via Roma, musicians began to play as the Feast of Saint Rosalia procession began.

"Back to work," Pablo said. "Lots to do for the feast."

The cross was returned to Cardinal Adamanto two weeks later. He sat at his desk and regarded the box. His thick brows tensed with worry. Cardinal Bonfiglio lay in the Vatican infirmary ICU on a

11

ventilator giving Adamanto no one with which to confer. His spirit troubled him. He tapped the box with his fingertip.

Bishop Clementi had performed the blessing and Mass for the Feast of Saint Rosalia in Palermo. He mentioned to Adamanto on his return to the Vatican the Epurazione Stagione—Purge Season—and the seven male bodies that had been discovered throughout the two weeks the cross was on loan. What disturbed him most was the Bishop's statement: …*And it was told to me over my torta setteveli that the seven men had betrayed the Family and were purged for their betrayal…*

He opened the box and considered the cross and its archaic tau rho design. There was some relief knowing that the Palermo Family would not seek out the relic again until next year. He snapped the lid closed. Most certainly, he was no longer going to permit the loan of the cross and the unclean cash, regardless of the positive affect the payment created. The idea that a symbol of the Lord would be implicated in murder, regardless of the probable wretched state of the victims' souls, plagued his conscience. Perhaps he should simply toss the cross into the Tiber, but since the cross did not belong to him, he dismissed the thought and the breaking of the commandment it would entail. He stood up and walked back to the reliquary.

As he closed the small wooden cupboard, he vowed that the cross would never be used in this unholy way again. He crossed himself and said a quiet Lord's Prayer. He had a year to consider how he would confront the Palermo Family when they came forward for it again. Still troubled after the prayer, he returned to his office and pulled out a pad of gray paper and his Conte chalks. Since the prayer had failed to soothe him, he once again relied on his artistic talent to provide focus to his troubled mind. As he had taught countless students over the decades, the action of drawing, painting, playing music, or any of the other arts closely aligned one's spirit with the greatest creator of all, and with that, sometimes came peace.

He made his way to the Basilica and took a seat on a marble bench across from Michelangelo's 'Pieta'. Adamanto's eyes followed the soft curves of Mary's hands that met sharp folds of marble. Opening his pad to a partial drawing, he sighed at his weak depiction of the glorious sculpture in beige and white and chalk. His lack of greatness was in part why he could only ever teach art and absent his calling to serve the Lord, would very likely have been a deeply bitter sixty-eight-year-old. He sighed and chuckled at his futile vanity.

But as he began to lay in a shadow of a deep fold in his drawing, he paused. His eyes shot between Mary and Jesus, mother and son. Family. The Palermo family. But. What if he could find a way to return the cross to the Flynn family? They after all donated the relic centuries back. A descendant would be a rightful heir. No commandment broken, and the vicious cycle of murder and dirty money would be permanently terminated.

As the administrator of reliquaries, he oversaw all acquisitions and research of holy artifacts. A team of historians and archaeologists at the American universities of Georgetown and Notre Dame was at his fingertips, not to mention a generous budget. It would take many months, maybe even a year, to arrange and perform the dig in Ireland to locate the good Bishop Flynn's bones. And if the Lord prevailed, the bones and DNA match to a living descendant would be found. The cross returned to a Flynn and the Vatican receiving the Bishop's bones—like a divine exchange. His spirit suddenly felt light.

Adamanto placed his Conte chalk back into its container and closed his drawing pad. He stood and crossed himself and bowed toward the statue, in part to thank the marble masterpiece for the inspiration. He walked rapidly back to his office with a sense of joy and purpose; there were many telephone calls and emails to send.

2.

"Welcome back to 'I Heart L.A.' Now turning to a more somber note—"

"And that's why I call him my Waddy, gang," the millennial hottie with her straight auburn hair and blue-green eyes said, pursing her full lips toward the camera.

"It's a tough job, but someone's gotta be your work daddy, Kitty," the man replied. His early forties, All-American handsome face under thick, sandy and silver hair, grinned broadly.

Kitty looked directly into the television camera lens once again.

"Really, Kurt? But our Hearties here aren't ready to be bummed."

"I think this guy is going to lift them more than those double lattes they're sipping right now, I'm sure."

The television camera widened to show Michael Dunphy sitting with his shoulders back, his salmon-colored shirt and navy polka-dot tie standing out against the blue-green screen behind the three of them. Bright light saturated the set and made his salt-and-pepper hair with its Caesar-cut sparkle as he nodded and smiled toward Kitty and Kurt. A chyron scrolled beneath Michael: 'The School Shooter Hero'.

"You're right, Kurt. And what a handsome hero, too," Kitty said.

"Ladies and gentlemen, for those of you who don't know, this is Michael Dunphy. He is the principal at St. Francis of Assisi School and was solely responsible for taking down that teen shooter three weeks ago who, thanks to this hero, never had the chance to injure anyone. Michael, welcome."

"Thanks, Kurt. And you, too, Kitty."

"So we know from your appearances on podcasts and Youtube that you happened to be at the right place at the right time," Kurt said.

"You know, I see that your appearance on Reality Bites has just hit the five hundred fifty-thousand mark," Kitty said. She looked up from her tablet, pointing. She raised it toward the camera, smiling and nodding.

"Shows how desperate we are for heroes, doesn't it?" Kurt said.

"Funny enough, I haven't liked all the attention over this. I'm not a hero. I owe it to my students to protect them in every way so that's what I did."

"I'll say!" Kitty said.

"When you stood there looking through the window of that classroom door, what went through your mind?" Kurt asked.

"Not much because my adrenaline pumped before I had the chance to think. That's why I say I'm no hero."

"Yeah but you didn't freeze and you didn't run," Kitty said. "You threw open that door and could have been shot."

"Thank hydrogen the kid made the bad judgment to have his back to the door and his assault rifle to his left side. I had him on the ground, his left wrist broken and twisted away from the rifle in what must have been only a few seconds."

"Thank *hydrogen?*" Kurt asked with a chuckle.

"It's the most abundant element we know of in the universe and it's my nod toward my beliefs, or lack thereof."

"So you're an atheist?" Kitty asked.

"Yes."

"An atheist principal at a Catholic high school? How does that work out?" Kurt asked.

"My administrative talents overshadow any concerns over that. Plus, I'm not in the classroom teaching so it doesn't really come into conversations with students."

"That's pretty forward thinking for this diocese, I'd think," Kurt said.

"They just expect me to keep it to myself while at work. They have told me that I'm the one going to hell, not them, so it's really not an issue."

"A lot of my Catholic friends tell me the same thing," Kurt said. "For different reasons, though. I know God has my back."

"Some of those 'New Order' nuts have been posting crazy stuff since it happened," Kitty said. "Have you gotten any threats?"

"Just a couple strange emails a few days after. Nothing since then."

"We really appreciate your being here, Michael. What is it you would want people to know that they haven't already heard from you?" Kurt asked.

"I thought about this a lot, Kurt. It's really the only reason I even wanted to come on the show."

Kitty reached out and patted Michael's shoulder.

"We so appreciate that you did."

"It's not really an earth-shattering idea or anything. In fact, I pretty much deal with it every day. I just would like parents to remember that they need to know what their kids are doing online, on their phones, and in every other way. Parents' presence matters."

"Sounds like a T-shirt to me!" Kitty said.

Kurt nodded.

"Thank you, Michael Dunphy. You're a hero in every way."

Michael noticed the television camera swing away from him and toward the weather lady. A man in the wings waved for him to get off the set. Michael

16

walked toward the man, paused for the stage manager to remove his lavaliere microphone, and then walked backstage. He nodded toward a couple of the stagehands, one of whom pointed out the exit. He hurried toward it since it was a school day.

Some days he was sure he couldn't face another twitchy mother who was convinced that her kid was not only Einstein but Meryl Streep and Mother Theresa, too. Michael had spent too many days at his desk arbitrating between indulged children and frazzled teachers. It was better he knew than to still be a history teacher to a gaggle of bleary-eyed 'tweens, but he wondered if all the time spent on his education doctorate only to be a principal had been worth it. For that matter, had anything been worth it? Other than his own kids, now young adults, and his wife, of course. They continued the long line of conventional and safe choices he made with his life, leading up to the education business—and it was a business; the calling long ago having faded, if it ever was there. He was safe, oh so safe, but the price was boredom mixed with disappointment and depression he now realized. And that boredom had led to this really unsafe choice he was about to fix. Had to fix or go over the precipice and into what? His months of early morning insomnia had banished any remnant of youthful optimism and replaced it with dark imaginings of nihilistic dread: the coming days of painful decline until death.

He toyed with the replica of the Rock of Cashel castle. His long fingertips extended from his pale hand and found their way to the top of the miniature keep. His uncle had brought him the souvenir when he was six or seven, Michael couldn't recall. That was after his uncle's fifteenth trip to research the Flynn family tree on his mom's side. The man had become obsessed with piecing together the family history back to the Irish nobility. Oddly and perhaps conveniently, he never could recall much of his life with his parents, Michael's

17

grandparents. They remained mysteries to Michael and the only other clue was that his own mother never spoke about them, either. A clue might have been that when his dad came out as gay when Michael was twelve, his staunchly conservative Catholic grandparents never visited California again. He could vaguely recall two visits when he was very little but after his dad's revelation, the visits ceased. Michael had only heard about their deaths when a note, postmarked Racine, Wisconsin, arrived. It was from the executor of their will notifying him of his grandmother's death. It also mentioned that he was not a legatee but included the address of the funeral home if he wished to send flowers.

His own interest in Irish history, for that matter, history and archaeology in general, extended back to The Three Stooges episode "I Want My Mummy" and was stoked by the Indiana Jones movies released while he studied at UCLA. He had yet to go to Ireland or any other of the dozen or so countries he yearned to visit. There were always financial concerns with the kids, and then student loans to pursue his PhD followed by business loans to get his wife Stephanie's business on firm footing. When he had summer months off from school, he still had to work. Like so many other interests or hopes he let go over the years, travel fell along the way. The strident noon bell interrupted his reverie. He sighed. A cherry wood desk intercom buzzed.

"Principal Dunphy?" a nervous older woman said.

"Phyllis, you can call me Mike, not a problem."

"You have a twelve fifteen appointment with Ms. Beauchamp. She texted to let me know that she just let her fourth period composition class out for lunch and will be here soon."

"Thanks, Phyllis."

Michael stood up, but forgot to push his chair back far enough. He struck his right knee against the underside of the desk as he went to stand.

"Shit!"

He rubbed his knee and then tucked in his salmon dress shirt. But then realized it was hugging his slight paunch. He tugged at the sides to loosen it a bit and adjusted his tie. Running a hand through his hair, he pulled it forward to mask the receding at his temples. He rubbed the back of his neck with his left hand, a nervous tick. As he gathered up the loose papers and files on his desk, he wondered if this was really happening. His heart sped up in nervous anticipation as he stepped around his desk and straightened the two brown vinyl armchairs. This was not going to be easy and he was committed to his choice. But was this going to be another proverbial ship in his life that sailed? The shadows of students played against the venetian blinds and their voices chirped as they passed his windows on their way to lunch. Oh, to be a stupid thirteen-year-old again. A chance to do it all over but with what he knows today. But this time, he would get to choose his mother. He glanced up at the crucifix hanging below the wall clock. He almost had the urge to say a Hail Mary. Almost. Faith and he were foul-weather friends at best. There was a knock on the door and it burst open.

"Well, well, did you do it yet?"

Gregory rushed up to his desk, raising his arms in the air with a big gesture of his lavender shirt sleeves. Michael glanced up at Gregory's light brown hair with blonde highlights. Gregory noticed and pointed toward his hair.

"Oh, get over it. I'm an art teacher—the kids expect me to be a little flamboyant. Sorry, creative. Besides, the color distracts from the fringe of cotton candy it's thinning into here." Gregory fussed with the cowlick at the peak of his forehead.

"Dude, she's due any second. Can you kind of disappear yourself for now?"

Gregory crossed his arms and arched his eyebrows. He sat down in one of the chairs and began to tap the desk.

19

"I might just stay here as a witness. That's what best friends do—not kick each other out."

"Unwad your panties! I'll catch you for dinner sometime this week."

Gregory stood. He straightened his shirt.

"Will that include Stephanie? I really miss our meaning of life and philosophical chats and rants but she kind of always has an answer for everything. I love her, but…"

"She *is* my wife."

"You have been selling me that line for years. You so want me."

A soft knock at the door interrupted them. Gregory gritted his teeth and smiled. Michael gestured for him to go. Gregory rolled his eyes and stood. He walked to the door and opened it.

"He's all yours," he said. Ms. Beauchamp's blue-green eyes flashed with confusion. As she walked past him, Gregory looked over her thick auburn hair. He wagged his finger and closed the door. Michael stepped around his desk and pulled out a chair for Ms. Beauchamp. He stepped over to the door and closed the blinds over the narrow, vertical window. Before he turned back around, Ms. Beauchamp had him by the shoulders and thrust her full, pouty lips toward him. Michael melted into the kiss but only briefly. He gently pushed her away.

"Not just yet," he said quietly. He guided her by the elbow back to the chair. She sat, adjusting her white, silk blouse over her well-shaped breasts. She reached for Michael as he stepped back around his desk and sat. He looked at her and sighed. He brought his palms together as if he were about to pray, touching his fingertips to the bottom of his nose. The wedding band on his left hand felt cool as it pressed against the ring finger of his right hand. How to start this—end this. It wasn't like he hadn't fantasized about finally consummating their affair and he knew she was ready for the next step. Never mind that as the principal of St. Francis of Assisi Parish School, an affair with a student teacher would most certainly result in his termination. He still loved Stephanie, and could not simply throw away thirty-one years of marriage and grown children in college for a fling with a student teacher who must have had a daddy-thing for him.

Ms. Beauchamp shifted in her chair. She dabbed at the corner of her mouth with her ring finger, wiping away a bit of coral lipstick. Michael avoided following the curves of her full lips. 'Be strong,' he thought. He looked down at his Rock of Cashel miniature castle and thought for a second: 'Give me strength, clan ancestors!' He shook his head and sighed.

"Natalie, this is really tough."

Natalie folded her arms. She leaned back in her chair, crossed her legs, and began to swing her left calf nervously.

"Am I fired or something?"

Michael chuckled. She was so young to think of *that* first.

"No. You're an excellent student teacher—that's all I ever hear. I'm talking about us."

"Oh."

She folded her hands and dropped them in her lap. She began to thumb wrestle, avoiding Michael's gaze and staying focused on her rose pink polished thumbnails. Michael stepped around and sat on the edge of the desk facing her. He reached tenderly and raised her chin so that he could look into her eyes.

"I'm sorry. It's over. I should have never led you on. This has to stop before it goes any further."

Natalie's eyes welled. She jerked her chin from his hand and wiped the tears as they fell.

"What did I do?" she asked softly.

"Natalie, I'm married. I'm old enough to be your dad. I should have never—"

"That's all? Those things aren't that big of a deal."

Michael's throat caught. He cleared it and spoke.

21

"I love my wife. I'm not going to divorce her. And I'm not going to continue cheating on her."

He stood up and walked back around his desk. Natalie stood and grabbed his shoulders.

"Please, I know this can work. You haven't even, we haven't even, well how do you know what you're missing with *me?*"

Michael plopped into his chair. He shook his head.

"Nothing good for either of us can come from it—just problems. Go find somebody else, someone younger and single."

"I'm not interested in anybody else. You are the one for me."

"No."

"You're one of the smartest men I have ever met. But you're also sensitive and sweet. And that's so rare."

"I'm not that rare or special, trust me. You're sounding a bit desperate and you're only what? Twenty-four, twenty-five?"

"Twenty-six."

"There you go. I don't even know how old you are; except that now I can safely say I'm almost twice your age. My daughter is graduating from Cal next year—she's only four years younger than you. You will find someone, trust that. Talk about intelligent. And you're beautiful, too."

It was Natalie's turn to clear her throat. She stood and swiped her tears.

"Is that all then, Principal Dunphy?"

"Natalie, really?"

"Ms. Beauchamp, please," she retorted.

Natalie walked to the door. As she grabbed the knob, she paused and said over her shoulder:

"You have no clue what you have missed."

She walked out and closed the door behind her. Michael felt a tension between his neck and shoulders. Natalie had no idea how much he felt that he missed in his life. Choices and consequences, actions, reactions, but there was no comfort in pure facts; just hard reality. The 12:45 bell rang and the clomping shadows of kids began to pass by his windows. He had the urge to throw open both windows like in the movie 'Network' and scream: "Don't miss out! Don't miss out!" Aside from the pure ludicrous nature of the impulse, Michael further dampened his urge on recalling the frightened faces of the social studies students a few weeks back and the drop-out wielding the assault rifle. No, bad idea to throw open a window and startle kids. Instead, he tapped the keep of his miniature Rock of Cashel castle. A sense of relief began to build in him. He had another urge and this one he would act on. He buzzed Phyllis.

"I'm going out for about an hour and a half."

"Princip—sorry, Mike. Don't forget to get back here by 3:00. Detective Mullen will be here to discuss the car break-ins in the employee lot last week."

"Yeah, I'll be back. Fine."

Michael drove Olive Avenue on his way to his home on Sparks Street in Burbank. The late winter sun warmed the interior of the Ford Fusion. Since he had neglected--or rather couldn't decide--to take the car in for the heater repair at the end of October, he had to rely on the sun to warm it. Leave it to Los Angeles to have a cold spell at the end of March when it's usually in the eighties. He couldn't decide whether to repair the seven-year-old system or replace the whole thing. And the cost for either was high so no help there to decide. Not to mention all the electronics involved with the heater and air conditioning. Now there's an expense for sure. He drove along thinking. And Michael was a thinker. And thinker, and thinker. Close to obsessive, he figured.

The fact that he had finally decided to end the affair with Natalie today had burdened his mind since the start of the dalliance nine weeks before. Now would he tell Stephanie? Could he? Would Stephanie scream, or hit him, or leave him? Could she divorce him? Would she run into the bedroom and grab the Glock 17 and blow him away? How they went back and forth about owning a gun at all. He supported California's gun control laws and especially liked the ability for one adult person in each household to own one registered gun for protection, just like he appreciated that ranchers and farmers were allowed to have one rifle and one handgun per person. It was all reasonable and based on regions where you lived rather than some thin constitutional rationale for stocking up on automatic weapons. Stephanie was completely opposed to private gun ownership in any context until Burbank had a spike in home invasion rapes. Then they bought the Glock 17 and trained at the Firing Line. Since she works from home, they both felt safer knowing she had some protection. But would that backfire now? Shot down in his late midlife by the gun he bought for her to protect herself.

No, she wouldn't go that far: the whole affair was pretty innocent since it was only a few lunch dates and one kiss--did that amount to true infidelity? He felt drawn to Natalie for the obvious physical reasons, and then he felt flattered that she would find his fading looks attractive. So there was that, too. But if he told Stephanie, what then? The kids would be fine—they were busy with their own adult lives. No worries there. But would Stephanie forgive him even though it wasn't consummated? Now the afternoon sun blared as he turned right onto Sparks Street. Would he get the heater fixed or replaced? He pulled into the driveway of their mid-century ranch home, but stopped the car just at the point where the driveway and sidewalk met.

Michael slid out of the car and closed the door quietly. Since Stephanie worked remotely as an insurance broker from the office that was once the boys' bedroom in the back of the house, he could easily surprise her. He would announce himself as he walked through the front door and into the living room. Stepping past the two thujas growing on either side of the porch steps, he made his way to the front door. Their orange-striped tabby appeared out of nowhere and softly meowed. He reached over and petted him, "Shhh, quiet Mo," he said in a whisper. "Where are Larry and Curly?" He looked around briefly to see if their other two cats were near. They weren't so he lifted Mo to carry him inside.

When he left the school fifteen minutes earlier, he felt unsure and lost. Somehow, taking action to end the affair before it got serious made him feel confident. Action rather than thought—now that was something worth thinking about. He slid his key into the deadbolt and cranked it open. As he opened the door and stepped into the living room, a chill went up his spine. It wasn't the cooled air but the sense that he was about to take a huge risk in confessing to Stephanie. For a second, he imagined running back out the door and into Natalie's arms again.

"Steph, I'm home. I wanted to surprise—"

"What the hell?" a male voice shouted. Michael looked toward the back of the brown leather sofa and saw an unfamiliar man's face. The man's eyes bugged out as he jumped up. Stephanie stood quickly. Mo jumped out of Michael's arms and ran toward their barking bulldog, Mildred.

"Michael!" she screamed and stood up. "It's not what you think."

His feelings went numb with indecision and incomprehension. He eyed both of them quickly, trying to take it in. The only thing that kept Michael from leaping on the man and beating the shit out of him was that he was still wearing clothes. Stephanie, for her part, was still fully clothed as well. Natalie and his whole reason for being home to surprise Stephanie flashed into his mind. He flexed his hands from fists to open palms. The irony of his own predicament further cooled his temper. He raised his arm and pointed toward the door. As the man hustled past him, Michael noticed his full head of gray hair and thick love handles pushing through his yellow polo shirt.

"What?" Michael said as the man closed the front door. "He looks as old as your dad."

"You almost gave me a heart attack. Michael, please!" she screamed at his back as he bolted out the door.

He wasn't going to chase down the man but instead, hopped into his car and roared out of the driveway. The image of Stephanie standing up and that gray-haired asshole played through his mind. How could I have been so stupid? How long had this been going on? He slammed his hands against the steering wheel as he turned right onto Olive Avenue. His heart pounded and he felt light headed. He pulled over in front of Carl's Junior. What am *I* running away from? Am I that unattractive now? Michael started the car again and continued down Olive Avenue. Should I just get on the 134 and head east? Is this my moment to make everything more real? He wasn't sure what he meant by that. His high school smoking and drinking best friend Dave Patchett popped into his mind. They had plotted running away to Tucson or Phoenix to become cowhands and chase loose cowgirls and slutty barmaids like in the western movies they watched on TV. That was right around the time he and Dave started gifted and talented college prep classes. Those dreams of running away faded as Michael excelled in an effort to please his mother. Maybe she would stick around more if he got straight A's, he recalled his motivation. She had been spending more and more time on her religious obsession after the divorce. His friendship with Dave faded, too, since Michael was becoming obsessively academic. But why would he think about that old teen cowboy dream right now: is that really what he wanted? A car horn blared from behind as he sat at a green left arrow. The turn would take him onto the 134 and on his way to Tucson or Phoenix maybe. He began the left turn but changed it to a U turn at the last second. The car behind him laid on its horn again. Michael flipped off the driver. The jackass didn't know how critical this moment was for Michael. I'm too fucking old to run away—I'm trapped and I better enjoy the cage. And after all, I came home to confess *my* affair—I have a lot of nerve feeling disgust with her. He let out a deep sigh as he changed traffic lanes and made his way back to Spark Street and Stephanie.

"Oh my God. I thought you left me!" Stephanie said as he walked up the front porch. Her face stained with tears, she reached for him, waving some papers toward him. He pointed toward the open front door. She nodded and went into the house and he followed behind.

Michael, now in a state of confusion, sat next to her on the couch. His mind whirled with conflicting thoughts of Natalie, the car heater, student reports, anger, odd relief, and hurt. He could not look at Stephanie.

"How long has this been going on?"

"Nothing has been going on"

"That doesn't make sense."

"It will in a second. This is the first time I have met him in person. It's been Skype meetings up till now. All work—he's a Farmer's rep."

Michael sighed with relief. Could this really be? He crossed over to the chair, kneeled, and took Stephanie's hand.

"What are you telling me?"

"He was here for a meeting to go over these actuarial reports and stuff. He had always been a little flirty but today he surprised me and made a pass."

Relief flowed through Michael. He nodded and swallowed hard, not sure what to say next. A pang of anger quickly softened into the deep compassion of a couple in love. He believed her and wanted to comfort her.

Stephanie continued. "But wait. I liked the flirting. So I must have led him on."

"You let him kiss you?"

"I had to sit next to him on the couch to flip through the stuff. He grabbed me just a few seconds before you walked in."

27

"Then I should go track him down and beat the shit out of him?"

"Oh, Michael. It's my fault, too. I liked the feeling of being wanted again. Things have gotten so odd and distant between us. Especially since the kids have been gone."

"Yeah, that's true," Michael said quietly. His nervousness was beginning to build.

"The empty nest thing is real. But you and I had lots in common and had lots of good times before the kids were born. Where is that fun couple?"

Michael took Stephanie by the shoulders. He nodded and wondered, too. He escorted her back over to the couch. He flicked away her tears with his thumb, struggling with what she just said and with his own moment of confession to come.

"You need to wash your face before I can kiss you—that old fart and all."

"He didn't *kiss* me."

Michael was now feeling an older sadness—this reminded him suddenly of the movie 'Jaws'. More precisely, how his father had sent him away that day to the Viceroy Walk-In movies when his father's AA-turned-golf-pal showed up and later that day, his mother kicking his dad out. And then the divorce, the sadness of missing the family, his dad, the whole thing. He stuffed the feeling—this was now and his own marriage was on the line. No time for that old crap.

"I have something to tell you," he said. "Goddamn it. There's no easy way to say it."

It was Stephanie's turn to be puzzled. She heard the angst in his voice and her compassion for the love of her life coursed through her. She clutched his hand.

"Okay. Tell me."

Michael cleared his throat. He rubbed the back of his neck and let out a sound somewhere between a sigh and a growl, fueled by disgust with himself. He spoke quietly.

"I almost had an affair with a student teacher."

Stephanie's throat closed in reaction and all that came out of her was a squeak like a hungry chick. She dropped his hand and leaned away from him.

"Wait. Wait, Steph. I broke it off *today*. Nothing ever happened but some flirting, a couple lunches, and one kiss."

Stephanie shrugged and nodded. It was her turn to feel relief and it welled up in her eyes.

"It's done. I don't know what I was thinking."

Stephanie's smile faded. Her brow with its slight lines knitted for a moment.

"Was this a first time or have there been any others?" she asked.

Michael gulped as the image of their Glock flashed into his mind.

"Yes, yes!"

"More?"

"No, no! I mean, yes, it was the first time."

Stephanie shook her head. She grabbed his hand once again. They sat quietly for a minute, both looking off in opposite directions like two guilty children. The sound of a dog barking in the distance became a roar in the silence between them as they both realized this moment was huge, almost overwhelming.

"We're a couple of clowns, you know?" she said. Her usual low-key wry tone had returned. "Do you think we should go see a therapist to work on this?"

Michael shrugged.

"I don't know. Work on what? I'd say we were both in the midst of a midlife thing. What the hell more is therapy going to help with?"

Stephanie nodded. She raised his hand to her lips and kissed it softly.

"Maybe we both should have talked about this a few months back before either of us got in too deep with all this flirting," she said.

"You're right," Michael replied. "Didn't we even put it in our vows somehow that if we were ever

29

tempted to stray, each of us promised to tell the other *before* it happened?"

"We both blew that one," she said.

She leaned in to kiss him. He shook his head.

"I don't deserve a kiss."

"Good. You should feel guilty. Really guilty."

"I do."

"But are we *bored* with each other?" Stephanie asked. "Is that what this is about?"

Michael slouched back. He rubbed the back of his neck.

"I'm bored with *me*," he said. "You're still an amazing work of a woman and I think it was just me feeling flattered. Escaping to youth, I guess. I'm so sorry."

Stephanie reached for his hand again and looked deeply into his emerald-green eyes whose beauty hadn't faded despite some lines and saggy lids.

"I just liked the attention, I think," she said. "I'm not the most exciting thing on two feet, either. I sell insurance for crying out loud. So much for those glorious dreams of law school and sitting as a judge."

"The kids took precedence over that, don't you think? And despite your lost ambitions, they turned out quite well. I'm proud of all of them."

"Are we just in a rut? Doing our own things and same things day in and day out? Have we drifted apart? I'm sorry, too—I can't bear the idea of you not being next to me the rest of my life. No one will ever know me and accept me the way you do. How could I have risked that over simple boredom?"

"Boredom at our ages may not be so simple. But we don't have to destroy our lives over mid-life crap."

"We were meant for each other, I'm sure of it," she said.

"I don't know—sounds a little mystical to me. I just know that we fit each other so well—always have. Like I said in my vows: your needs, wants, and desires will always come before mine."

"Yours, too, my Midee love."

He knew he was secure and safe when she called him by her pet name for him, 'Midee', a contraction of 'Mike D'.

"Your desires before mine. So do you want me to go chase down dad and let him do you?"

"You're a putz," she said.

"Can I kiss you? In fact, more than that. If you want some *extra* attention."

Stephanie smiled and stood up quickly.

"Now *that* doesn't sound boring," she said.

"Don't be too sure about that. I'm pretty out of practice."

Stephanie laughed over her shoulder. As she got to the hallway door, she turned.

"So tell me one more time, and mean it, that you never did anything but kiss her one time."

The question hit Michael like a lightning bolt, and he felt he deserved it. And Stephanie meant it that way since her trust in him was now deeply fractured.

"Yes," Michael said almost in a whisper. "Nothing but a kiss."

"I believe you. Both of us were on the edge. I'm not sure either of us would have made it back."

"Me more than you," Michael said. "I don't think grandpa's pass at you is a quite as bad as my stupidity."

Michael stood up. Stephanie stepped to him and took his hand. She led him to their bedroom.

As they lay in each other's arms later, Stephanie raised her head from Michael's chest. He brushed away a few strands of hair from her face.

"So I *am* going to tell you one thing," she said.
"Uh-oh."

She playfully slapped his chin.

"No, no. Don't get excited."

"Too late for that, anyway."

Stephanie raised the sheet and feigned a look toward his penis.

31

"That's for sure."

"Hey!"

Michael grabbed the edge of the sheet and pulled it up under his arms. Stephanie giggled.

"You were saying?" Michael said.

"I felt pretty again. That's the whole thing right there for me."

Stephanie lay her head back down. Michael stroked her hair.

"What about you?" she asked.

"I always feel pretty."

She pulled on a few hairs of his chest.

"Ouch!"

"You know what I'm saying."

Unlike Stephanie, who could cut through to the crux of any situation, Michael's mind as usual swirled with different possibilities. Most often, one idea would be the complete opposite of another, ad infinitum, never settling.

"Thinking."

"Shit. I don't want a diatribe. Isn't there a *main* motivation you can point to?"

"Working on it."

"Now is a moment I wish I smoked so I could light one up while you cogitate."

"Got it!"

Michael actually felt proud that he found the most likely cause of his wandering.

"I felt young."

That made sense to Stephanie. She nodded and kissed his cheek. It was a kiss of understanding. Forgiveness would have to come later.

"This makes me think of that song in 'Putting it Together.' "

Michael, not much of a fan of musicals, shook his head.

"The Sondheim DVD Gregory gave us for Christmas a couple years back."

"Okay."

"Carol Burnett sings it to George Hearn in 'Putting it Together': '*Hey, old friend, what do you say old friend…you and I can continue next week…*' "

"Is that how it goes?"

"Not exactly, but the point is the older couple is singing to each other about going on together no matter what."

"We do go on, don't we?"

"Wait, wait. Oh, shit, the other song is a tearjerker: '*I am unworthy of your love, darlin' darlin'…let me prove worthy of your love…*"

Stephanie's voice cracked. Tears began to flow.

"Oh, Midee, Midee…we almost screwed it all up."

"I'm sorry, Steph. Please forgive me."

"Give me some time for that, Midee."

Michaels' eyes welled. He pulled Stephanie closer to him as she cried. Yes, he realized: how fragile it all was, one action away from destruction. To give up complete acceptance, appreciation, and love for some futile attempt to feel young again. He shuddered with relief.

When they stopped at the valet kiosk, Michael sheepishly handed over his Ford keys. Stephanie was already standing outside the car, looking past the wrought iron entrance gate toward the rambling Mediterranean ranch house and the breaking waves tinted persimmon by the sunset off Lunada Bay. Michael stepped up to join her. Something was so odd about being on the edge of a life abyss yesterday and today showing up for the annual fraternity reunion. All of it odd as usual, Michael thought.

"I don't think they have much of a view or anything—the huge house just blocks too much of it," she said.

"Let's just go in and say 'hi' to Paul and Sharon, grab a drink and shoot the shit for a few minutes with any other of the frat bros that might be here," Michael said.

"I knew 'SC grads had places like this but I thought you UCLA guys always had higher intellectual callings."

"Higher intellectual callings usually equals lower savings accounts."

Michael placed his hand on Stephanie's bare back. His eyes followed the sapphire satin line of her dress as it pressed softly against her smooth skin, and then up to her neck just below her hair she wore in a French twist updo. While some of his fraternity brothers like Paul had hit it big, none of them could boast a wife as gorgeous as Stephanie. That was some comfort as they stepped through the front doors of the estate and flutes of champagne seemed to appear in their hands from thin air. An orchestra of voices and clamoring bodies engulfed them while everything sparkled with the sumptuous beauty of wealth.

"You made it, old guy!" Paul yelled. The crowd parted to let the paunchy, balding host, with a smile that seemed to stretch across his face, greet Michael. Paul threw his arms around Michael, and then paused to kiss Stephanie on the cheek.

"And still the most gorgeous of alumna!" he said.

"This is quite a big shindig," Michael said. Party crowds tended to mute his conversational faculty.

"None of the guys from our class have made it here yet," Paul said. "Night's young, though. I see you got some bubbly. Come on out to the terrace and check out the sunset. Seems some gray whales are passing by, too."

Paul smiled once more, squeezed Michael's upper arm, and then disappeared back into the crowd. Stephanie pointed toward what looked to be a large Jackson Pollock on one wall and then toward an Andrew Wyeth on the other. They stepped over toward a niche that held a sculpture of a woman with a water vase on her shoulder fashioned from porcelain. Stephanie leaned in to examine the statue.

"Oh, God. That's Limoges. Just never mind."

She took a sip of her champagne.

"Whales from the terrace then?" she asked.

"Sure."

They crossed the terra cotta floor, past several more niches and a few more remarkable paintings. Just through a set of distressed glass-paned doors in the Monterey style, the terrace opened up before them. Paved with local Palos Verdes stone, it ended at a low wrought iron railing that seemed to be positioned on the edge of a cliff. Over left was an infinity pool and off right, a tennis court. White miniature lights buffeted by a soft ocean breeze made the terrace look like fireflies had invaded. Michael pointed out the chamber orchestra that played some sort of classical string piece next to a long stone-faced bar.

Stephanie leaned against the railing and squinted. She shook her head as the breeze tossed a few loose strands of her hair.

"I don't see the whales. Sunset is amazing, though."

Michael nodded. Stephanie recognized his glum reaction.

"We don't have to come to these things if you're going to feel bad," she said.

"It's just that I was always smarter and more talented than Paul and yet he's the one with the goods."

"Yeah, well Paul started out from wealth and just made more."

"What he did still counts."

"You started with nothing and made something. And you got me and the kids, too."

"It's hard not to compare."

"No—the word you're looking for really is 'compete'. And that's a waste of time. Think about it this way: aren't you better now then you were then?"

"Yes. I guess."

"'Guess?' Really?"

"Okay. Yes. What's your point?"

"Point is it's a loser's game to compare and compete with other people. If you can always look at yourself and say that you are better now than before, you won't have time to worry about what anybody else is doing or has."

"Right as usual. I'll work on it."

"And Sharon fell from the top of the ugly tree and hit every branch on the way down. No kids, either."

"Now who's comparing?"

"It's not comparing. It's being catty. I'm entitled to that."

"Sexual harassment?" Michael said the following Tuesday afternoon. He sat at the walnut table in the dining room of the rectory at St. Francis of Assisi parish. Branches tickled and scratched the outside windows as a mild Santa Ana blew. Spring was definitely coming, or maybe even Spummer—summer heat in late March. Father Griffith, the pastor of the parish and superintendent of the school, sat across from Michael. He nodded his white-haired head as he removed his horned rim glasses and wiped them with a handkerchief.

"It's all there in the letter Ms. Beauchamp's attorney sent the diocese," Griffith said.

Michael snatched up the document and began to read. His face grew red with anger and then embarrassment. He tossed the letter back on the table.

"There was no harassment, Father. It was mutual and consenting."

Griffith grunted.

"You're the principal of the school. You are in a position of authority over her as well. We are all more sensitive to that these days. But you see it doesn't matter, since in either event, you are married."

Griffith reached over to the heavy-carved buffet and grabbed a manila folder. He placed the folder down between them.

"Does she want money? What?"

"Her attorney explained that if you are terminated, she will drop the allegations. It seems to be the best and only course given the circumstances."

Griffith pushed the folder over to Michael who nervously ran a hand through his hair and went to open the folder. He fumbled it and the pages fell onto the desk. He paused, so tired of his clumsy nature, and just stared at Griffith. Father Griffith scooped up the pages, put them back in order, and handed them to Michael. As he read, he shook his head.

"So you're asking on her behalf that I resign. I'm fired basically."

"The resignation suits her purpose and the diocese's. If you prefer for us to fire you, then we will have to put the sexual harassment accusation into your file. Under state law, we are required to disclose such a termination to a new employer if children are involved. I don't want to do that."

Michael stood up. He rubbed the back of his neck.

"So six years of service and I don't get some sort of fair hearing?"

"Michael, you committed adultery as principal of a Catholic high school. You have admitted that. Seventh Commandment broken, you are no longer suitable to be employed by the school. It's the morals clause in your contract. It's just that simple. You were on thin ice with your declaration of atheism on that morning show as it was, but you did credit us with looking the other way on that issue for years. This, though, is quite a different matter. Go ahead and sign. The envelope inside the folder has three months severance pay."

"The affair was never consummated. Does that matter at all?"

Griffith shrugged and shook his head.

"Intent, Michael. The Lord knows the intentions of our hearts."

Michael glanced around the room with its dark cherry walls and shelves of china and silver. His eyes landed on a painting of Jesus looking skyward, hands folded. Griffith cleared his throat.

"You have a pen, Father?"

Leaving the folders and papers on top of his desk, Michael grabbed up his redwood pen holder from a trip up north when the kids were small, his coffee mug with a quote from physicist Lawrence Krauss in white on black, and his miniature Rock of Cashel. As he loaded them into a box, he didn't feel sad as he expected but something odd he hadn't felt in a long time: anticipation. This may be all for the best, he thought. But you're fired and no matter the reasons, you failed. His anticipation darkened over by the cloud of failure. This, too, was a new feeling. He hadn't failed in anything until now. But can you fail if you have always played it safe, he wondered. Where's the risk when the choice is safe and easy? Would they have to sell the house and downsize? What—to a condo? Falling backwards. And he might lose his cracker box of a house in Burbank? Paul's house in Palos Verdes from the reunion the other night flashed into his mind. Loser, he felt, loser. And then he thought about the frat brother with his place in Bel Air. The only thing that lifted him at that second was recalling that the Bel Air frat brother lost his house as a result of a cocaine addiction. Nothing better for bitterness than the sweet failure of another, he thought. Wait—according to Stephanie, I'm better than I was before. So I'm succeeding, he tried to comfort himself. Still gotta work on believing that one, he sighed.

"Here's your sheepskins and that sweet picture of you guys with the kids," Gregory said. He paused and lightly dusted the framed photograph.

"It's going to be hard not to see you everyday," he added. His voice strained a bit. "Are you sure you don't want to fight this?"

Michael placed the frames into the box carefully so as not to scratch the glass. He folded the box closed as he considered Gregory's question. Fight the Catholic

Church and its tenets? That's what was really at stake. From a reasonable standpoint, if one could apply reason to religion, Michael's actions were in direct violation of the faith. In this national atmosphere of the alleged attack on religious freedom, and despite the relative liberalism of California, this whole thing could wind up in federal jurisdiction. He didn't have the time or resources for such a thing.

"Nope, Gregory. I'm going to have to find a new admin position in a charter school, maybe. Or something else entirely—I don't know. I have three months of severance and about a year and half of savings to figure it out."

"At least you're a two-income family. That will help."

"Yeah. Stephanie's insurance brokerage has taken off so we're okay till next year."

Gregory leaned against the desk and folded his arms. He sighed.

"You know, I'm really beginning to like her more."

Michael picked up the box. He leaned over and kissed Gregory on the cheek. Gregory smiled.

"You haven't liked her since our Phi Lambda days at UCLA. She confirmed that I'm straight since you never believed me."

"Bitch stole you from me!"

"You already know that if I had been gay, you would have been my guy. Now put your fangs away."

"Wait. Take one more look around," Gregory said.

Michael shrugged though he felt the pang of an ending.

"What?"

"Like I teach my burgeoning artists—you have left something more beautiful and better than you found it."

"Please tell me you're talking about the school and not you."

Gregory waved his hand in the air mimicking a slap.

"We haven't had a good philosophical bullshit session in a long time," Gregory said.

"Measles epidemics, PTA complaints, teachers walking out—that's about all I can think about these days. We're getting old."

"Speak for yourself! It has been well over a year, though."

"I'll call you for dinner after this dust settles down a bit," Michael said. "Next week, probably."

"I guess you can bring *her* if you have to."

"Even after three decades, that joke never gets old. It's a good thing she loves you as much as I do."

Michael stepped out the door. Gregory paused at the jamb. He glanced around the office, noticing the sunset through the blinds as his cocoa brown eyes glazed with tears. He looked around to be sure no one could see him and wiped them away.

While Gregory stood in his office wiping away tears, Michael made his way to his car. He had already said his goodbyes over coffee and marble cake in the teacher's lounge earlier. Just get in your car, turn on the engine, and don't look back, he thought. But if not looking back, what exactly am I looking toward? He argued with himself. What happens after we go through the severance and savings if I don't find a job? Will Stephanie make enough to cover that? But aren't I a loser if we have to depend on Stephanie? As usual, his mind was set in motion. The thoughts, counter-thoughts, recriminations, resolutions played through his mind as he reached for the door of his car. The sound of crushing glass startled him.

Michael glanced over and saw two young men and a woman at the side of Mr. Vogel, the math teacher's, VW Passat. All three wore dark hoodies and he couldn't make out faces in the dusk light. He set his box on the hood of his car and hollered as he ran toward them.

"What the hell are you—?"

He saw a flash of light as a dull thud hit the back of his head, and he could only hear the sound of breaking bones and teeth as the world spun from dusk to dark strangeness. What Michael couldn't know then as he lay unconscious and bleeding was he hadn't simply stumbled on to a car burglary. Had he miraculously snapped awake and saw the printing on the attackers' hoodies, he would have understood more: 'New Order 2.0'. These three kids who were about to get away with assaulting him were part of the Facebook group of anti-government fanatics. But worse yet for Michael, their compatriot in their terrorist group was sitting in a downtown jail cell about to be indicted for the school shooting plot Michael had interrupted a few weeks before. Michael might have become a hero and instant local celebrity but not to these three reprobates; they kicked and stomped his limp body in violent revenge. Michael lay in darkness when the pummeling stopped thanks to the holler of a teacher, causing the attackers to flee in separate directions.

A new kind of light burned Michael's closed eyes. But stranger still were the mosaics of light he could see on his inner eyelids. He focused on a part of his eyelid and saw something he couldn't understand: what he recognized as corpuscles from biology class years ago he could see coursing through what appeared to be an artery. He trained his vision on one of the corpuscles and now could see molecules that comprised the cell. As if he were on the old ride Adventure Through Innerspace at Disneyland, his field of vision was filled with the dance of molecules. Burning white light hurt his eyes as he shot them open.

"Michael? Midee?" Stephanie spoke his pet name softly. "You're awake."

Michael turned his head to the right and it felt heavy. He could barely turn it against what felt like a blanket of force resisting his movement. His mouth felt stuffed and dry and he realized he didn't have the energy to speak. With all the energy he could muster, he raised his right hand and pointed toward his mouth.

"Water?" Stephanie asked.

He slowly nodded once. There was no energy for more than a single nod. A plastic straw pushed at his lips and he parted them. As the cool water flushed his mouth and then cascaded down his parched throat, he thought he could taste blood. He kept drinking until Stephanie pulled the straw and what he now saw was a blue, plastic cup from his lips.

"You have to take everything slow right now. "

No worry about that, he thought. My whole body feels stiff, lifeless. His vision adjusted a bit more and he looked around.

"You're in the hospital, Midee. Providence. You were mugged in the school parking lot."

Whatever else she said, Michael missed it. He fell into another deep sleep.

Two weeks later, Michael had fully recovered from the attack and what he learned were slight fractures--depressed and linear--to the back and side of his skull. The side fracture resembled the tip of a boot. His three broken ribs ached but were beginning to mend, and he had an appointment with his dentist the following week to fix his broken teeth. Stephanie and a nurse helped him slide out of the bed and into a wheelchair. Along with his severance, his health insurance was extended for three months so this was all covered. That was a relief to him.

"How long will this scan take?" he asked.

"Just a few minutes, Mr. Dunphy. We just need to confirm the bleeding has subsided. You'll be released tomorrow or Friday if all looks good."

"Lucky me."

"Midee, you're sounding more like your smartass self."

Just as Michael slid into the wheelchair, his hospital gown parted so that his left buttock felt cold against the vinyl material. A high-pitched sound screeched in his ears. His head began to vibrate and as he looked at the nurse, he saw through her skin, past her vessels, and into her molecules. Worse, he looked past her and it seemed he could see slow molecules in the walls and even the wavy particles of sunlight. If Stephanie was afraid, he could not tell because she too was just an outline surrounding molecules of different sizes and densities.

"Midee?" was the last thing he heard before his vision went dark.

He woke up to find himself inside a CT scan tube. The whirring sounds as the x-rays passed around and through his head were almost peaceful. Whatever they were looking to find he couldn't recall, but he did remember being in this machine a couple previous times recently. He also recalled what he had just seen: molecules and particles of everything in the nurse, Stephanie, and the hospital room. One of his strange thoughts occurred to him as the CT scan hummed along: was I able to see the particles in everything? If so, wasn't then everything, living or inert, truly connected to everything else by virtue of the source: exploding stars, dead comets, gas, dark matter, gravity, and time? No intelligence behind it, just simply the infinite and unknowable power of the cosmos. He caught himself: who am I? Carl Sagan for Christ's sake? He really wished he had a notepad so that he could write down these thoughts. But those hallucinations were something bizarre and new, to say the least. He would find out soon what was causing them.

"Just about done, Mr. Dunphy," a female with an East Indian accent said from somewhere near his feet.

Moments later, the diminutive X-ray tech helped him into his wheelchair. Her thick, gorgeous raven hair brought his Stephanie to mind. He grabbed his hospital gown from below and held it tight as he realized he just shot the X-ray tech a moon.

"Sorry about that. I haven't been able to get my boyzilian done in awhile."

"I have seen it all, Mr. Dunphy. Nothing new under the sun. Or with your moon."

She chuckled and patted his shoulder.

"They called me 'Assquatch' in high school," Michael said with a shrug.

"Everything looks okay for now," she said. "Your scan, I mean. Dr. Berg will review and let you know officially, however."

"Is there a notepad or Post-Its around?" Michael asked.

The X-ray tech looked at him quizzically. She shrugged and looked around. As she opened a couple drawers in the lab, Michael grew anxious that he wouldn't remember the thoughts he wanted to capture.

"Oh, here we go," the X-ray tech said. She closed the drawer and handed him a pad and a black Bic stick pen. "Oops, forgot this."

She handed Michael a tarnished silver chain from which a dog-tagged shaped medal hung. Michael took it from her and slid it back over his head.

"I know Catholic patients sometimes wear Saint Christopher medals but I never saw a 'Mother Harriet' medal before."

"You can get one if you go to one of my mom's conferences. Blessed by her."

The X-ray tech shook her head in confusion.

"Mother Harriet is my mom. She gave me this medal for my eighteenth birthday."

"Very sweet," the X-ray tech said.

Michael shrugged and pulled the cap off the pen and began to write furiously: *All connected and one from the Big Bang forward. But no intelligence behind it. Great darkness, big explosions of lonely stars and us eventually. God bias and male patriarchal dominance as a result from time immemorial. Truth is there is no great truth to be had.* Satisfied, he tore off the page and handed the pen and pad back to the X-ray tech. The X-ray tech glanced at the sheet but Michael folded it quickly.

"Anniversary coming up soon or something like that you need to remember?" she asked.

"Something like that."

The next day, Dr. Berg stopped by Michael's hospital room. Stephanie sat in the gray vinyl visitor's seat. She poured Michael some water as he ate his meager hospital breakfast of scrambled eggs and bland oatmeal. Michael dropped his spoon and reached for the notepad and pen next to him on the side table. A stack of handwritten notes lay next to the notepad. He didn't notice the splash of oatmeal the spoon ejected onto his neck when it landed in the bowl. Stephanie smirked. She picked up Michael's napkin, moistened it with her saliva, and then dabbed away the oatmeal blotch as Michael wrote.

"More inspiration?" she asked.

"Yeah, yeah," he said scribbling quickly. He tore off the page and laid it on the stack of notes.

"When do I get to see this tome?" Stephanie asked.

Michael chuckled.

"Not for some time. Gotta get it together and written cohesively."

"Hi folks," Dr. Berg said.

He pulled over another visitor's chair. His smile revealed a crooked front tooth and dimples that seemed to arc back to his ears. He scratched the top of his head with its silver, tight curls.

"Well, aside from the couple of seizures, the bleeding has stopped and your healing is coming along. We should be able to release you by tomorrow or Friday morning as long as we have these seizures under control."

"That's good news," Stephanie said. She rubbed Michael's shoulder.

"No more molecules or light particles, huh? I kind of like seeing all that."

"Just visual hallucinations. You may start having odd dreams from time to time as well. The area of your brain that was affected is an old part of the brain and tends to be involved with dreams and beliefs. We're

45

mapping brain regions everyday and finding out more. And flashing lights and colors are very typical with brain injury seizures. "

"It's not just flashing lights, doctor. I'm seeing molecules. I think I'm seeing the elements in everything. And amazing new ideas about, well, existence."

"You must not believe in God," Dr. Berg said.

"How's that?" Michael asked.

"Do you tend toward science, agnosticism?"

"Oh yeah," Michael said. "Read all I can understand at least on cosmology."

"That's what I figured. If you had faith in God, the Bible, that sort of thing, you'd most likely be hallucinating visits with Jesus or helping Noah build his ark. Happens all the time with my patients who have faith."

"I think I get it," Michael.

"I don't," Stephanie said. "What the hell are you guys talking about?"

"Your husband here is having hallucinations based on his belief bias. What he already believes, he sees. We're finding more and more how the brain does this so in that way, your husband's cerebral injuries are adding to our understanding."

"Neuroscience!" Michael rubbed the side of his jaw.

"Mouth pain?" Dr Berg asked. Michael clenched his lips shut and nodded.

"Your pain meds should be helping with that, too. You want me to amp up the dose?"

"No, it's already easing up, doctor," Michael said.

"You ought to get yourself to your dentist as soon as we release you. Shattered molars are not just painful but infectious."

"Week after next as long as he's out of here," Stephanie said.

"He will be," Dr. Berg said. He reached into his lab coat and handed Stephanie a prescription form.

"I do have another prescription here, though. This is for Tegretol. It's going to prevent the seizures."

Stephanie flipped the prescription over and back again. Her brow wrinkled.

"How long does he have to be on this, doctor?"

"We need to get his brain and skull fully healed. No more than two to six months. Any questions for me?"

"What if I don't take it?"

Dr. Berg shook his head and stood. He placed his hand on Michael's shoulder.

"Seizures are not something you want to toy with. We need to get you to the point where the threat has completely subsided. Take the meds and check in with my office for a follow-up in two weeks."

Dr. Berg nodded toward Stephanie.

"And good luck with the teeth."

He turned and walked out. Stephanie reached for Michael's water cup and began to pour. Michael thought about the molecules again.

"I guess seeing the molecules is just a symptom," he said.

"Yup. Sorry you're disappointed," she said.

"But wouldn't it be cool if somehow my brain is now able to do something bizarre as a result of the injuries?"

"Michael, you heard Dr. Berg. You're not suddenly X-Ray man. Eat your eggs."

"I'm just saying that maybe I can now see things the way they are, the way they *really* are, the actual elements. Like a modern seer, a reality profit."

"You can't mess around with the seizures. You're not a 'seer'. You're starting to sound like—"

"Well there's my boy!" a throaty woman's voice said. Stephanie reacted with a start as Michael's mother walked through the door. She gestured with a wave of her long-sleeved, white blouse with its diaphanous silk cascade toward two other plain-dressed and doughty women. Mrs. Harriet Flynn Dunphy didn't step toward the side of her son's bed but seemed to float like an

47

angel in a wind tunnel. Her silver hair was piled like a candle flame atop her head and it was dotted with small daisies. She stepped around Stephanie and picked up Michael's hand.

"Hail Mary, full of grace, the Lord is with thee..." she prayed. The two ladies prayed along with Mrs. Dunphy.

Michael pulled his hand away.

"Hi, Mother. Good to see you, too."

He rubbed his jaw.

"What's wrong?" Mrs. Dunphy asked.

"A few of his back teeth were broken in the attack," Stephanie said. "Causing some pain. They'll be fixed next week."

"My poor boy" Mrs. Dunphy said. She reached into her white, soft leather purse and pulled out her rosary. She raised the rosary to her thin lips and kissed it. The skin around her seventy-four-year-old mouth was still taut with minimal lines. Except for the crow's feet around her squinting olive-green eyes, her porcelain skin drew smooth across her high cheek bones.

"I hope this doesn't mean you have lost your faith in the Blessed Virgin, Michael."

"I'm not particularly concerned about her. You remember Stephanie, my wife and mother of your grandkids, Mother?"

"Nice to know you still have your wit about you. Hello, Stephanie darling."

"Hello, Harriet. Can I take your purse and set it over on the other chair? It's probably a good idea to avoid germs and all. "

Harriet jerked the purse toward her bosom and shook her head. Stephanie noticed Mrs. Dunphy's initials in gold and fine script near the clasp of the Hilde Palladino white alligator bag: 'H.F.D.' Harriet reached up and gently touched Stephanie's hair and face. Her bare nails were manicured short but ending in sharp points extending from her thick fingers.

"You are so lovely, darling. I can see worry has creased your brow a bit of late, though. The children are all well I hope?"

Stephanie smiled and nodded, her mouth tight with restraint. Her mother-in-law had not contacted the family since she took off to heal children in Africa, claiming to be the only living person in direct contact with the Virgin Mary. While she may have helped some starving children over the years, she had neglected her own grandchildren. Not to mention Michael's teen years spent with her as she withdrew into her veneration of the Virgin Mary after the divorce. There was a lot Stephanie wanted to say but she bit her lip. She took the visitor chair in the corner of the room, behind Harriet.

"How did you find out I was in the hospital?" Michael asked.

Harriet turned back toward Michael. The ladies that accompanied her stepped outside the door. She pulled over one of the visitor chairs and sat.

"I called the school to let you know I would be in town for an interview on 'The Talk' about the Blessed Mothers work we're doing in India. You know, Sharon Osbourne was Catholic."

"India?" Stephanie said. "I thought you were in Africa."

"Oh, we finished that mission last year. We have been working in the slums of Bombay, bringing the vision and word of the Virgin to those polytheistic heathens starving in the streets."

"How charitable, Mother," Michael retorted.

"While you have been educating the masses of sinners here in Los Angeles, the Blessed Mothers have raised millions to save children. Is that so much to scoff at?"

"Yes, because you do so suggesting that you are in sole contact with the Virgin Mary. I *know* you can't posssibly believe that."

"You can't possibly know the depth of my veneration or what lies in my heart. The Truth I have come to know will be revealed soon."

Harriet smiled oddly then patted Michel's hand. Her eyes stared in that way Michael had come to accept: the outside world shut off from the delusional confidence of her zealot mind. It was fueled by her faith in some great truth she was convinced she possessed but for which the world was not ready. He had grown up and become inured to the unblinking stare he had known since she first told him she loved God and the Virgin Mary more than him. The old pang of missing his mother made him shudder.

"So anyway, I'm on the mend. Ribs are healing, seizures under control. In case you were curious. Jesus, thanks for asking."

Harriet reached up and pinched his cheek. Stephanie reacted with a start.

"Ouch," Michael said.

"Don't use the Lord's name in vain. I *am* your mother and I *never* stop caring about you. I gave you life. And when you were old enough, got out of the way and let you live it. "

Twenty-dollar bills left on a counter and peeled-back foil covers of TV dinners flashed into Michael's mind. Ditching his confirmation catechism to smoke and drink beer with his best friend, Dave Patchett, caused the previous memory to fade. It was Michael's turn to keep tight-lipped but oh how he wanted to slam his mother and her insidious, dubious faith.

"Yes, and Wendy, Marie, and the Colonel all saw that I ate properly. I don't think you cooked me a meal once after I turned thirteen. You were too busy chasing after the Virgin Mary. Appearances in trees, on walls, and on pieces of toast a couple times."

"I made the world aware of Her presence."

"And yourself famous and I suppose rich, too."

Stephanie mimicked holding a purse and pointed toward it. She nodded, making a '$' symbol in the air. Harriet followed Michael's gaze and turned around. Stephanie dropped her hands and straightened her blouse, smiling.

"And let's not forget about Father Fingers who you thought would be the best person in the world to stay with me on your first trip to Mexico for one of your 'sightings'—completely trustworthy."

"How can I forget that you broke his hand when you slammed your bedroom door and leaned on it, I believe?"

"Funny that even now, you think about his hand as opposed to how afraid I was of him. And you never even asked if he had ever gotten to me after the news busted him."

Harriet turned her face away and crossed herself.

"Don't worry—he never even got close. By the way, speaking about other people you drove away with your obsession, Dad died last year."

"Mike, you need to rest. This isn't the time for all that," Stephanie said.

Harriet's mouth grimaced and she stood up. She stepped over to the window and looked up toward the sky. She nodded.

"Your father was a grave sinner," she said over her shoulder. "He left his marriage bed to commit the sins of lust and adultery, while breaking the laws of Leviticus our Lord confirmed were righteous. Again, you have no idea the depth of my heart and pain after our marriage ended. I am grateful every day to the Virgin Mary who lifted me up from that ruined life."

"She took you away from me and ruined my life, too," Michael said through clenched teeth. Stephanie reached out and grabbed his hand. Harriet turned away from the window and the sunlight created a halo around her. She regarded Michael for a moment.

"You know, this sunlight makes you look even more like your father now than you did as a child. So handsome really, both of you. But as your dear Stephanie said, it isn't time for all that. I'll be in town for Easter. Maybe we could enjoy a brunch."

51

"Easter, really Mother?"

"Rest and get better, son. I will pray for you."

Harriet turned and walked out the door.

"Now! *And* at the hour of my death!" he hollered.

Stephanie put her hands on both of his shoulders and pushed him gently back against his pillow. She kissed his forehead. After she made sure Harriet had left the floor, Stephanie spoke. She noticed his sad and pensive expression.

"It sucks she still gets to you so much."

"It's not her—please. Just thinking about Dad."

Stephanie took his hand. She stroked his knuckles with her thumb.

"Oh, Midee. I miss him, too. He was just so funny and smart. And damn how tender and good was that chicken piccata. Speaking of which. You okay if I hop downstairs for a sandwich? That cold oatmeal is starting to look good."

"Yeah, of course."

"And you're for sure okay?"

Michael nodded. Stephanie kissed him and left the room.

"Dad," he said softly. "Dad, Dad, Dad…"

Michael fought the image of his dying father's hollow face and let his mind wander much farther back. The fall sun cast long shadows that Sunday as he walked out from the doors of the UCLA Catholic Center after mass. He had been attending mass again during his first semester at the university. It had been more than six years since he last bothered with church and he didn't really know what compelled him to start again. But he did feel some sort of comfort, though dubious, that a father in the sky might be looking out for him after all. The actual mass, prayers, the priest's sermon, none of it really moved him one way or another. The crucifix with the tortured body of Christ creeped him out as it did when he was a kid. Still, there was something peaceful and warm he felt sitting in the chapel on Sundays.

When he got back to his dormitory room some minutes later, he noticed the red message alert light blinking on the Panasonic answering machine. His dorm mate was home for the weekend and he figured the message was probably for him since so far, he had not given his number out to any new friends he had made. He paused and rubbed the back of his neck, then decided to go ahead and retrieve the message.

"Michael, it's Dad. Your mom was nice enough to pass me your number. It's been a long time and I wanted to see if we can get together—"

Michael stopped the playback. His heart pounded and his throat began to tighten. He hadn't seen his father since the divorce. An odd sweat began to break out on his temples and neck. He restarted the message and jotted down his father's number.

"So mom wouldn't let you see me?" Michael asked. He and his father, Taylor, sat in a corner of the Sproul dining hall later that night. The dining hall was only half full thanks to weekend student commuters who had yet to return.

"It was part of the divorce decree. My sexual orientation and lifestyle were not viewed by the court as a suitable environment for a teenage boy. "

"I wouldn't have cared. You're my dad."

Taylor dabbed spaghetti sauce from the corner of his mouth with a paper napkin. He took a sip of Diet Coke.

"It was more than that, though, Mikey. Do you remember before all the shit hit the fan that when I wasn't working, I was drinking? I didn't have interest or time for your mom, but not you, either."

Michael swallowed a bite of spaghetti quickly. He slurped some Diet Coke but he could barely speak.

"I remember all that. I just wanted you to play catch with me or maybe sometimes go to the park."

Taylor grabbed his son's hands and squeezed them. Tears formed in his eyes.

"I can't just say I'm sorry and make all that better, Mikey. I can tell you that I stopped drinking years ago, and I would love the chance to make up for all that lost time. I am sorry, so very, very sorry."

Taylor released Michael's hands and wiped away the tears from his face. Michael stood up, starting to feel weepy himself, and felt his body almost go limp. He stepped around the table and threw his arms around his father.

"It's okay, Dad. It's all okay now."

After a minute, Michael released the embrace and kissed his father's cheek. He stepped back to his seat and noticed a couple of students staring from across the room. Taylor snorted and wiped his eyes. He cleared his throat.

"Just one more thing," Taylor said.

"Yes, Dad. I'd be happy to meet your boyfriend."

"Okay. But that's not it."

"What, Dad?"

"Don't expect to play catch. But I will take you to some good shows at the Mark Taper and Music Center."

Tears flowed down Michael's face as the memory faded and the brash light of the hospital returned. He recalled how he and his father rebuilt their relationship from that point forward. He also remembered the moment not long after he realized that it was his own father who he yearned for in all those Sunday masses, and having him back in his life made church irrelevant to him. That was also his first step away from faith.

"Egg salad," Stephanie said as she walked back into the room. She held it toward Michael. "Not bad for cafeteria crap. Wanna bite?"

3.

As Harriet drove away from the hospital, her son healing from the attack that could have killed him, she felt the pang of her maternal love umbilicus stretch tight once again. It had never broken in all the years and even if Michael had grown to be a serial killer, she knew nothing could severe it. So though she prayed to the Virgin once again to bring the light of the Lord's love to her atheist son, even his blasphemous and arrogant beliefs were no match for her own love. But the psychological acid that spewed from him seemed just as eternal. She knew she stirred up sad memories for him, but any time she saw or spoke to him, she suffered her own painful walk down memory lane.

'Who do you love more, Mom? He asked her on his sixteenth birthday. 'Me or God?'
She remembered the shock the question brought to her. She also recalled that whatever her answer was going to be, he would just roll his eyes and head out the door with his friends. The same as he had his last three birthdays since the divorce. How she missed the days when Michael would insist on them watching "The Brady Bunch" right after the divorce. She got the point that Michael missed their family but didn't know how to break it to him that there was little chance she would find a Mr. Brady with kids and

remarry. Since he asked, she figured he was ready for the truth.

'No one before the Lord or the Virgin. That is commanded of all of us.'

Michael's mouth, surrounded by a dark peach fuzz moustache and dotted by a few red pimples, tightened for a moment like it did as a child just before he would cry. Instead, he let out a wisp of a sigh and shook his head.

'Don't wait up,' he said. 'Going to see "Saturday Night Fever" and I might crash at Dave's.'

He ran a hand though his air-blown, chestnut hair, as thick and shiny as his father's. She had the impulse to fix the crooked part Michael had just mussed. But she stood still.

'Don't stay up too late. We're heading out to the gun range for your birthday tomorrow.'

The door had slammed before he heard that. The gun range was the only thing they still shared it seemed. And she had bought a gun and trained to use it only because she felt vulnerable as a single mother living in the duplex near Western and Third Streets. Michael had really wanted her to buy an antique Smith and Wesson, maybe two, along with a holster. She sighed and glanced back at the light blue princess phone and the rumpled loose leaf list of donors. Even those dozens of strangers who supported her charity and believed in her visions of the Virgin would most likely answer their own children the same way. The work of the Virgin on behalf of all mankind eclipsed any one mother's love for one child. She believed in her visions and in her calling; no one and no force on earth could stop her from acting on her faith. The Virgin guided her every decision and she prayed about every problem of any magnitude. The truth of any problem was always revealed to her.

Beyond her faith, she also knew that her son held her at fault for the divorce. He had no idea how much his dad was her knight and prince, long before her first vision and mission foundation work. Her first

56

and only love in high school and after. And before the moment that ended it all.

Taylor Dunphy had been in recovery for his martini habit for a month. When his nightly habit began to include lunches and afternoon martini breaks and started causing him to miss work at his design firm, they both recognized he was in trouble. She didn't know what was troubling him. He came from a strong family with average challenges but no tragedy. She wondered if the stereotypical Irish drunk gene might somehow really mean something. He didn't even express any concern with her growing devotion to the Virgin—everyone needed a hobby he said to her some time back. Her prayers to the Virgin led her to suggest that he try a recovery program at the church. Things had been going well for the last month. His new friend from the recovery program, Jerry, a handsome blonde older man in his early forties with light crow's feet around sparkling blue eyes, had spent a lot of time at the house, sometimes even showing up with Taylor's sponsor on really bad days. Both Taylor and she felt supported during this hard time. She leaned against Jerry's broad shoulders in more than a couple moments of despair and admittedly, a little guilty pleasure.

To celebrate the one-month sober anniversary, Harriet had picked up a box of Betty Crocker cherry chip cake mix and a box of cherry frosting mix on her way home from her job as the St. Athanasius rectory housekeeper. Father Cooke had taken her under spiritual guidance when her visions of the Virgin had begun a couple years before. She had gone to seek his help recently to cope with Taylor's alcoholism and though she could not mention it, the end of their sex life as well. She wondered if his month of sobriety might bring her knight back to their bed for more than just sleep. She missed his touch and blamed herself a little bit for the thicker hips she had been unable to lose since her thirty-fifth birthday. As she drove her red Pinto wagon home in the dimming afternoon light, she switched on the headlights and dashboard lights. She turned up the radio when Kiki Dee and Elton John began to sing.

Don't go breaking my heart…I couldn't if I tried…

Harriet asked the Virgin if the song she liked so much was now an omen. She got her answer as her heart welled with hope in her husband and marriage. She began to sing along and loudly.

When she pulled into the driveway under the carport that swelled with wisteria blossoms, she noticed Jerry's rust-orange Camaro parked at the curb. The exotic and tropical rich jasmine scent of the wisteria filled her nose as her heart fell to her ankles: Taylor must have been in crisis. Disappointment stirred up as well—he couldn't make it a month without the gin? She threw open the door of the Pinto and ran toward the kitchen door, leaving the grocery bag with the cake mix behind. She dreaded the slurring words and the nonsensical laughter that was inevitably about to occur. As her low heels clomped against the linoleum kitchen flooring, she heard a groan and something like a gasp.

'Taylor!' she screamed running down the hall to her bedroom.

When she reached the open door, a sudden flash of gold and brown sheets, male buttocks, and flailing arms whirled around her in a crazy nude tornado. When it subsided, Taylor stood nude with only a pillow blocking his genital area. Her breath left her body as she saw Jerry's bare chest though a robe of crumpled bed sheets. He stood off to the side, looking down toward the floor. She turned away, her heart pounding.

'I'm just going to go bake a cake,' was all she could manage.

She reached the kitchen and clutched the dimpled white counter tiles. Panic arose.

'Wheeerrreee's Miiichaeelllll?' she screamed back down the hall.

' "Jaws" ' came Taylor's choked replied. 'At the walk-in seeing "Jaws." '

Harriet gathered herself and went back out to the car. She sat staring until she heard the engine of Jerry's Camaro as he drove away. A strange sense of numbness settled over her and for the first time, she found herself unable to pray to the Virgin. She was too ashamed to invoke her help: how could she have failed Taylor so much? How could her knight have fallen to this? Sleepless nights over endless weeks began that day. She would send Michael to the movies any chance she could as she pored over legal documents while having telephone conversations with an attorney. None of it made sense and all of it did as her life fell apart, more like exploded.

The day she walked out of the Hall of Justice in downtown Los Angeles, just after the judge signed off on the divorce papers, the February sunshine made the skyline sparkle. A rare blue sky above seemed to remind her of the Virgin's veil. Assured of a moderate income for her and Michael, she realized that she could continue her work for the Virgin and moving forward, would dedicate her life's purpose to that end.

"A suicide bomber took thirty-eight lives, including seven children, outside a grammar school in Tikrit today." The radio news report on KFWB brought Harriet out of her reverie. The traffic on the 134 continued at a crawl as Harriet drove away from Michael and Providence Hospital in Burbank toward her home in the south Santa Monica bay town of Rolling Hills. She prayed to the Virgin for the thirty-eight people who died in the bombing, again as she had numerous times recently. She also asked the Virgin to consider appearing to some of the jihadists and perhaps convert them from their sinful Islam and away from violence. She didn't approve but she did understand the jihadists' motives: serving God with any method made sense to her, and if lives were lost as they had been over the course of history in honor of God, then so be it. But she asked the Virgin again to perhaps end the violence by

bringing the terrorists toward the Virgin and the Lord. Violence might just end, she thought.

The traffic opened up and the drive down to her gated home in Rolling Hills took less than an hour, which was quite fast for Los Angeles traffic. Harriet retrieved dozens of pieces of mail from an over-sized black mail box that shared a stone column with an electric gate control pad. She punched in the security code and the black wrought iron gates swung open. She admired the Sterling and Simplicity tea roses that burst with lavender tones as she drove the circular driveway past her front lawn and sprawling mid-century ranch house with its low-eaves and diamond-shaped window mullions. Two mourning doves startled her as they burst into flight from the outstretched arms of a three-quarter scale lawn statue of the Virgin Mary. She slowed and eased the car into the carport next to the garage.

Moments later, Harriet stepped into the side door of the house, pausing to unset the alarm. She entered a dark hallway that led off to the right, toward the living room. The bright afternoon light did not make it past the heavy, sapphire blue velvet drapes of the living room. When Harriet switched on two wall sconces that surrounded a red brick fireplace, they cast a yellow glow that seemed to be swallowed by the burnt chocolate brown of the walls. Harriet removed her diaphanous white coat, which flowed like a long robe, and placed it gently across the back of a black leather tufted sofa. She picked up a small remote control and clicked it several times. Dozens of battery-operated tea lights sparked to life in blue glass jars, forming a trapezoid-shaped table of lights that cast their glow on a porcelain statue of the Virgin Mary and Christ as a baby that sat on a pedestal above. The tea lights and statue dominated a large corner of the room. Framed paintings, cameos, mosaics, and numerous other representations of the Virgin Mary hung on the two walls behind the over-sized statue.

Harriet crossed herself then lowered herself onto a kneeler, its ornate dark wood supporting an upper arm rest and lower knee rest, both also covered in sapphire blue velvet. Harriet considered the subtle flickers of the tea lights as they made the statue's eyes almost sparkle with life. She folded her hands.

"Blessed Mother, I ask for your guidance. How shall I heal my son of his pain and sinful ways?"

Harriet closed her eyes. She began to breathe deeply and rapidly.

"Please enter my heart and give me the guidance I seek."

Her breaths grew more rapid. Her face began to contort and her teeth gritted together.

"Daughter of the Truth," Harriet said, but now her voice was an octave lower as if she were in a trance.

"Your son must come unto me of his own accord. Of that step forward, will come his reward…No love of a mother for a child may come before, that Truth and Light in which you and all are adored…"

Harriet's hands crossed so tightly that her nails dug into the backs of her hand. She trembled and her rapid breaths turned into a moan. Her eyes shot open.

"Hail Mary, full of grace, the Lord is with thee…" she began to pray. Tears flowed down her cheeks and dropped silently into the white folds of her gown, each reflecting a slight yellow highlight from the tea lights.

4.

"I almost forgot," Stephanie said the next day.

"My Archaeology issue—woot!"

"I don't know how far you'll get since you're going to be released tomorrow, but at least you can enjoy it till then."

He glanced at the cover and pointed eagerly.

"This is the article about the translation of the Maya codex found at Chichen Itza last year—I can't wait."

Stephanie raised her eyebrows and nodded. She clearly had no interest. But she was encouraged to see him feeling good enough to be interested in his favorite hobby next to baseball. Michael flipped open the magazine and pointed toward the side table.

"Would you toss me my close-ups?"

Stephanie reached over and picked up the wire-rimmed reading glasses. She opened them and slipped them over his ears. He mouthed a kiss and smiled.

"I'm going down to the cafeteria for some coffee and fresh air. Do you want me to bring you back something?" she asked.

Michael shook his head slowly, already absorbed in an article. As Stephanie stepped toward the door, her phone text tone beeped. She read it.

"Looks like Marissa aced her medieval history midterm!"

"Marzi-Marzi-Marzi! Tell her I'm proud of her," he said, not looking up from his magazine. Stephanie's thumbs danced across the phone keypad. Her text tone beeped again.

"She sent a kiss emoji, tell Daddy I love him. The Dan Jones Plantagenet book really helped. She'll call you later."

"That's my Berkeley whiz kid."

"Forgot. The boys were by Sunday and they mowed and raked. The yard looks great."

Michael looked up over the edge of the magazine. The dark bruises around his eyes had faded to vague shadows.

"Antoine helped? Really?" he asked.

"I was as surprised as you."

"You forgive them, then, for not coming by to see me?" he asked. "I wouldn't get anywhere near a hospital either if I could help it."

"That they finally showed up to help at all took them off my shit list. Sons are weird."

"Yeah—I was one, once."

Stephanie read another text from Marissa and her eyebrows knitted. She glanced at Michael as he read the magazine. She slipped her phone into her jean pocket and stepped back over and kissed Michael's forehead. He feigned a kiss as he read. She shook her head.

"I'll be back," she said as she walked out.

What Stephanie hadn't told Michael is that their daughter, Marissa, had just suffered a panic attack in the middle of her anthropology class and was texting from the student medical clinic. Marissa was like her dad in this way: always so concerned about other people's feelings, but especially, about what she thought they felt about her. Stephanie had tried on more than one occasion to help her daughter understand, like Michael, that not only could they not read other people's minds, but also that they were wasting a lot of their own energy and mental health trying to do so. Marissa had texted that she had 'freaked out' because she couldn't stop thinking about Dad and wanted to fly home immediately.

Stephanie stepped outside on to the tiny hospital cafeteria patio and saw she had a decent cell signal. She dialed Marissa.

"Mom, Mom, why isn't he out of the hospital yet?" Marissa said each word with a rapid breath.

"Hello to you, too Marzipan. Now just stop a second and take a deep breath."

Stephanie could hear her daughter's inhalation and exhalation. "One more," Stephanie said. "And one more."

"Okay, okay, but I'm so scared, Mom. I couldn't think anymore and all of a sudden, I felt my throat close up and the lecture hall closing in on me. I had to run out."

"Take another breath and listen. Dad is doing just fine."

"But didn't you say that they think the shooter he stopped and the people who attacked him might be all a part of 'New Order 2.0'?" Her breaths increased once again.

"Marzipan, everything is just theory right now. But no one thinks anybody is out to get your dad. Breathe again, sweetheart."

Marissa took three deep breaths.

"You're right, Mom. The whole 'New Order 2.0' thing is just another crackpot Facebook group. Like all the others out there, they scream revolution but don't have anything to replace democracy. They don't even know democracy has been the best result of all revolutions."

"See. There's my little political scientist."

"And you're sure dad is okay? Do you need me to come home?"

64

"No. We have this managed. Let's just stick with the plans and we'll see you for the barbecue in a couple weeks."

"Just hearing your voice makes me feel better, Mom. I don't know why I let it all freak me out."

"It happens. Believe me. Where are you now?"

"Just outside the campus clinic."

"Did you get to see a doctor yet?"

"Yep. Just did."

"What did he tell you?"

"*She*, Mom."

"Okay. One ding on my feminist card."

"Anxiety. Panic. She'll give me Lexapro if I want it. Cognitive Therapy referral. Blah blah blah."

"Sounds reasonable. What do you want to do?"

"Screw the meds. No way. And it's not like I have panic attacks all the time."

"But you have had few since your teens, Marzipan. It might be time to start thinking about meds or even cognitive therapy."

"No meds and no time for therapy right now, Mom. This whole thing with Dad just weirded me out."

"So you're okay, then?"

Marissa began to answer, but her throat caught. She tried to stifle tears.

"I'm just so worried about Daddy."

"Are you worried about me, too?"

Marissa snorted.

"Oh, Jesus no. You're titanium or some shit."

"So you're okay right now?"

"Yup. Feeling better. I'm going to be more like you from now on."

Stephanie chuckled with relief.

"I probably should get back up stairs to Dad."

"Yep. Talk to you in a couple days. And SEE you in couple weeks!"

"I love you, Marzipan."

"By the way, I might be bringing someone. Okay gotta go!"

"What?" Stephanie said into the dead phone. But she knew Marissa liked to stir things up and leave her hanging with questions. She wouldn't indulge her own curiosity but would take the high-mother-road on that one. The little shit, she thought.

Stephanie also went the high mother road with not letting Marissa know just how worried she was about Michael's 'visions'. The doctor had explained them satisfactorily, but Michael seemed to continue to take them seriously, imbue them with some sort of cosmic meaning. That's where her worry came in: was this brain injury a sign of some sort of delusional mental illness starting? Was he showing signs of an embryonic charismatic nut job? His own mother was dubiously stable but Stephanie had never seen Michael show any worrisome mental traits.

Aside from what some might label a tendency to think, over-think, recursively as being OCD, a mental trait she had seen and admired early in their college days, Michael had never exhibited any inability to accept and live in reality. Many a night she had listened to him 'why' an idea into abstract absurdity, but an idea and reality are two different things he always could distinguish quite efficiently. They had both come to agree in many conversations over their years together that thought experiments or metaphysical 'what lies beneath' questions still had to yield to the facts on the ground. The 'how' of things. And that meant they could let their minds imagine, expand, fly, even, but that their skulls and brains were still vulnerable to crashing back onto concrete.

She paused her rumination and dropped a few coins into the coffee machine. The popping of the paper cup and the foamy whirring of the machine's stream distracted her for a moment. Her nostrils were abused with weak, instant coffee aroma.

So if he believed he was really seeing molecules and particles, the 'reality below reality,' how would their lives proceed? The question puzzled and worried her. It certainly wasn't a question for her daughter with her mild anxiety disorder (weren't OCD and anxiety linked?). She sighed. She grabbed the paper cup that teased her fingertips with heat until she unfolded the paper handle. She walked toward the elevator.

Michael finished the article a few minutes later. A subscription card dropped from the back pages of the magazine. He sighed with annoyance. He flipped to the back of the magazine to see if there were any other subscription cards. His eyes landed on the advertising pages, but most specifically, the research digs. The banner ad explained that one could take a vacation by joining a research dig as a volunteer and one only had to pay for roundtrip transportation.

"Hmmm," he said to himself.

He slid his finger down past digs in South America and South Africa. And then he paused. The ad for the dig read: *Join Monsignor Daniel Leahy of Georgetown University in Limerick, Ireland for the month of May. The dig will focus on recovering relics of the Siege of 1651 and attempt to locate the remains of Blessed Terrence Flynn and others near the ruins of the Dominican Priory. Volunteers still needed. Please contact Nancy Fitzgerald at Georgetown University, 202-687-0100.*

Michael recalled from the family tree research his uncle had given him, along with his Rock of Cashel miniature, that Terrence Flynn, his great uncle nine times back, had been the Bishop of Emly before he was executed in 1651. That had grabbed his attention more than any trace of supposed royal blood, the main purpose of his uncle's search of their ancestry. And now it appeared the Catholic Church wanted to locate the bishop's remains. Michael's heart pounded with excitement. It wasn't discovering the Ark of the Covenant or the Holy Grail like Indiana Jones, but with the link to his family line, it was pretty compelling.

Stephanie walked back in sipping her coffee and noticed Michael smiling broadly. She set down the cup

"I haven't seen you smile like that in a month. What's going on?"

Michael held the opened Archaeology magazine toward her. She shook her head.

"What?"

Michael pointed. She removed his close-ups and held them up to her eyes and read.

"An archaeological dig?

"Do you remember before the attack we talked about a vacation?"

"Yes. But we have some big medical bills to deal with. I can't take time off—"

"I got severance till the end of June and we have savings. No one's going to be hiring education administration personnel till the end of summer so it's not like I'd be missing job opportunities. Plus you can work remotely."

"But an archaeological dig? It's not exactly sipping a mai tai on St. Maarten."

"Not just any dig. The guy they're looking for is a dead ancestor. At least as far as Uncle Patrick's family chart is concerned. This is a big chance for me. I may never be able to do this again."

"Okay, but three things."

"Name them."

"We upgrade the accommodations if they're tents or something like that. And I have to have Wi-Fi to work."

"Done and done."

"And we give it only a few weeks. A month at most."

"Agreed."

Michael leaned forward and pulled Stephanie toward him. He winced.

"Careful, Mike. Your ribs."

"I have a lot of sore bones."

Stephanie kissed his face and shook her head. She sat up and placed the close-up glasses back over his ears.

"There's plenty of time for that after you're released," she said.

Michael leaned back and folded his hands behind his head. He smiled.

"This is going to be the adventure of my life."

"Digging up a dead ancestor? At least it's not skydiving or something like that."

"So I like quiet adventures."

"I hope they know how to make Mai Tais in Limerick."

"Just wait till she gets her baby teeth," Stephanie said. Her daughter-in-law, Camryn, laughed and stroked her three-month baby bump with her elegant smooth, brown-sugar-colored hands.

"I know. Mom said I was a terror when I was teething, too," Camryn replied.

"I gotta call your mom and put together the shower soon. Or should I say your sister. God, she's so gorgeous."

Stephanie picked up the pitcher of iced tea and went to pour some into Camryn's glass. Camryn waved her hand and shook her head.

"No caffeine—it's chamomile. Safe for my grandbaby."

Camryn pulled her hand away and smiled.

"Then pour away, girl," she said.

"Ouch!" Michael hollered as a baseball popped loudly into his baseball glove. He and his oldest son, Phillip, played catch in the yard off the patio where Stephanie and Camryn sat with plastic tumblers of tea.

"Sorry, Dad!"

Michael gestured it was okay. He tossed the baseball back to Phillip.

"Take it easy on your dad, Phillip," Stephanie said. He's only been home for three days.

"It's okay, Steph," Michael said.

"Is Antoine going to drag his lazy ass out to see us today?" Phillip hollered.

"No, your brother is in a pre-production meeting for some sort of project," Stephanie said. "But your sister will be here with her new beau."

69

"See, that's what I'm talking about," Phillip said. "Marissa driving down from Berkeley. There's nothing lazy about that girl."

The loud pop of the baseball hitting his glove startled Phillip.

"Jeez, Dad! Getting even?"

Michael broke out in a wide grin and nodded.

"Come get some iced tea, guys," Camryn said. "Phillip, why don't you get the barbecue warmed up, too? Those ribeyes we brought aren't going to grill themselves."

He looked at his dad and shrugged. His eyes were his mother's color of hazel and almond-shaped, too, and made Michael smile. The only thing Michael had given him it seemed was his thinning, wavy hair.

"Honey-do, honey-do," he said under his breath.

"Just wait till the baby gets here. Ribeye?" Michael said. "Big spender."

Michael slapped Phillip's back lightly then reached up and clutched his son's shoulder. They joined the ladies at the glass patio table under a turquoise umbrella. Ice cubes clinked into glasses as Stephanie poured the tea.

"Seriously, though, Dad," Phillip said as Michael slowly slid into a patio chair. "You are going to join my softball team this year, right? Could use a great third baseman."

"Just give your dad a little time," Stephanie said. "I'm sure he will."

"Steaks?" Camryn said.

"All right, all right," Phillip said. Everyone else chuckled.

Phillip opened the lid of the barbecue. The ticking of the igniter gave way to the 'swoosh' of the gas jets igniting. He closed the lid daintily, turned toward Camryn and feigned brushing dirt off his hands. He reached up and scratched the top of his thinning, sandy hair.

"That didn't look so hard," Camryn said.

70

"Well lookee who's here!" Phillip hollered. He pointed toward the side metal gate as it clanked open.

Marissa bound through the gate like a blonde gazelle. Following behind was a young man of olive complexion, just barely her height if at all. He looked down toward the ground, making his jet-black, close-cropped beard appear to join the shadow he cast.

"My girl!" Stephanie hollered, jumping up and causing her chair to make a metal screech against the stone patio. Michael turned and stood too quickly, knocking his tumbler of tea and ice cubes onto the table. He looked at Camryn in despair, gesturing at the mess.

"I got this. Go see your girl," she said.

"That's why you're my favorite daughter-in-law!"

"It's easy when I'm the only one."

Marissa practically leapt into her mother's embrace. Stephanie kissed her cheek repeatedly and pulled her close. Michael stepped up to join them.

"Marzi-Marzi-Marzi!" he said.

"Daddy-Daddy-Daddy!" she replied.

Marissa pulled him into the embrace and he kissed her opposite cheek. Marissa pulled back.

"Daddy, you're a little wet?" Marissa said.

"The iced tea and I just got into a fight and it won."

"As usual," Marissa said.

Marissa hugged her parents once more. Stephanie paused and looked over Marissa's shoulder.

"This must be—"

"Adeel. Adeel Bukhari," Marissa said. She pulled away from her parents' embrace as she ran a hand through her thick corn silk hair. She straightened her pastel sundress with its faded sunflower print.

Adeel raised his chin and Stephanie was struck by the beauty of his round, almost black eyes. He looked like a twenty-something Omar Sharif. She held her hand out to him.

"Welcome, A-deel. Is that correct?"

71

He smiled and grew impossibly more handsome, revealing sparkling white teeth.

"Yes, Mrs. Dunphy."

"I certainly can tell what my daughter sees in your looks."

Adeel looked down sheepishly.

"Nice to meet you," Michael said. Adeel took Michael's hand and shook it strongly.

"Please call me Stephanie and this is Michael. Makes us feel less old if you use our first names."

"Oh, Mom!" Marissa laughed.

Stephanie stepped between Marissa and Adeel, put her arms over both their shoulders and walked them toward the table. Phillip stepped over from the barbecue and they paused. He nodded and offered his hand to Adeel.

"Phillip Murphy. Glad to see someone will take this blonde wart off our hands."

"Blow me, Phillip," Marissa said.

Adeel laughed.

"I thought you only talked like that around me," he said.

"That's my girl," Stephanie said. "Taught her to take no crap from anybody."

They all laughed but Adeel dropped his head again as they approached the table to join Michael and Camryn. Marissa noticed his posture.

"Adeel, no need to feel shy. That's my sister-in-law with dad."

Adeel looked up and his eyes brightened when he saw that Camryn was African American. He smiled and nodded.

"Hi, I'm Camryn. Phillip's wife."

"Hello, I'm Adeel."

Marissa stepped up to the chair next to Adeel. He pulled it out for her. Stephanie, who was now sliding into her chair, exchanged glances with Camryn. They both nodded.

"I miss that," Camryn said.

"It's not the manners I learned at home," Adeel said. "If I were at my family home, the guys and I would be sitting at a separate table. It's an orthodox Muslim thing."

"A Muslim!" Stephanie said smiling. "Well, we're an integrated and diverse family. We're atheists, Camryn is Baptist, obviously African American, our screenwriter son, Antoine, is gay. You're welcome at our table as a Muslim, too."

"Gotta check the steaks," Phillip said.

"He really does have to check the steaks, Adeel." Camryn said. "He's not leaving the table because you're Muslim."

"Rare steaks up in five!" Phillip hollered. "Hand count. Who wants 'em?"

Stephanie and Michael raised their hands. Marissa, Adeel, and Camryn looked at each other with grimaces, shaking their heads.

"See if everyone just sat at tables having steaks and tea, there wouldn't be as much to disagree about," Adeel said after he took a swig from a Stella Artois. He cut into his steak and gestured with his fork.

"Take my parents. Trust me, I love them and appreciate they're paying for my doctorate. But they're very strict Muslims and only like that I'm studying technology because they see wealth in it. That's it."

"Do you have faith?" Camryn asked.

"I believe in God, or something overseeing all of this. I just think all the holy books are full of confusing contradictions because they are all the word of man. Just let people believe what they want to believe and leave them alone to do it."

"I think we have to give up on politicians fixing this and just do it one steak dinner at a time," Marissa said.

"That would take a lot of steak. Steak comes from cattle. There goes the carbon footprint," Phillip said.

Phillip held a large chunk of steak up for emphasis then chomped it down. He smiled as he chewed.

"You're too linear and narrow thinking," Marissa snapped back.

"That's such a female argument," Phillip retorted.

"All the neuroscience data suggest that women are only different from men based on about two percent of our brains—that's it, Phillip." Adeel said.

"But hormones are a huge part of that," Stephanie said.

"Ok, men and women are different, fine," Marissa said. "That's really not the problem. It's that men have made women inferior for their differences and subservient, too. Barefoot and pregnant because men have more powerful bodies."

"Carrying life in your body is pretty powerful, too." Camryn added, patting her baby bump.

"We're on to something," Stephanie said. "Maybe men have always felt inferior, so they built cultures and institutions asserting masculine brutality. The whole Me Too phenomenon is just the latest reaction to that exploitation."

"The women are in control of all of that, Mom. They could have spoken up sooner." Phillip said.

"Eat your steak!" Camryn snapped at Phillip. "That's not the point. The point is men asserting power over women again because they can."

"Men have been asserting power over other men for eons. It's what men do, talk about differences that need to be accepted." Phillip said.

"The point is why can't we just be partners, equals, bringing our different strengths together?" Stephanie said. "Isn't time to get past shrugging and saying our biologys dictate everything?"

"And get past the rigid roles built on those biologys while we're at it." Marissa added.

Michael grew tired from the conversation, bored really. It was all a mess from beginning to end and nothing was going to be solved at this table. That thought led him to feel aloof and removed. All this talk of men and women, child bearing, God or no God and he suddenly wondered what his life would have been without his wife and children. He couldn't define himself by his kids or their achievements, that much he at least knew; their lives were theirs to enjoy or screw up. And what was the point of any of it since the universe was just fading away, anyway? He felt guilty somehow and rubbed the back of his neck.

"Neck aching, Midee?" Stephanie asked. "He didn't sleep well again last night."

"It's that new medica—" he said but suddenly, Stephanie became transparent and he could see her vascular system pulsing with life.

"Michael!" he heard Stephanie holler. "Get him on the ground and get me some garlic, Marzi! Kitchen counter—there's a basket."

Michael glanced toward Camryn and not only could he see her vascular system, he could also see the baby's. The baby's heart beat wildly fast as he now saw the molecules of blood and other cellular material coursing through the baby's system.

Stephanie's face broke through the visual hallucinations. The scent of raw garlic overwhelmed him and he realized Stephanie held a raw clove under his nose.

"Midee!" she hollered and dropped the clove. "It worked!"

Michael could feel the pressure of the stone patio pushing into his left shoulder. Stephanie carefully rolled him onto his back.

"The nurse was right. The garlic stopped your seizure," she said.

As Michael's senses came fully back, he saw his children and Adeel forming a horseshoe of worried faces above him. He took a couple deep breaths.

"Everything okay?" Phillip asked.

"Yep," Michael said.

"I think your father missed his dose of medication this morning," Stephanie said. She rubbed Michael's chest and patted him. "It's taking some getting used to."

Phillip and Adeel helped Michael back to his feet. They guided him back into his chair.

"I'm going to get your pill now," Stephanie said and walked into the house. Marissa took the chair next to Michael, wrapped her arm around him and laid her head on his shoulder.

"I told you my parents weren't boring, Adeel," she said.

Adeel and Camryn chuckled. The sweet warmth and comfort of his daughter further soothed Michael. And while he understood that his seizures included bizarre biological hallucinations, he felt ill at ease when he recalled the baby's fast heart rate; it was a like a hummingbird's wings. Phillip patted Michael's back, then took his seat back next to Camryn. Michael smiled at both of them, restraining the urge to tell them about the baby's heart. Everyone waited quietly for Stephanie to return with his medication.

"That's gotta be it!" Michael said late that night. He had been home from the hospital for over a week but was still not able to sleep through the night. Something about all the drugs, blood drawing, and ambient noise had messed with his circadian rhythms. The best he was able was four hours straight through and then boom! Awake. Rested. Ready to think. He grabbed a pad and pen from the nightstand and crept quietly to the bathroom. Stephanie needed her sleep especially since she had work in the morning. Michael closed the toilet lid and sat.

'Human disease and suffering is linked to inbreeding similar to canine genetic disorders,' he wrote. *'Humans are meant to breed across all races, continents, and cultures. Keeping tribal within our segregated cultures has fomented diseases like Sickle Cell and Taysachs. Evolution and survival demands us to*

76

no longer limit our human breeding to local or limited gene pools but spread and share our genes throughout the human gene ocean.'

He paused and held the tip of the pen against his lips. After a moment, he wrote:

This really is one species and old constructs of cultures and faiths are relics. Where they once were a salve and bulwark against barbarism and anarchy, they are now the sources of violent nationalism and extremist savagery. We have the knowledge, the technology, the resources to move us forward all as one living species.'

Michael continued to write until an hour later when Stephanie tapped on the door.

"You okay in there?" she asked, her voice slow and thick with sleep. "Your appointment tomorrow got you on edge?"

Michael cracked the door. He held up his notepad and smiled.

"Writing again, huh?" Stephanie said. She stretched and yawned.

"I'm going to go transcribe this and submit it to HuffPo to see what happens."

"Sounds good. Glad you're happy with it."

"It's not done yet. Got a long way to go."

"Can I come in?"

"Why?"

"Uhh…to pee."

"Wait, I gotta tell you something else," he said.

"What? I really gotta go."

"Okay, go pee and I'll tell you through the door."

Stephanie nodded and yawned. She stepped past him and closed the door.

"So the seizure I almost had today?"

"Yeah."

"This will sound even weirder than other stuff I have told you I see."

"Worse than my veins and blood cells?"

"Yes. I looked over at Camryn right after you and I not only saw her vascular system, but I thought I saw the baby's too."

"Michael, really?"

Stephanie flushed the toilet. A moment later, Michael heard the sink faucet run briefly. Stephanie opened the door and leaned against the jamb.

"So what did you see?"

"The baby's heart beating crazy fast. I mean, dozens of beats a second."

Stephanie sighed.

"Michael, this is a hallucination. You got that, right?"

He nodded.

"And even if it weren't, you're not a pediatric cardiologist. So what the hell would you even know a healthy heart rhythm from one with a problem?"

"Okay. I guess you're right."

"Besides, Phillip and Camryn already had the baby's heart checked out. Just before your attack, don't you remember the fetal echocardiograph appointment? I went with Camryn and her mom."

Michael shook his head, vaguely recalling something.

"Camryn and the baby are already on meds for it—supra-tacka something. It's congenital. Turns out it runs in her family. Everything is going to be fine."

Michael sighed with relief. His grandchild was going to be okay.

"Now I do remember," he said. "Wow. My brain must have concocted the hallucination around that like Dr. Berg said back at the hospital. Wait"

"What?"

"Now I'm thinking that hallucinations must have been happening since the human brain evolved to its current state. That's tens of thousands of years ago."

"Okay," Stephanie said. She stifled a yawn.

"But back when things like the Upanishads, or the Old Testament, or any of the other creation-based texts were written, people were having hallucinations then, too."

"Makes sense. You finished?"

"Wait. They didn't have neuroscience, any science at all, to help them recognize that their hallucinations, their visions, their dreams or anything else were probably just brain injury or disease."

"Midee, I gotta get some sleep."

"Or people who thought they saw spirits might have floaters in their retina like you have. Not necessarily revealed truths."

"Okay," Stephanie said. She patted his back. "I think you're over-thinking all this. Coming back to bed then?"

Michael shook his head. Stephanie kissed him and climbed back into bed.

Some time later after he surrendered the bathroom to Stephanie, Michael clicked away on his keyboard, adding strong historical references where he needed to undergird his arguments. By the time the morning spilled soft, blue light through the office window, Michael finished the grammar and spell-check. A few minutes later, he emailed the submission. After he read it over one last time, he felt satisfied and exhausted. His oral surgery was in a few hours so he had some time to catch a couple hours sleep and he didn't care that he would be groggy for that, anyway.

Michael slid into the seat of the rollercoaster next to his mother. He scooted forward and wrapped his bent elbows around the grip bar in front of him. Harriet waved her hands in the air as the rollercoaster started up hill.

"You really should hold on, Mother," he said.

"The Blessed Mother holds me always."

"Okay but just till we get to the top of the hill because you're believing in the lion that ate the little boy caveman's mom. That started everything."

"What on earth? Just have, faith, son."

The rollercoaster rumbled and rattled up the first hill. Michael grew increasingly nervous that his mother left her hands free instead of clutching the safety bar.

"When the caveman boy saw his mom killed and dragged off by the lion, he ran back to the cave to tell everyone that a strange creature stole his mom and disappeared like the fireball in the sky."

"Michael, cross yourself. We're almost to the top and we need the Blessed Mother's protection."

"No, Mom. Hold on! The boy made up this whole story about the lion sprouting wings and flying away. No one ever saw the lion again. But everyone believed in it because his mother disappeared. His brain made it all up because there was nothing else they knew then."

The rollercoaster stopped at the top of the hill. Michael's heart thumped wildly in his chest. Harriet now stood and began to say a 'Hail Mary'.

"No, Mom. Stop believing. You don't need to believe anymore. Believing in *anything* is the problem! It's simpler than all that!" he screamed.

But the cars of the rollercoaster began to tumble over the crest of the hill. Michael reached out for his mother with one hand.

"Pray, dear, pray!" she screamed.

"No! It's just your evolutionary mind construct, Mother. Hold on!"

But she remained standing and as the rollercoaster crested the hill, she fell. And now the rollercoaster roared down the hill and the tracks began to separate. A chaos of speed and confusion pulled Michael from his seat.

"I can't—"

"Michael, Michael!" a woman's voice pulled him out of the dream. His eyes popped open and he realized he was in the dentist's chair.

"Evolutionary Mind Construct," he said softly.

Carmen, the oral surgeon's gentle assistant with doe eyes, patted his shoulder gently. She wiped his mouth with a wet swab.

"Evolutionary Mind Construct" he said again, but his anesthetized lips caused him to fumble the words.

"You were dreaming. Happens sometimes as patients come out of propofol. You're all through. I'll go get your wife."

Michael, confused about where he was, looked around the office, at the tray with the blue cloths over it, and out the window toward the Verdugo Hills crisp and brown from drought. The right side of his mouth was nothing but numb thickness. He recalled that a broken molar had to be removed surgically. Stephanie walked in and the full sense of fluorescent-lit reality flooded him.

"You okay there, Midee?" she asked gently.

"Just a little numb," he said.

"That was the last step. We're good till next month when those temporary front crowns get replaced. Do you want a little water?"

Michael nodded. As Stephanie filled a small paper cup with the spit fountain just to his left, the phrase rolled through his mind again: 'Evolutionary Mind Constructs'. Where had he ever heard that before? And why would he think of it now? Stephanie handed him the cup. As he went to sip, Stephanie reached for his dental bib and raised it beneath his chin.

"Careful, Mike. You're still numbed on the right. Can you sip from the left?"

He twisted his lips to form a small pocket on the left. Tipping the cup, he let a bit of the water flow into his mouth. His tongue was immediately refreshed but most of the water dribbled onto the dental bib. He handed the cup to Stephanie and dabbed at his face with the bib.

"I'll wait till the Lidocaine wears off."

"Good plan," she answered.

"Have you ever heard of Evolutionary Mind Constructs?" he asked.

"What?"

"It's this idea from a dream I just had. I can't recall where I heard of it before."

"That makes two of us."

81

"Okay, well you're almost ready to go, then," Carmen walked back in carrying a small bag and a prescription form. "You feeling okay?"

Michael nodded. "Fine. Maybe a little hungry."

Carmen opened the bag and began to explain Michael's after-care. Stephanie listened pointedly but Michael's mind wandered away from Carmen's soft Armenian accent and back to his dream phrase. He understood the concept but would Google it later to locate the source of it.

"That all make sense, Michael?" Stephanie asked.

"Yeah, yeah," he answered. Stephanie smirked, recognizing full well in his tone that he hadn't heard a word.

The Lidocaine wore off a few hours later but Michael only felt a slight gnawing discomfort. He had resisted taking the Vicodin though the oral surgeon had suggested he take it before the Lidocaine wore off. His system reacted sensitively to any drug, including aspirin. Even alcohol hit him hard. A lightweight didn't begin to describe his tolerance level, which always made him question the Irish stereotype. Or did it just skip a generation if it indeed exists in the Irish population? Unlike his father, he lost the interest in alcohol midway through his undergrad years. One too many hangovers probably helped, too.

He finished a quick email reply to Detective Kurtz, the LAPD officer who was investigating his attack. But checking his email or Facebook posts was not his goal when he logged on. A Google search for 'Evolutionary Mind Constructs' was his aim. He typed the words into the search filter but Google only returned hits from each of the three words. The phrase itself didn't produce a result. Still, he scrolled through several screens until he ended up on a construction contractors' referral website. Dead end.

As he leaned back in his chair, he began his litany of self cross-examination. Why does this matter at all? Did I land on something no one else has thought of? But if there's no research, evidence, or proof, it's just another idea with no foundation. Remember your theory of gene-based disease in humans being linked to ethnic in-breeding similar to purebred dogs with genetic disorders. You're no Richard Dawkins so how dare you think about such things? Am I just an anti-religious zealot in the way my mother is a Virgin Mary zealot? Is that what this is all about? Like a teenage rebellion against my mother? Since I never had the chance to rebel in her absence, am I making up for lost opportunity?

"No luck, huh?" Stephanie asked from behind. Stephanie rubbed his shoulders. Michael could smell the soft coconut aroma of her hair conditioner.

"I've made up another theory—so I'm an original if nothing else. Not that there's any science to back me up."

Stephanie sighed. She reached to Michael's left and held up several manila folders.

"Don't go reorganizing my office. I have to work on these three accounts tomorrow."

"I just moved them off your keyboard. That's all."

"Tell me *this* theory of yours."

"Okay. Our brains evolved to recognize patterns and to create patterns where sparse information exists."

"Is there any proof of that idea?"

"There's a lot in anthropological studies. Neuroscience is starting to back it up, too."

"Duh. What was I thinking?"

"Steph, don't be a smartass. Recognizing patterns was one of the ways we survived the caves and our great migrations out of Africa. Trouble came when random stuff happened that we couldn't explain. Again, we connected up sparse information and then started telling stories about it. This propensity was successful, and we passed it on over generations and eons."

"How was it passed on--you mean like genetics?"

"Sure. Nature and nurture, I'd say. Pretty soon this survival tool morphed so that we not only created gods to give us meaning in the random, wild world, but we also began creating constructs like truth, love, even culture. Evolutionary Mind Constructs."

"What the hell?"

"That's what I'm calling them. They still exist and are evidence of the older parts of our brains. But see, they helped us before but now are traps. We need to free ourselves from these old mental barriers. They're like a cross on mankind's shoulders. It's not mystical or magic—it's the evolved organ asserting itself."

"I can't agree or disagree with you because you're not offering anything to back up your idea, Midee. But I do have another question."

"Go 'head."

"Did you take a Vicodin after all? Is that what's going on here?"

"Funny. No, I did not."

"Then are you hinting that this is the new career direction you want to take? Evolutionary Biology or something? I mean if it is, you're going to have to do a lot of catch-up in the physical sciences, not to mention that—"

"I'm a bit long in the tooth?"

"No. You're short of a few teeth right now. Remember the implants?"

Stephanie nodded, smirked, and shrugged.

"Oh that's funny."

"Well…" she said quietly.

"Let's not forget that I'm unemployed currently and would have to take out a second to get another graduate degree. I think not. This trip to Ireland is all I really want—stretch my archaeology and history legs a bit."

"So why are you fixated on this evolutionary mind idea?"

Michael pointed at the back of his head. Stephanie shook her head in confusion.

"I think this knock on the head rattled an old part of my brain or something. Like with the seizures and seeing molecules. New ideas are coming rapidly. About...well...existence."

"We're not talking religious awakening here are we? Like mother like son?"

"Actually, it couldn't be more opposite. No, I'm seeing reality, elementally, and sensing the source."

"Michael you've always been grounded in reality."

"It's different than that, Steph. Like the reality below reality."

"Hitting the pause button here, Michael. Doctor Berg already explained all this. You are NOT seeing the molecules and elements."

"Okay, Okay. Agreed. That was brain injury."

"Then what the hell are you talking about with all this?"

"It's the ideas that are springing from my hallucinations."

"You sound like some sort of prophet to me. It scares me a little."

"I'm not losing it, Steph. I'm just intrigued. Plato, Aristotle, Aquinas—all of the great philosophers would have conceived ideas quite differently if they had our science at their disposal and didn't have to rely on a god to explain things once they reached their limits."

"I gotcha. Phew. I was getting a little nervous."

"Don't be. I just want to dig deeper into cosmology and line it up somehow with evolution and our brains. Simple."

"Oh, yeah. A snap to understand."

"The point is, Steph, God isn't necessary with a universe that probably sprang from gravity and particle fields."

"Can't wait for Easter brunch with your mom!"

"Oh, that's going to happen. Right."

Michael turned back toward the computer. He typed in 'flights to Ireland' and chuckled when the Irish airline name came up.

"Ah, hah. Aer Lingus. Sounds a bit nasty, doesn't it?"

5.

"Sounds like something I might have done once or twice," Gregory said a few weeks later. "Aer Lingus. I need to look that up."

Stephanie turned and slapped his shoulder. She stood up and grabbed his breakfast plate along with Michael's. Mildred lay on her dog bed in the corner of the kitchen between the refrigerator and the pantry. Her head on her paws, she watched every move Stephanie made.

"Rude," she said through a laugh.

"Not at the frat with Michael, of course," Gregory said.

Michael shook his head and grabbed up Stephanie's plate and a basket of sweet rolls and brought them to the counter.

"We didn't talk much back when you came out, remember?" Michael said.

"*Much?*" Gregory said. "You gave me the cold shoulder. Worst three weeks of my life until my break-up with Phil. You were so homophobic."

"Excuse me," Stephanie said. "I believe that when you told him you were gay *and* thought you were in love with him, you were lucky he didn't deck you. Most guys I knew then would have. Times were different."

"He decked my heart," Gregory said.

"I worked it out, Michael replied. "We were best friends and pledge brothers—I loved you in every way, *except* sexually, so it was tough on me. And I wasn't sure if by loving you as a friend, it would lead you on."

"You could have given me the chance to reassure you."

"It was just a shitshow, but I needed time to figure out you were never going to jump me or push things any further. Also, it wasn't the worst thing to hear someone was hot for me."

"That's what I'm talking about!" Gregory said. "What's so bad about that?"

"It's a good thing I was over all my Catholic crap by then, too."

"It was *no* big loss. We had to shower together as frat pledges before I came out, in case you don't recall."

"Oh, I remember. And the bottle of Nair you left me in my sock drawer for my butt, too. I should have realized you were gay at that point."

"I was way ahead of my time with manscaping."

"Boys, boys, why are we going over this ancient history again?" Stephanie asked.

Mildred groaned. Gregory went to her side and petted her.

"Little Millie girl, you know daddy and mommy are taking off soon?"

"She watched us pack and at one point, stepped into the open suit bag and laid down," Stephanie said over the clatter of dishes being rinsed and stacked in the dishwasher.

"Well Uncle Gregory will be here with you the whole time so there's nothing to be afraid of. God is still looking out for you and me."

Gregory looked over his shoulder toward Michael and sneered. Mildred looked at him then laid her head back on her paws. She groaned again.

"Oh, baby—wanna just come home with Uncle Gregory and we'll let the Three Cat Stooges fend for themselves? After all, you did spend your first adopted night with me before I gave you to these apostates for their anniversary."

A van horn blared. Gregory stood up.

"That's our ride," Michael said.

Stephanie closed the dishwasher and rinsed her hands. Michael left the kitchen and went to the front door. Stephanie, Gregory, and Mildred followed, the nails of Mildred's paws clicking lightly on the hardwood floor. Michael opened the front door and the van driver in his navy blue uniform grabbed up their luggage. As Michael and Stephanie picked up their carry-on bags, Gregory bent over and picked up Mildred. He grabbed her right paw and started waving.

"I feel like Anne Bancroft in 'Home for the Holidays'. I never think I'm going to see friends again when they fly."

Stephanie smiled and rubbed his shoulder. She kissed his cheek.

"We'll be back. Thank you again for staying with our babies."

"Be safe, hon," Gregory said through a choking voice.

"Here's something to remember me by," Michael said.

Michael wrapped his arms around Gregory and Mildred. He landed a big kiss on Gregory's mouth.

"We'll be back—this is just a few weeks and a little adventure."

"Says you," Gregory said.

Stephanie and Michael stepped out the door and down the porch steps. Gregory waved Mildred's paw more vigorously. Mildred looked at her paw, up at him, then back to her paw. She groaned. Gregory dropped her paw and wiped his tears away.

"Crying again, old girl," he said. "I may need to get my testosterone checked." He kissed the top of her head.

'The apple doesn't fall far from the tree,' his mother said. 'Nooo, I'm nothing like you at all!!'

Michael woke with a start, his neck cramped and his teeth gritting. His thoughts were muddled since he was unable to sleep in the coach seat that barely reclined. Why was he dreaming about his mother again? The plane dropped altitude suddenly.

"Your hand is so cold again," Stephanie said. "We've just got another hour and a half or so."

Michael clutched her hand with his left and braced his legs against the bulkhead in front of him as the airplane dropped and shook. Several other passengers cried out, which didn't comfort Michael.

"Is this turbulence ever gonna stop?" he asked.

His head felt tight. Adding to his flying phobia was a sense of dread that he might never find another school administration position, let alone a principal position. What the hell was he really doing going on this trip? Shouldn't he be home posting his resume and following up every lead? The airplane thumped and dropped again.

The turbulence triggered anxiety in him, but at least not nausea. Not yet. Through most of the flight, his gaze fixed on the fasten seatbelts sign, waiting for it to go out. During the last eight hours of the flight, Michael figured the seatbelt sign had been lighted for at least four hours. Once the plane made its way over northern Canada, the turbulence started, and then over the north Atlantic, it increased. In his earlier Catholic days, he probably would have been doing the rosary, at least in his mind. Now the only comfort he felt was in his glass of pinot grigio that was having its effect. But even the flight attendants, the wine and coffee service halted long ago when the heavy turbulence started, sat strapped into their narrow seats in the galley, chatting casually. Michael did notice that when a rumbling jolt of turbulence hit, without missing a beat in their chat, both stewardesses reached down and grabbed their metal seat handles. Passengers remained fairly quiet unless a strong drop occurred, causing them to shriek in

90

unison, followed by the captain with his thick Irish accent reassuring the cabin that while the latest drop was a doozy, all would be well again soon.

When the plane began its descent some time later, it was swallowed up by gray rain clouds. The raucous turbulence of the north Atlantic gave way to a rumbling, slight vibration. Michael released Stephanie's hand and leaned to look out the window. With one final thump of a drop, the plane cleared the clouds and Michael could now see the renowned verdant green in all directions and murky blue of the River Shannon estuary. The seatbelt lights flashed on and the Captain announced that the flight crew should prepare for landing. As the engines roared and died back and then roared again, Michael's heart seemed to keep rhythm. For whatever reason, descent and landing always calmed his nerves.

"The good news is Limerick is only about fifteen miles away so we can catch a taxi after grabbing our luggage," Stephanie said.

"Yep. All good," Michael said. He kept his eyes trained on the thatch roofs and stone walls forming tic-tac-toe grids as they grew closer. "But you know what?"

Stephanie smiled as she heard the sarcasm in his tone. His anxiety was easing up and it was a relief to her, too.

"What?" she asked.

"It's a long way to Tipperary."

Once the plane's landing gear slammed and bounced and the plane slowed on the runway, Michael's mind, freed from the prison bars of flight anxiety, conjured up an urgent idea he had to jot down. These urgent ideas had badgered him since the parking lot attack.

"Steph, you got a notepad in your purse?"

Stephanie sighed. She recognized this new state of mind and wasn't going to fight him on it. Something in all of it was compelling to her, and might he have become just a bit sexier again with all these new ideas flooding into his mind? His intelligent, probing mind

91

was one of his traits that made her fall in love with him in college, and in some ways, she felt he was not using his full mental potential as a school principal. The boredom they had talked about weeks back could probably in part be attributed to this underuse of his mind. She leaned over and snatched up her purse from below her seat. She snapped it open and handed him a notepad and pen.

"Finally!" he said.

"Snippy-pants!" she retorted.

Michael once again scribbled frantically to the sound of passenger seatbelts unclicking. Stephanie popped her seatbelt open and watched him write. Michael nodded to himself for the couple minutes he wrote. He tore the pages out of her pad and handed it back to her.

"You wanna hear the new idea?"

"Sure, we got time while everybody rushes the exit."

"All right, all right. So Buddha is to Hinduism what Christ is to Judaism."

"Okay."

"Buddha distilled all the teachings, myths, legends, documents, and whatever to the core important issues—he synthesized it through his own life experiences."

Stephanie nodded. She reached into her carryon and applied some lip gloss.

"Or most likely, some ancient Hindu or group of them did the distillation and made up the myth of Buddha since they lived in a time when there was no alternative to supernatural creation—he needed some sort of god to pin the ideas onto. Like we talked about before."

"A few times."

"You don't need to get snarky."

"Sorry. It's the long flight and my damn lips are so dry."

"Okay. So just like the Buddha idea, a similarly bright and imaginative ancient Jew probably created the myth of Jesus and was smart enough to incorporate mythical elements like virgin birth and resurrection that had been around forever. "

"Yup," Stephanie said. She was sliding on her sneakers and tying them.

"And they added some eternal reward for living a good life, a good life by their particular definition, and blah-blah-blah."

"Like the Rainbow Connection?" Stephanie asked as she sat back up.

"Huh?"

"The song: *Somebody thought of it, and someone believed it...*"

"Pretty much. The human mind and capacity for imagination hasn't changed much over the last fifty thousand years so it makes sense. And it most likely all comes from our evolved minds, from evolved lower organisms, and ultimately, from the evolution and destruction of stars since the Big Bang."

"So are you going to start writing some sort of history of religion and philosophy book or something?" Stephanie asked.

"I don't know."

"And don't forget—you have billions of people all believing in some sort of religion. Who's going to be interested in all this? Basically, you'd take away their hope."

"Maybe they should stop hoping and start working on this life as one species. There's a thought."

"No. They're mostly thinking about death and the heavenly reward, or at least, relief."

"I'm not worried about what happens when I die. If there is a God, I'll just have to tell him—"

"Her."

"It--that I was wrong."

"Let's get off the plane now, Michael. We can talk about this later. We're the last two on the plane and the flight attendant is staring at us."

Just outside the airport, the highway turned into a rural greenway, surrounded by pink-flowering shrubs. Tom, a jovial and chatty Irishman, pointed out sights and historical points along the way in his thick Irish brogue. He slowed and pointed toward a Celtic cross just off the road on the right.

"That's one of the soldier graves from the feckin' English civil war—all Irish. You'll see more a' those as we get closer to Limerick proper."

As they passed the 'Welcome to Limerick' sign and merged their way onto the Limerick Southern Ring Road from the M7, Michael and Stephanie could see the top of yet another castle peak over the tree line. They had seen several ruined keeps and battlements along the way, but this castle appeared to be more complete. Like the other ruins they had passed on this drizzly day, the castle seemed to disappear into the gray clouds. Tom noticed their gesturing.

"That's the roof of King John's Castle, 'tis. What you can see of it today, anyway. She's in quite good shape and that's where all that hell broke out during the feckin' English Civil War."

Tom pulled a map from his console as he whipped the car over to pause. A horn honked from behind and Tom waved them on as he studied the map. His finger traced a route.

"Pery's Hotel on Glenworth, that right?"

"Yes," Michael said.

"What made you choose that one, might I ask?"

"The university chose it for us," Michael said. "It's within walking distance of the dig sites. Is there something wrong with it?"

Stephanie clutched Michael's knee.

"You one of them gonna be diggin' round again, I see. 'Tis fine—clean and no bugs. It's just I usually drop yanks off at The Strand or The Absolute. More amenities, as they say."

"Michael, do you suppose—"

Michael shook his head. He was not about to budge with their meager budget.

94

"The Pery is near everything and has what we will need for four weeks," Michael said.

"Four weeks! I'll say it's got everything—'cludin' a ghost or two. Some say even a banshee."

"We'll take our chances," Michael replied.

Tom pulled the van up to the front of the Pery. Stories of red brick and minimum windows rose several floors above them, creating a façade that would have been as appropriate for a prison as a boutique hotel. In the gloomy weather, the red brick took on a bloody aspect.

"Here we are, folks."

"Lots of brick," Stephanie said.

"Twas a Georgian thing. All round Pery square you'll see the red brick. Feckin' English."

Tom stepped out of the van and to Stephanie's side. He opened the door for her and then walked around and did the same for Michael. As Tom pulled their luggage from the back of the van, a porter in a navy vest and navy pants greeted them. He grabbed up the luggage and loaded it onto a brass luggage trolley. Michael shook Tom's hand and handed him a tip. Tom nodded his gratitude.

"Be on the look out for the ghostly head of Mayor Dominic Fanning," Tom said. "His house was here long before the Pery. Beheaded after The Siege. Feckin' English."

As Tom made his way back to the driver's door, Michael and Stephanie looked over at the porter. The porter shook his head.

"The only thing hauntin' us here is some bad water pipes," he said.

"The water pipes make some sounds here and there," the check-in clerk said as she handed Michael the room keys a few minutes later. "I'm sure it's no goblin or banshee," she added, grinning.

"Thank you," Michael said.

The porter led them behind the luggage cart to a small elevator. Michael and Stephanie then made their way down a narrow hall that ended in a large window that barely let in the blue-gray light behind its sheers. The wheels of the luggage cart squeaked as they led the porter. Gold and yellow pillars meeting crown molding arches spaced every ten feet, along with the soft salmon wallpaper accented with tiny red roses made Stephanie think of a gaping whale, Monstro, on the Storybook Adventures ride at Disneyland. So Victorian, to be sure, but rather than comforting, it made the hall foreboding. Stephanie grabbed Michael's elbow when they reached room four sixty-two.

"Maybe this place is haunted," she said.

The porter smiled and went to open the door. Michael stopped him.

"It's fine. We'll take it from here if you'll just leave the cart."

"If you're sure, sir," the porter said. Michael was sure. He only had one euro left since tipping Tom the driver and mistakenly converting only seven US dollars before they boarded the plane in L.A.

"I'm sure," Michael said. He handed the porter the euro. The porter arched his jet black left eyebrow and his thin lips pinched tight.

"Thank you, sir."

"That's all I got left right now. Is there a currency exchange around?"

"Yes. Down on St. Brigid's near the castle."

"I promise I'll catch you up when I get more Euros."

The porter nodded and walked off.

"That was smooth," Stephanie said.

Michael pinched her arm.

"I'm starting to feel like a typical American tourist jerk," he said. "First that joke with the stone-faced customs agent who didn't find me funny and now no money to tip."

Michael slid the room key into the digital lock that looked odd on the carved walnut door. He opened the heavy door and heard:

"What the fuck?"

A young man with sandy hair in his mid-twenties jumped up and pulled his pants up quickly. Michael jumped back and put his hand instinctively over Stephanie's eyes as she let out a shriek. The quiet drum beat of a pornography score played in the background. Worse than the young man's bare butt Michael just saw was the extreme close-up on the TV flat screen. Whatever genital flesh it was, he closed his eyes in embarrassment. The TV popped off.

"Get the hell outta my room! Get the hell out!"

Michael nudged Stephanie back and slammed the door. He grabbed the luggage cart and wheeled it down the hall. Stephanie followed quickly, hollering back over her shoulder: "Sorry. Sorry. Enjoy yourself!"

"You can plainly see, sir, that only yourself is listed."

The young female clerk held out the Georgetown itinerary a few moments later. Her thin, pale and freckled fingertip pointed to the top of the itinerary.

"I should have checked that—my mistake," Michael said. "But what do we do?"

"The university has only let twin rooms and each volunteer shares with another."

"So that guy was supposed to be my roommate?" Michael said. He grimaced and shook his head.

"Yes. You were *supposed* to share a twin room with that *guy*. I understand he is a doctor of philosophy student from Georgetown."

"Doctor of reproductive physiology more like," Stephanie said under her breath.

"Ma'am?" the clerk said. Stephanie waved her hand and shook her head.

The young woman folded her thin arms. She looked like a ship mast with a navy-colored cross beam crowned by titian hair pulled back into a severe bun. Stephanie stepped up to the counter.

"Clearly we have a problem and my husband here was a bit negligent. Men, you know."

The clerk's expression froze. Not a freckle twitched in response. Stephanie cleared her throat.

"Is there any possibility that we can reserve a king or queen room?" she asked.

As always, Michael admired Stephanie's quick ability to handle business issues. Such things flustered him and it was one of the myriad of strengths of Stephanie's that offset his weaknesses. The clerk began fluttering her fingertips across the computer keyboard. She paused, shook her head, and fluttered away again. She looked up and fixed her steely gray eyes on Stephanie, clearly dismissing Michael's presence.

"We have only one double room with ensuite. It's available the entire month."

Stephanie held up her laptop case. She patted it.

"Does the room have a desk or any sort of counter where I can work?"

"Aye."

"Wi-Fi will still be good?"

"I might say Wi-Fi is so-so. 'Good' would be misleading ya'."

"How much?" Stephanie asked.

"One hundred fifteen euro."

Michael touched Stephanie's elbow. Clearly the budget was about to get blown. He shook his head.

"Can you help us at all with the rate?" Stephanie asked.

"I'm willing to apply the forty-five euro for half of the twin room to the double room rate. It was pre-paid and we're not going to be able to fill a twin at this time."

Stephanie sighed. Michael dropped his head, unsure.

"The next inns or hotels with rooms are probably four kilometers away. But they're going to cost you quite a bit more than one hundred fifteen. Also, you can walk to the digs and town centre from here."

"Give us a moment, will you?" Stephanie said.

Stephanie and Michael stepped over to a small bench. Stephanie pulled out her phone and punched in some info.

"Thirty days at seventy Euros a night, plus room tax," Michael whispered. "That must be two thousand bucks or something."

"Twenty-three hundred and eight cents to be exact," Stephanie said and held up the phone. Michael shook his head. He placed his right foot on the bench. The clerk cleared her throat loudly and Michael quickly placed his foot back on the floor.

"This was only supposed to cost us our flights. I can't get my head around adding another two thousand bucks," Michael said.

Stephanie heard the dejection in his voice. She tucked her phone away and gently took his arm.

"I can't believe I'm saying this because I wanted to run back to the airport when I walked into this dump. Midee, you said it before. This is an adventure of a lifetime. I haven't seen you this excited about anything in years. We'll put the room on a card and make ten-dollar payments for the rest of our lives. This is *too* important. You need to do this, and with all the shit lately, *we* need this time."

Michael pulled Stephanie to him and kissed her deeply. She giggled beneath the kiss, surprised by his gusto.

"Wow," she said.

"And you won't complain about the bathtub being grungy or the color of the bedspread?" he asked.

"Let's not get crazy here."

"The Wi-Fi is going to make me a bit crazy I think," Stephanie said the next morning.

She lifted her laptop from the laminated oak desktop and carried it over to the matching laminated nightstand. She lowered her close-ups onto her nose and checked the Wi-Fi signal. She shook her head.

"It's not any better here. Fine. Back to the desk."

Michael sat in a chair covered in stained turquoise rayon and tied his shoes. When he finished he stood and went over to Stephanie. She sat once again in a rickety wooden chair and scanned her emails. The portable printer on her right began to rattle to life. Her phone buzzed with a call.

"If you're all set, I'm heading out," Michael said. "I think it should only be a twenty-minute walk or so to Bishop Street and the convent entrance. I'll use my cell GPS to get there."

Stephanie nodded and picked up the phone. Michael snuck in a kiss before she started to speak. He held up his phone to let her know he had it with him and she nodded. She mimicked taking a pill and he nodded to let her know he had taken his Tegretol.

"Hi, Alex. Those actuarials are not..." she said as Michael closed the door.

When Michael stepped out the front entrance of the hotel, he felt the chill and moisture from the overcast sky. As a southern California native with thin blood, he needed to zip up his jacket and get some relief. There was a bit of traffic on the street but few pedestrians. Patting his phone keypad to add the address of St. Mary's Convent of Mercy, he began to follow the GPS directions. Most people he passed looked down at their phones or past him. He expected the friendly joviality of Tom the van driver but assumed that people had work or worry on their minds. Or maybe they could somehow perceive he was American. He had hoped that when he stepped off the plane and onto his ancestral soil, he would feel a sense of connection. He didn't. It was dozens of generations and millions of mixes of genes that separated him from Ireland. He wasn't necessarily drawn to this experience by his thread of an ancient relation to Terrence Flynn, who was really just a name on a genealogy chart, but rather by the excavation, sifting, research, and archaeology of it. And he knew full well that the supervising archaeologists would get to do the fun stuff; he and the other volunteers were glorified ditch-diggers.

But what would he feel if *his* shovel turned the dirt that revealed old, Uncle Terrence's bones? Some thrill, to be sure.

The structures and buildings he passed on his walk were mostly of few stories, modern, and dour under the gray sky. Occasionally, a periwinkle blue or lemon-yellow door would pop out from the gray facades. Antiquity was well covered and hidden by the squat modernity, with only a four-cornered church steeple up to the left hinting at the past. He made note of the location of the church as a possible place to tour on a weekend, especially if it had an old graveyard next to it. As he made his way from Patrick Street onto Bridge Street, he came upon The Locke, a bistro set in a two-story corner building right where the two streets met. That would be ideal for a lunch prior to checking out the old church, he decided. Soon Bridge Street took him to Athlunkard Street. Just before Athlunkard crossed Bishop Street, he spotted what appeared to be a medieval building with a plaque high above an extinct wall fountain. Michael was obsessed with reading all signage at museums, to Stephanie's bored chagrin, but he was even more intrigued with plaques on historic buildings. Too curious to pass it up, he looked left and right and hustled across the street. He hopped the curb just as a car blew its horn and sped past. Oops, they drive on the left here, he reminded himself for the umpteenth time.

The pine green plaque sat under an arch in the stone wall and stood out like an emerald set in tarnished silver. 'The Bourke House-1641' it read, along with details about the structure that seemed to reach back to the days of Donal Mor Flynn. He wasn't sure who Flynn was, and he would check his genealogy chart later, but he did know that this house pre-dated The Siege of Limerick, and therefore his ancestor's execution, by ten years. It might even be conceivable that Terrence Flynn passed this building on daily routines. Since the convent and Dominican Priory ruins where the digs were scheduled to locate his remains lie

101

just up on Bishop Street, Terrence might even have been carted past the wall after his execution. A pang of sadness hit Michael and he reached out and patted the bowl of the wall fountain and then continued on to the convent.

Just past a modern, four-story building on the right that looked to be composed of concrete with inlaid gravel, Michael saw a passenger van letting people out to join with a small crowd. He checked his GPS and saw that this must be the front gate of the convent. As he walked past the building and started making his way along a white-painted, modern metal fence, he noticed what appeared to be an ancient wall from which sprouted wild ferns and grasses. Arches that opened to light and air graced the sides of the weathered stones that stretched fifty or sixty feet. But instead of being inspired by the ruins, Michael's mind began to whir: *Arches as empty and archaic as the Bible that inspired them and the dead Romans who spread the superstitions throughout their empire. Why do I really care to dig up an old ancestor whose life was dedicated to primitive, tribal, exclusionary, oppressive ideas? Should I turn and walk back, pick up Stephanie, and occupy my time with something more definitive and decisive than chasing a faded image of myself from youth? Indiana Jones, right.* The thoughts made Michael pause and he took several deep breaths. These ideas and the flow of them made him anxious at times of late, and even made him question his sanity when they surfaced. He looked back down Bishop Street in the direction he had come and had the urge to run. A few more deep breaths and he turned back toward the convent.

As Michael approached the open gates of the convent, he saw a sandwich board that read "Georgetown University-USA Archaeological Dig." Several people were presenting their passports to a pouty-lipped young woman who looked over their identification through a pair of retro-styled horned rims before making checkmarks on a clipboard. Michael stepped toward her and noticed her baby-blue eyes smile toward him. Her paper name tag read 'Nancy

Fitzgerald.' Too pretty to be a history major, Michael thought.

"Part of the dig?" she asked.

"Yes."

"Name?"

"Michael Dunphy."

"USA I take it?"

"Yes."

"Great," Nancy said. "When Monsignor Leahy and Professor Hood finish the introduction and presentation of the project, you'll join Professor Hood on the west side of the excavation. Do you have any idea if Yorick Kinnaman is here yet?"

"I have no idea who that is," Michael replied.

Nancy's eyebrows furrowed briefly and she flipped a few pages of the clipboard pad. She pointed at a line of information.

"But this says you and he were assigned to the same room at the hotel."

Michael laughed.

"Oh, no. I did meet him briefly, well, out of his briefs, anyway."

"I'm sorry," Nancy said quizzically.

"Never mind. My wife is with me so we changed to a double room."

"All right," Nancy said. She was still a bit puzzled. "Can I have the room number? We need to keep the volunteers organized and we may need to call you with assignments as we go along."

"You have my cell?"

"Yes. This is just for back-up."

Michael reached into his jean pocket and pulled out the folded cardboard room holder. He held it up to her. She glanced, nodded, and made a note.

"Thanks," she said and stepped over to two other people. "As soon as Mr. Kinnaman arrives, I'll introduce you. He will be your partner in the dig."

"Oh, great," Michael said quietly.

Michael took a moment to look around. They had gathered just inside the gated parking lot of a modern, angular building that must have been the convent. Michael was aware the convent was over a century old so it clearly had been rebuilt. As he surveyed the flat, gray façade, he noticed nuns in full black-and-white habits keeping watch out two windows in the opposite dormers. He waved but got no response. The chill of the morning tickled his cheeks once again and he considered moving in closer to the group for warmth. But the dozen or so twenty-somethings had paired off and were fixated on their phones, mumbling occasionally to each other. Michael glanced past them and toward three priests: two in long, black robes and red skullcaps and a third in the usual black suit with white collar. A wild shock of silver hair and thick, Harry Potter glasses he removed and polished made Michael think that was Monsignor Leahy. The other two priests spoke quietly in Italian under stern, dark eyebrows to Monsignor Leahy who smiled and nodded. Dr. Hood stood off from the priests in a brown windbreaker. His chin was raised as he looked through his wire glasses at what appeared to be a catalogue. His black tie flapped a bit in the breeze and Michael figured he didn't stand much over five-two, if that. But something was commanding in the way he regarded the catalogue.

Nancy finished with what seemed to be the last two volunteers. She flipped the pages on the clipboard and looked around and then back toward the street. Michael knew who she was looking for: his bare-assed, almost-roommate and now partner. Was that clown wanking off again and going to hold everything up? Michael grimaced as he thought about spending a month in a cramped hotel room with a young guy who probably would be jerking off several times a week if not, a day. His discomfort was tempered with envy and nostalgia, however. Nancy waved Michael back over to her.

"If he doesn't show, you can team up with Dr. Hood and me. We'll be handling one of the pits."

Just as Michael nodded and turned to his left, he felt a push from the right. He jerked his head toward Nancy.

"I'm here, I'm here," a young male voice said, slightly out of breath.

Michael's mood sank a bit. He had hoped to join pretty Nancy and Dr. Hood.

"You needed a couple extra minutes of in-room movies this morning?" Michael said.

The young man, who Michael figured was no more than twenty-five, tensed his mouth and blushed up to the edges of his van dyke beard. His eyes narrowed under sandy-blonde eyebrows.

"Mr. Yorick Kinnaman, this is your partner for the dig—Michael Dunphy." Yorick extended his hand and Michael noticed the vines of tattoos winding toward his wrist.

"You can call me 'Yor'. My dad is an English professor at Stanford. Shakespeare expert, to be exact. "

"You wash that thing, Yor?" Michael said. "I didn't recognize your…face. But maybe if you turn around."

"Oh," Yor said. But instead of shrinking into an embarrassed heap, he started to chuckle.

"If you had just waited two more minutes—hotelis interruptus."

"Okay, everybody," Nancy hollered. "Please gather round so that Monsignor Leahy may speak about why you're all here. Dr. Hood and I will follow with the logistics of the dig."

"Ladies and gentlemen, I'm Monsignor Leahy, and I would like to introduce their excellencies Cardinal C'Dealva and Cardinal Fratelli. Their excellencies are the emissaries from the Vatican curia, specifically, the collection of holy reliquaries.

"Many of you may not know that Blessed Terrence Albert Flynn, whose remains we hope to recover in the coming weeks, is a beatified personage, the first stage to sainthood. He was not only the compassionate and caring Bishop of Emly, but spent many of his later years here in Limerick. In doing so, he bravely joined the insurgents and encouraged what he saw as a defense of the homeland and Catholic faith against the British during the siege of Limerick.

"The citizens of Limerick eventually surrendered after starvation and disease took their toll. As part of the surrender agreement, the leading city officials along with Catholic clergy, including Bishop Flynn, would be subject to being tried under English law. You can well imagine that most all were found guilty and sentenced to execution by hanging.

"Just a mile or so over on Old Clare Street and Pennywell, all were executed, including our beloved Bishop Terrence Albert Flynn. In sight of the steeple of St. Mary's, he uttered a final speech in honor of God and his native land. Nancy is now distributing binders that contain a more comprehensive recounting, along with historical footnotes and bibliographies, of the Siege of Limerick, the players in that siege, and the victims and martyrs as well. You'll do well to read it through and in these materials, you will come across Bishop Flynn's final speech.

"I now turn to Dr. Hood, the lead archaeologist who will guide this most important of efforts. Dr. Hood."

"Ladies and gentlemen, thank you for joining us on this exciting research. Without your brains, but mostly your brawn, we wouldn't be able to carry out this effort. I am truly grateful. Also, in your packets of information, you will see coupons for Tiger Balm ointment. You'll need them."

The group chuckled.

"Seriously, though, you have all been paired off and the outside of your folders has a large number on it. This is the number of the pit you have been assigned to. We will be exploring ten pits, all of which based on research and ground sonar readings, have the potential to yield the remains of Bishop Flynn.

"We know from research and the available literature that the Bishop was buried somewhere along the outside walls of the Dominican Friary—the ruins you can see around us. As you have no doubt seen, there are three sets of existing ruins: east, just outside the gate of the convent here and to the left; west—across the convent grounds; and right where we stand.

"I will now yield to Nancy who will go over the specifics of who's working where and she will distribute the shovels, brushes, sieves, and sorters. Nancy?"

When the orientation concluded, Michael and Yor walked over to the east side pit. Just below a large rust stain on the ancient stone wall, near the convent fence, stakes and plastic tape marked a four-foot by eight-foot rectangle. Yor moved for the shovel and picked it up. He tossed the brush and small trowel to Michael. He grabbed up two pairs of work gloves and tossed one pair to Michael as well.

He slid on the work gloves. "Since we have to dig down seven feet, six inches at a time, it probably makes more sense for me to do the digging."

Michael picked up the work gloves and slid them onto his hands. He glanced down at the brush and trowel that lay on the ground.

"Why exactly would that be?" Michael asked.

"Really?" Yor asked. "Let's start with you're probably old enough to be my dad."

"Your point would be? I go to the gym. Sometimes."

"I go to the gym sometimes, too. *After* I have spent an afternoon rock wall climbing," Yor answered.

"Why don't we just take turns digging, hmm? Seems fair to me," Michael said.

Yor shrugged. He let the handle of the shovel go and Michael caught it.

"Have at it, dad," Yor said.

Michael jammed the spade into the ground that felt heavy with moisture. The black soil, riddled with peat, pushed against the shovel blade.

"Just six inches, pops. You're gouging in past that."

"I think I know what six inches is," Michael said over his shoulder as he slid the shovel blade horizontally and picked up the first load of soil. He dropped it into the sifter.

Yor held up his thumb and forefinger and made a gap of two inches.

"It's more than this, pops," he said laughing.

"Just do your sifting and sorting, smartass."

"This shit is almost wet mud," Yor said. "It's pressing through the sifter like Playdough."

Michael brought over a shovelful of soil a couple hours later, having dug out the first couple of inches across the entire plot rectangle. He dumped the soil into the sifter and watched as Yor pressed the wet muck through the sieve, his hands black and thick with mud. Michael wiped the sweat from his brow and watched as Yor's tattooed arms swirled around the muck. It was almost as though the black soil had crawled up his arms, the ink was so thick. He became mesmerized by Yor's movements and tattoos.

"Looking tired there, pops."

Michael nodded and leaned against the shovel handle.

"So why all the tattoos?" he asked.

"Once I got started with one, I just had to get another. You should try it some time."

"No—skin is too old and saggy where it isn't dimpled. No good. Did you make up the designs?"

"Nope. But they tell stories, the mythology of my life. Like wearing my own cave paintings. And when I'm old, I'll be able to look at them and they'll remind me of who I was. Make sense?"

"About as much as anything else people believe."

"I have no idea what all this is about but I'm pretty sure no one else does, either," Yor replied. "Ready to switch off, pops?"

6.

Michael walked slowly into Pery's Hotel. His face grimaced with pain as he passed by the reception desk. The receptionist noticed him.

"You're still in a bad way, aye?" she said.

"Everything aches. But I can't let the punk I'm working with know it after all this time."

"Are you using anything for the aches?"

"Tiger Balm and Advil. Not much help, though."

The receptionist waved him over to the counter. She reached under and pulled out her purse. She withdrew a black velvet pouch, opened it, and placed a light green, ceramic pill bottle with a crude cork in front of Michael.

"This is an ancient balm made mostly of arnica and some other herbs. Rub it on your sore muscles and you'll surely feel the better for it."

"At this point, I'll try anything," Michael said.

"It's a little white magic."

Michael noticed her name tag read 'Chakranna'. The silver stud in her tongue made a clicking sound when she pronounced certain words. She leaned over the dark oak counter to speak quietly as if she might be overheard.

"I'm a member of a coven and we specialize in healing potions."

"Oh," Michael said. "Thanks, Chakranna."

She leaned back and tucked a strand of her strawberry blond hair behind her ear. Michael noticed an earring that appeared to be a narrow strand of sterling silver that traced the edge of her ear and ended at her lobe with a spiral. At its center stood the shape of a star.

"I hear your tone, sir. Limerick has had a coven of good witches since the days of Florence Magee, White Witch of Limerick."

"Hey, whatever floats your boat. I'm Michael, by the way."

Michael reached for the jar and the receptionist grabbed his wrist. He pulled his hand away.

"Please listen, though it sounds a wee odd, I know. Florence was tried and executed for placing a love potion under the pillow of her maid servant who was unmarried and with child. When the maid servant lost the child, she accused poor Florence of black witchcraft."

"I didn't realize witch hysteria had ever touched Ireland," Michael said. He was making a mental note to google Florence Magee.

"Yes, it did as early as the fifteen hundreds. The witches were always accused of pacts with the Devil but no one ever considered the white magic some witches did for good, healing, and love. But Florence. Who do you suppose was the chief clergy at her trial?"

"No idea," Michael said.

"That old, supposed saintly bishop you're all trying to dig up. That's who."

"I guess that makes sense for the time. Thanks. I'm going to get going here because I really hurt."

"Just mind yourself because Maggie cursed that old pious bastard."

Michael reached for the jar. Chakranna held it and cleared her throat.

"Yes?" Michael said.

"Hopin' you can spare a few Euros. Witches got to earn a livin', too."

Michael dropped four Euros on the counter and picked up the jar. He nodded to thank her.

"Maggie's Curse, mind you!" she hollered as the elevator door closed.

"I can't believe I still need you to massage my back after two and a half weeks of this dig," Michael said some time later.

He lay on the bed in the hotel room as Stephanie rubbed the witch balm into his bare back. She flexed her right hand into a fist and began to rotate the flat side deep into Michael's back just below his right shoulder blade.

"Oooowwww…shiiitttt!" he hollered. Stephanie paused.

"Do you want me to stop?"

"No. That's the knot that started two days into the dig."

Stephanie continued the knuckle massage and Michael gritted his teeth. She finished and rubbed his muscles gently.

"I'll just be glad to have decent Wi-Fi again," she said. She grabbed a couple of facial tissues from a box on the night table to wipe her hands. "I'm tempted to leave this stuff on my hands—smells so nice of lavender, and is that oregano?"

"Maybe the arnica?" Michael said. "I'm not kidding—I expected the receptionist—sorry, 'Chakranna'--to peel off her outer skin and reveal Maria Ouspenskaya. She was that creepy, whispering about the whole thing."

"Ooh, hope she didn't lay a hex on ya'!"

They both chuckled.

"Maybe the curse is the reason we haven't found the Bishop. And there's only four days left," Michael said.

"You know, my hands feel really soft—I'm leaving this stuff on," Stephanie said.

Michael rolled over onto his back and then sat up. He winced a bit. Stephanie lay down next to him and placed her arm across his lap.

"That doesn't hurt, does it?"

"No, it's fine."

"Even though this is turning out to be a dud, I have to tell you something."

"Oh, shit."

"No, no nothing like that. I get that you're having aches and pains as you try to keep up with that punk, but something much more important is going on."

"Uh-oh. You are going to talk about *all that* again."

Stephanie slapped his stomach gently.

"No. I don't ever want to talk about *that* again. Ever. We trust each other. Maybe even more than before all that. We do, don't we?"

"Of course!" Michael said.

"What I'm talking about is your attitude. It's like you have your spark back."

"No job prospects, though."

"Cut the job sulking crap for a second. You have been more joyful and excited than you've been in years. You remind me of that kid I met in college."

"You're probably right—you always are with the psychology stuff. But I have to tell you something important, too."

"Anything, my love. What?" she asked.

"That back rub kind of got me a little frisky," Michael said.

Stephanie stood and rolled her hands onto her hips. Her left eyebrow arched with incredulity.

"Hmm. Are you sure you're up to it?"

"Let's give it a try."

"Why don't we try just scooping the last layer as quick as possible? We gotta be close to seven feet, anyway, and nothing." Yor said the next morning.

112

He stood in the pit and raised his soiled hands over his head. Since he stood six-feet-one, it did appear they had reached the depth limit. Michael glanced in the sorting box at everything they had found over the three and a half weeks: a silver button; 10 shards of different shades of porcelain and a handle of a teacup; four small musket balls; and four beads from an onyx rosary. Michael touched the rosary beads. He wondered who had handled them and what lives they had lived. The shadow of failure began to creep over him. A bunch of crap and nothing close to a human bone. Almost three weeks away and just this? And now he had to face the reality of his life in a little over a week.

"Dude, wake up," Yor said as he approached with a huge shovel of soil. "I think I saw something shiny in this batch so maybe gold or silver?"

"Probably just another button from a—"

"Doctor HOOOOOODDDDD!!!" a female screamed from the west side dig area. "BONES!!! BONES!!!!"

The stamping of feet and the clanging of dropped shovels as volunteers rushed to the west side of the dig met their ears. Yor raced ahead of Michael. Michael hustled past the two Vatican priests who had been sipping coffee at the table in the convent parking lot. They brushed off their cassocks and made their way behind Michael and Yor. Michael caught up with Yor and the entire crew of volunteers along with Monsignor Leahy surrounded a pit. Michael and Yor elbowed their way into the group. Immediately, Michael noticed the pit was maybe five feet deep, at most five and a half. Clearly, he and Yor had worked harder and faster. But he like everyone else stood silent as Dr. Hood, who was on his knees at the bottom of the pit and clearly unconcerned about his white dress shirt, brushed away some soil. Michael gasped along with everybody else.

The ivory and yellowed bones of a human hand and arm began to emerge. Dr. Hood paused and removed some caked-on soil with a trowel, revealing more of the bones. He stopped and stood up.

"I need the volunteers who were working this pit to join me with their hand trowels and brushes. Also, bring along one spade."

"We're right here, Dr. Hood," a thirtyish looking woman said. Michael thought he recognized her voice from her scream moments ago. Another woman, young, closer to Yor's age with corkscrews of red hair pulled back into a loose ponytail also stepped up. They both climbed down into the pit.

"We will need the rest of you to help move soil up and continue to sift. It appears to me that we may have three sets of remains. We'll know soon."

By the next morning, three skeletons, as Dr. Hood suspected, lay exposed. All three were headless. Fragments of fabric that must have been either clothing or the burial shrouds created a nest around the remains. Dr. Hood clipped a few samples of the cloth and placed them in separate, small plastic bags. Volunteers shook the sifters and chatted quietly as Michael walked up and joined them. When he looked down to see the headless skeletons, a deep sense of sadness overcame him. He had to step away.

By early afternoon, a couple of news reporters with cameras were on the scene along with dozens of onlookers. All of the volunteers, including Michael and Yor, stood off near the reporters. A few uniformed police officers stood near the rediscovered grave as Dr. Hood was questioned by a constable. Once Dr. Hood finished, he stepped toward the reporters.

"Good afternoon, ladies and gentlemen. I am Dr. Marcus Hood of Georgetown University, United States, department of archaeology. While it may be premature to speculate exactly who we have discovered, preliminary review of the remains along with various artifacts uncovered in recent weeks suggest this is a seventeenth century burial of three men. No coffin remnants, coupled with the fact that the remains are missing skulls, would imply this group burial was a hasty one done after executions. Further, the historical record would seem to support that these are the remains of Bishop Terrence Flynn, Father James Wolfe, and the Mayer of Limerick at the time of The Siege, Dominic Fanning.

"Once research is done here at Trinity College in companion with Georgetown, and the financial support and supervision of the Vatican, we will perhaps know better who these remains might be. For now, may I answer any questions?"

"Why would the heads be missing?" one of the reporters asked.

"Typically, in that period, the heads would have been removed after a hanging execution and would have been put on display in the city as a warning to other would-be rebels. At the point of the maximum decomposition, the heads were probably discarded in the river."

"If these are the three people you say," the other reporter asked, "how will researchers confirm the identities?"

"Our researchers will comb the genealogical records at various archives to see if we can locate possible descendants, then compare DNA samples. Similar to the Richard the III discovery and confirmation."

"How long do you estimate that will take?"

"We will first need to find usable DNA—mitochondrial or Y—from the remains. That's the easy part—a few days to a week. Combing through the records to locate descendants of each of the remains may be the longest delay since--

"I'm right here!" Michael hollered.

Dr. Hood, the reporter, and the crowd all looked toward Michael.

"I'm supposed to be a descendant! Of Bishop Flynn!"

Dr. Hood and the reporters stepped toward Michael. Dr. Hood scratched his head.

"No one mentioned this to me," he said.

"Sir, may we ask your name?" one of the reporters asked.

"Michael Dunphy. But I'm a Flynn through my mother."

As the reporters asked Michael a few more questions, Dr. Hood stood off to the side looking enthused. It wasn't just the crowd that heard the revelation. Stephanie had taken a break from her work to pack and had turned on the TV in the hotel room. She paused and sat on the edge of the bed to hear the rest of Michael's interview.

"Yes. This dig interested me mostly because I wanted to get back in the field and have an adventure. I was aware of the possible relation."

"You're an archaeologist?" the reporter said off camera.

Michael paused. His face went expressionless for a moment. Stephanie wondered if he was going to either have one of his philosophical rants or a seizure. Had he taken his medication this morning, she wondered. She rolled her hands together nervously.

"I'm not sure what I am right now," Michael said.

Stephanie noticed his face relax and eyes open in such a way that he looked twenty-three again. Dr. Hood stepped up and began talking about mitochondrial DNA and she switched off the TV. She knew he was down when he left this morning and she figured it was because the dig was at its end and there was no success. But now it seemed he might be the key to identifying the dead bishop and also, his own ancestor. There was no question she was fed up with the bad Wi-Fi and the inconvenience of working the last month at the hotel. Here, though, was the climax of this whole experience for him. Something that had lifted him out of his middle age boredom and renewed his confidence in himself. She could not stay any longer, but neither could she take him away from this great moment. Sitting on the edge of the bed, she knew what she would tell Michael when he got back from the dig. She sighed and went back to packing, but this time, just her own suitcase.

When Michael arrived a couple hours later, Stephanie greeted him with a big hug and lingering kiss.

"Wow. What was that for?" he asked.

"My Indiana Jones."

"I'm all dusty and dirty so we shouldn't do much more of that, if you know what I'm saying."

When he placed his wallet and watch on the dresser, he noticed the packed suitcases. He pulled out a chair and sat.

"I only packed my bags, Michael."

"That's fine. I have time but I have news."

Stephanie stepped around him and sat on the edge of the bed. She grabbed his hands and rubbed the inside of his palms gently with her thumbs.

"Ooh. Calluses?"

"My calluses have calluses that have their very own little tiny calluses."

"It's kind of sexy. Sort of butch somehow," she said. "Reminds me of when you played on that night league softball team when we were first married."

"Haven't thought about 'The Colts' in awhile. So you think I'm damn seeexxxy?" Michael said with a cartoonish Scottish accent.

"Easy, Fat Bastard. Here's the thing. I saw you on the news."

"Uh-oh. So you know, then?"

"You're the star of the hour."

"Yup. Big around Limerick, Chakranna tells me."

"Isn't it going to take them some time to get DNA from the bone? And then more time to test it against yours?"

Michael raised Stephanie's hands and kissed them. He let them go and leaned his neck on the back of the chair, slumping.

"The priest from Georgetown says that they will happily pay to extend my stay here until the DNA results come back. He's not sure how long that will be."

"Why would you need to stick around?"

117

"No clue. But it doesn't matter. I told them I leave tomorrow night."

"*I* leave tomorrow night. You *need* to stay and see this through."

"You don't mean that, Steph. Really?"

Michael sat up and scooted to the edge of the chair. Stephanie grabbed his hands again. She looked deeply into his eyes.

"I was going to say that *before* you mentioned they will continue to cover your costs. Stay and do this, Michael. You have to."

"By myself?"

"You're a big boy, now."

"It's just we have never spent more than a couple nights apart. This might be a few weeks. I'm going to miss you."

"I'll get lonely, too. But it'll be easier knowing you're having the adventure of your life."

Michael jumped to his feet. He rubbed the back of his neck and then his eyebrows shot to the top of his forehead.

"We can Skype or Google hangout—everyday!"

"Don't make promises this Wi-Fi can't keep."

"Point taken. Then we'll email and text and all that stuff."

Michael paused and raised Stephanie's chin so that their eyes met again. He smiled.

"And *I really* will miss you," he said.

"One other thing, Midee."

"What?"

"Don't let them push you around."

"Who's going to push me around?"

"It's just that without me around, a lot of times, you're worried about how people feel about you. That's when they best you."

"I like to be liked."

"Yes. Just don't spread that around. Makes you vulnerable."

"I'll be fine, Steph. I'll miss you like crazy, but I'll be fine."

As Michael watched the plane taxi down the runway the next morning, thick, gray clouds hung low over the treetops in the distance. The sun broke through in anemic patches. The plane now paused at the end of the runway and it was strange to think that the most precious aspect of his life sat in that white and green aluminum tube. They really did find their trust in each other and their marriage once again. He also understood that while he'd most likely never have the ambition and enthusiasm of his youth that in part drew Stephanie to him, he did recognize a rekindled confidence and sense of purpose developing within him. Whatever path he eventually chose with his next career move, he knew he could handle and manage just about anything. The engines roared to life and Michael had the strange sensation that his stomach was being pulled from his body. He kept his eyes on the end of the runway as the plane lifted off and in a few seconds, disappeared into the dreary sky. Aloneness in a way he hadn't felt since he was a teen gripped his heart and throat. He turned from the window and wiped tears from his eyes.

Stephanie stared out the plane window, back toward the terminal gray and wet from the overcast. She didn't like the feeling of leaving him behind. They had spent no more than a few nights apart total in their marriage, and those were due to her tough, c-section deliveries that required hospital stays. She was capable and fully independent but she knew he was not. Without her, he would lapse into making sure everyone liked him, even jerks and bullies. It wasn't exactly being a people-pleaser as much as being popular and liked by everyone. She had supposed and he agreed at one time that it was probably a by-product of his mother's self-absorption and neglect of him. At age fifty-one, he was still motivated by it.

She recalled the first time she witnessed it in college. It wasn't his most defining trait or even something that raised a red flag. It actually brought out her protective instincts as she realized he was often blind to other people's insults, and blind to his own need to make a friend of everyone.

"Murphy, you know you're still a pledge until midnight." Chad, the fraternity treasurer whose gruff, deep voice belied his GQ looks, said over Stephanie's shoulder.

Michael and Stephanie paused their dance. Stephanie turned and faced Chad.

"What's your point, Chad?" she asked.

"This is my dance," he said. He pulled Stephanie toward him, pushing her breasts firmly against his chest. Stephanie pushed him away.

"For your information, this is the Pledge Active dance," she said. "They were already initiated last week so get over yourself."

Chad reached for her shoulders but Michael stepped past her. He thumped Chad in the chest with his index finger.

"My lady is right and she doesn't want to dance with you."

Chad paused and stared at Michael. Since they were the same height and of equal muscular build, it was a stare-down. Chad flinched then cracked his neck to one side. He touched Michael on the chest lightly.

"Not cool, bro. Really not cool over a chick."

Stephanie recalled that moment with warmth and excitement—Michael was tough. Or so she thought.

The next Thursday she stopped by the fraternity open-drinking night, and when she found Michael, he was standing in the doorway of his frat room with Chad. They were laughing and clinking Corona beers. She crossed her arms and stood, puzzled.

"And right then-bam! Right in my fuck marbles!" Chad said. He grabbed his crotch for emphasis. Michael burst out laughing.

"I swear my voice was falsetto for a week. She bruised the little fellas. And--"

Chad noticed Stephanie. He gestured toward.

120

"Old lady's here. There goes the party." He stepped past her, licking his lips lasciviously. Stephanie pointed toward the direction he walked.

"Fuck marbles?" she asked.

"He's got a knack for the testicular euphemism, doesn't he?"

"What's going on? You King Asshole pals now?"

"He's okay, Steph. Besides, I can't let a bro have bad feelings about me."

"And what's with this?" Stephanie said.

She pointed toward Michael's two top shirt buttons. Each was off by one buttonhole, making his collar and shirt front crooked. He unbuttoned and buttoned the shirt correctly.

"I think too much and get distracted sometimes. I have tripped over my own feet, I kid you not."

Stephanie couldn't help but laugh, though she found the whole thing completely charming.

"There's my girl!" Gregory hollered and ran up to Stephanie and Michael. He threw his arms around Stephanie. She recalled his perfectly styled hair, sparkling eyes, great clothes, and Polo eau du perfume.

"You sure you want this guy?" Gregory said.

"Now here's someone worth your time," she said toward Michael.

"Strawberry margaritas in my room. Who's game?" Gregory said.

"I'm in!" Stephanie said.

"Uhhh," Michael replied.

"I didn't say 'who's gay', Michael. *Game. Game* for margaritas!"

The roar of the plane's jets drowned out the memory of the blender whipping up the margaritas. Stephanie recalled the tequila hangover the next day. But more so, she remembered the protective feeling of Michael born that night she discovered his odd habit of making friends of jerks and missing buttonholes on his shirt. Somehow that brought the cute Pery's

121

receptionist, Chakranna, to mind. Stephanie had never found out if she was married. Why did she care? Shit, she realized. She was going to need more time to trust Michael again. Should I book a return flight right back and keep an eye on him? She dismissed the idea as crazy, but the residual effect was worry. One more pang of worry enveloped her: would he be preoccupied and cross the wrong side of the street, forgetting he was in Ireland? Or just trip and fall off a high curb? He was just that much of a klutz. He's a big boy now. She resigned herself and began to relax. She glanced out toward clouds that began to press against the plane window. She reclined her chair and slipped on the Bose noise-cancelling headphones.

7.

"Even more exciting news than just the bones, your Excellency," Monsignor Leahy said.

Cardinal Adamanto adjusted the telephone receiver to his left ear. He continued to adjust the microfiche knob as he reviewed issues of the Giornale di Sicilia from decades past. He had already found three articles detailing mob purges that correlated with donations and loaning of the cross.

"What would that be?" Adamanto asked.

"We may have a descendant of the Bishop here in our midst."

Adamanto paused.

"Really? Tell me more."

"He's a volunteer from California, of all places." Monsignor Leahy chuckled.

"Name?"

"Michael Dunphy. We're going to extend his stay in Limerick a few weeks while we have his DNA tested here at Trinity."

As if he were receiving instant illumination and grace from the Lord, Adamanto's heart lightened with relief and anticipation.

"You must inform me of the results prior to any announcements. Including informing this Mr. Dunphy if he is a descendant. Are we clear?"

"Yes, your Excellency."

"Bless you and ciao." Adamanto hung up. He saw no reason to go further with his research because the unholy record was clear: the church had been making money from loaning the cross to the mob for decades. And it was also clear that he would be the faithful one to end this pattern and rid the Vatican of the now cursed relic by returning the cross to the rightful heir. He could only guess at who else in the Vatican was aware of this evil arrangement and he didn't care. When the next spring arrived, the Palermo Family would leave the Vatican with nothing in hand except their tainted Euros.

A few days later, Michael sat in the rear seat of a Lincoln Town Car with Monsignor Leahy and Cardinal C'Dealva. While they spoke quietly in Italian, he glanced out the window at the bustle on Leinster Street in Dublin. The aged granite of Trinity College began to appear, and it reminded Michael of the buildings at UC Berkeley. There was an air of scholarly dignity and austerity in the ancient structures. As he wondered which building housed the Trinity Institute of Genetics, Monsignor Leahy turned toward him.

"The cardinal tells me that the Vatican chief of reliquaries is quite interested in meeting you, if it turns out you are Bishop Flynn's descendant. The cardinal says he has been instructed to arrange a flight and short stay at the Vatican if you are interested."

Michael smiled toward C'Dealva but was met with a slight scowl beneath his dark brows. His smile faded.

"I don't know what to say other than of course. What's not to like about a free trip to Rome?"

"And Cardinal C'Dealva will be your escort."

Michael nodded. C'Dealva, who was growing into his new shadow, cracked the most meager of smiles. The driver veered left and the historical architecture of the college gave way to a set of modern buildings with sharp angles of glass and steel. They passed the Dublin Dental Hospital. The driver slowed the car to a creep and looked from his navigation system up to his right and then back down. The car stopped.

"I believe the Genetics Institute is this first building on the left. I'll be minding about some parking, so I'll drop you all off at the entrance here."

Leahy, C'Dealva, and Michael slid out of the car and walked through the glass doors of the institute. Michael's legs and lower back were stiff from the nearly three-hour car ride so he was glad to walk the few yards. After they were greeted by a receptionist, Michael noticed the cavernous atrium over her shoulder. Despite the omnipresent gray overcast of Ireland, the atrium was ablaze with light coming through three stories of plate glass. Mustard yellow and muted moss green walls gave an aura of technology and the future. This was no dour Georgian foyer. Even the air had a crisp dryness that Michael did not expect since he had grown accustomed to the damp air of Limerick.

"Afternoon, gents," Michael heard over his shoulder. He turned and saw a forty-ish slender man in a lab coat with salt and pepper hair and crystal blue eyes smile through his scruffy van dyke beard as he shook Monsignor Leahy's hand.

"I'm Dr. Seamus Reilly and I will be heading up this project."

He reached for C'Dealva's hand but C'Dealva simply nodded. Dr. Riley nodded back and turned toward Michael, reaching out his hand once again.

"You must be our guinea pig, so?" he said. "Just a swab and a poke and we'll have what we need. Follow me gentlemen."

Dr. Reilly led them up one flight of stairs. Students sat at several tables in the atrium and several glanced up toward them. Michael thought of his daughter and smiled back at them. They followed Dr. Reilly through two sets of glass doors and then a third security door. Dr. Reilly placed his thumb on a small digital screen, and it opened with a hydraulic gust of air.

Two rows of glass office cubicles, each lined by white lab tables and stools above which sat glass shelves and cabinets, stood on either side of them. Several people in lab coats hunched over microscopes as they reviewed slides or handled pipettes. This might have well been a movie set if Michael didn't know better. Dr. Reilly stepped through a single glass door and held it open for Michael and the others to follow.

On three lab tables in the center of the room lay the headless skeletons from the dig. They looked like dirty wood to Michael. He paused at the edge of the table. He pointed toward the center skeleton.

"That's gotta be my ancestor. Same boney calves passed down."

He chuckled. Dr. Reilly grinned but Monsignor Leahy and Cardinal C'Dealva looked at him quizzically. Michael cleared his throat in embarrassment.

"My office, gents," Dr. Reilly broke the awkward silence. "We'll handle the samples in here."

Dr. Reilly patted a blood-drawing chair with its small side table for a left armrest. Michael regarded the black vinyl chair cushions, sighed and sat. He rolled his shirt sleeve and laid his arm on the table. Dr. Reilly nodded for Monsignor Leahy and Cardinal C'Dealva to take two seats a few feet away. Dr. Reilly slid onto a round stool. He patted Michael's shoulder and then pulled on vinyl gloves.

"Just think, you are making history by revealing it. Quite exciting, so?"

A moment later, Dr. Reilly drew Michael's blood. To the doctor's credit, Michael barely felt the poke. As soon as Dr. Reilly stored the blood vile in a short test tube stand, he tore open a sealed plastic bag. He withdrew something that resembled a single cigar case, twisted it open and pulled out what looked like a flat, grooved Q-tip.

"This is the easy part. I'll just take a buccal swab of your inner cheek for a moment and we'll be good. "

Michael opened his mouth as C'Dealva spoke quiet Italian to Leahy.

"Cardinal C'Dealva asks, and I wonder, too, how long is all this DNA work going to take?" Monsignor Leahy asked. "It took six months to identify Richard the Third."

Just as Dr. Reilly finished the swab, Michael said: "Yeah. Me, too. How long?"

The doctor placed the buccal swab into its case and placed it next to the vile of Michael's blood. He pulled off the gloves and tossed them into a metal medical waste receptacle.

"So the English took six months to identify Richard the Third," Dr. Reilly said with a note of disdain in his tone. "We are a far more advanced lab. Without boring you with the details, we will have Michael's DNA extracted and compared to the three bone samples in three weeks, four weeks at most."

"Extraordinary," Leahy said. He translated the answer for C'Dealva. C'Dealva's eyebrows raised and he almost smiled. He spoke quietly to Leahy.

"Cardinal C'Dealva says that it must be God's blessing on this lab in such a good Catholic country. I heartily agree," Leahy said as he nodded and smiled.

"Not to mention the efforts of these scientists who came up with the rapid DNA analysis," Michael said.

Leahy's forehead wrinkled in confusion as he was taken aback. He shook his head.

"Sir, we are hosting this experiment under the auspices of the Church. That includes your room and board for your extended stay."

Dr. Reilly began to chuckle. He looked down and made a note on a file.

Michael began to see the arteries in Dr. Reilly's hand, and the corpuscles of blood flowing through them. Monsignor Leahy and Cardinal C'Dealva morphed into spinning molecules as if he saw them through a kaleidoscope.

"Forgot my Tegrot…"

The white light almost blinded Michael. His head felt faintly heavy and his mouth parched. He felt someone patting his right hand. He blinked to clear his eyes and saw a doctor and nurse standing on either side of him.

"What the hell?" he strained to say.

"Mr. Dunphy, you're in St. James Hospital emergency. You had a convulsion. Do you recall anything prior to the episode?"

Michael sighed. He recalled molecules and atoms exploding across his vision. He took a deep breath and he remembered bones. That was it—the bones on the table.

"Yeah, yeah. The bones on the table. They're testing my DNA."

The doctor nodded and patted his shoulder. Michael now saw the doctor had a shock of red hair over spectacles through which milky green eyes smiled approvingly.

"Good, good," the doctor said. "We were able to contact your wife and found out that you must have missed your dose of Tegretol. We adequately dosed you and the seizure resolved itself."

The doctor nodded toward two nurses, a male and female, in blue scrubs. They approached either side of the exam table.

"These nurses here will help you to your feet. Monsignor Leahy is waiting in the lobby to escort you back to Limerick."

As the nurses gently grabbed Michael's arms and helped raise him to a sitting position, he felt slightly dizzy. He also wasn't looking forward to the hours in the car with Monsignor Leahy and most probably, Cardinal C'Dealva.

"May I have some water, please?" he asked.

The water cooled his dry throat. He let the coolness of the second sip linger on his lips. Just as he finished the last sip from the small plastic cup, the nurses were back at his side.

"Let's give it a try, so?" the male nurse said.

Michael leaned forward and let his shoes touch the floor. His legs felt heavy but, in a moment, he stood firm. Both nurses held tight to his elbows as he stepped toward the blue curtain of the cubicle. The female nurse slid it aside quickly to allow him to pass. She held his elbow and they walked together down the hall, past the other emergency stations with blue curtains. At the double doors, she paused.

"The Monsignor and Cardinal are seated in the waiting hall just down to the left. Mind yourself, then."

She nodded goodbye and made her way back down the hall from which they had just come. Michael pushed against the handles of the double doors and they opened automatically. The doors snapped shut with a metal clank behind him as he looked left and saw Monsignor Leahy and Cardinal C'Dealva. They both stood as he walked up to them.

"Glad to see you're better," Monsignor Leahy said. Cardinal C'Dealva muttered something and nodded. "The car is waiting for us out front."

The car ride back to Limerick was nearly silent except for the occasional bursts of quiet Italian conversation between Monsignor Leahy and Cardinal C'Dealva. Michael was lulled by the soft cadence of the conversation and drifted off to sleep. He woke with a start when the car pulled up to the front of Pery's Hotel. He looked over and saw that neither Monsignor Leahy nor Cardinal C'Dealva were still in the car. The ordeal in the emergency room must have really wiped him out—he couldn't believe he had slept through their drop-offs.

"You doin' okay there, so?" the driver asked.

Other than feeling the thick and heavy-headed feeling of needing sleep, Michael was okay. He clicked open the passenger door and shifted his legs toward the curb. They too felt burdensome. He thanked the driver and made his way to the hotel door, feeling as though he were wading through a pool of molasses, his legs straining against the inertia of a long car ride. He sighed as he considered how very old he felt and pulled open the lobby door.

"Call your wife, aye?" Chakranna said. "Where ya' been?"

Adrenaline jolted Michael. He hadn't checked his phone for hours. He plucked it from his pocket and saw nine voicemails had been left. A long series of texts from Stephanie showed as well. The flow, like a river of information that always seemed to get him caught answering the wrong email in an email chain, or posting a Facebook comment out of context, usually fatigued him and sometimes, inundated him. This time was no exception. Once again, he felt old and slow. He sighed and picked up his pace toward the elevator. Chakranna kept a concerned eye on him.

"You look a wee tired, then. I got a tonic for that if you might be interested."

"No, I just need some rest."

The elevator door opened and as Michael stepped in, Chakranna kept talking. He held the elevator door open to let her finish. He had learned over the weeks with her and many other Irish people he encountered it was best to let the chat run its course.

"Given it might be hard on you with your wife home and all, maybe you'd enjoy a nice tea with my husband and I tomorrow night? Sure you haven't had any home cooking in some time."

Michael rubbed the back of his neck. He sighed with fatigue but the kindness touched him. And he *could* use a homemade meal.

"Yes. Dinner tomorrow night sounds good."

"Really?!" she said.

"What time?" he asked.

"We'll leave straight away after my shift ends at six thirty. No bother with an Uber—you can ride home with me."

"Sounds good."

"And will you not be eating any sort of thing? No type of meat or what not?"

"I eat everything."

"That's good. So you go get yourself a good night's rest, then."

"Thanks, and you, too."

Michael dropped his hand and let the elevator door shut. He leaned back against the wall, the fatigue once again overtaking him.

"Dinner with the witch, then?" Stephanie said. Her image shifted in and out on Michael's phone as they Facetimed later.

"And her husband."

"Are we thinking eye of newt stew or raven claw pie?"

"Might be better than a lot of this Irish fare I have been eating. Just how many ways can you make cream gravy and pork, anyway?"

"Yes, but the steamed cabbage is an excellent cruciferous veggie. And you know you need those with your brain still healing."

"Please, not my brain again. I already set Siri with a Tegretol alarm every morning at eight. I won't miss it again. You have anything else to say? I need to get to bed."

"Oh, yeah. Your mom showed up on Pat Robertson's YouTube Channel. I watched until I couldn't take it anymore."

"I thought evangelicals like him think Catholics are all going to hell."

"I guess they're both affiliated with some sort of mission in the south. Maybe a truce for now? I don't know."

"She never ceases to amaze me," Michael said shaking his head. "Where is she going to pop up next?"

"Just as long as it's not our house, I'm good. The funniest part of the YouTube video was her holding that damn Rodeo Drive purse in her lap. What the hell does she keep in that thing?"

Michael shrugged and shook his head. His mother remained an enduring enigma to him so her penchant for mystery was just another level of the unfathomable.

"Okay. We done?"

"Yep. Love you. Get some rest. And take your Tegretol!"

"Love you, too." Michael raised the phone to his lips and kissed it just as the call ended. He needed to get rest for his big evening with the witch.

"Are you going to rev up your broomstick?" Michael asked Chakranna the next day.

He stood at the reception counter as she closed out her station. The male evening receptionist stood near, nipping at the skin of his middle fingernail. His dark chocolate, almost black eyes darted between Chakranna and Michael. Chakranna lifted the wooden partition of the counter and stepped around to Michael.

"No broomstick. But my VW Bug is almost as small."

They walked to the glass doors. Michael stepped ahead and opened the door. Chakranna smiled and walked out. As Michael passed through the door, he heard the male receptionist holler:

"Enjoy yer date, so!"

Moments later, the VW Bug sputtered along. It passed the convent and digs. Michael could see that the pits were all refilled and only the slight mounds of coffee-colored dirt betrayed their locations. Chakranna shifted the car into neutral as they waited at a red light. With one quick gesture, she pulled out a hair pin, releasing the bun and causing a strawberry blond cascade to fall down her shoulders. She reached for the stick shift once again and they chugged along.

"Such a relief," she said. "I like to be made up for my husband when I walk through the door."

"Oh," Michael could think of nothing to say, surprised by the rather casual and conventional sexism.

At the next stop light, she shifted to neutral again and pulled out a tube of lipstick. In two quick strokes, her lips turned violet-black. Streetlights reflected off her lips as they drove along. The car went on another mile or so, and at two more stop lights, she was able to apply deep violet and brown eye shadow to her left and right eyelids. They pulled up in front of a series of plain stone row houses. Chakranna stopped the car and turned off the engine.

"Home, sweet home," she said.

But before they exited the car, she reached into her purse and pulled out a tube of eyeliner. She raised her chin and, with a well-practiced finger, pulled gently to tighten each eyelid as she applied thick lines. Closing up the tube of eyeliner, she glanced over at Michael. She was, in a word, goth, Michael thought.

"A wee different from my counter face, so?"

"I'll say."

They slid out of the car's cramped front seats. Michael felt a light pull of his abdomen muscles against his still-healing ribs. He hadn't felt that pain in awhile and he winced. Chakranna didn't notice, though, because she had already walked ahead and passed through a short, iron gate She stood at the porch sprinkling something from her purse. As Michael joined her, he watched her bring her palms together as if in prayer. Her eyes closed briefly until she noticed Michael.

"Sage to keep out evil," she said, pointing toward the ground leaves scattered like green powder across the brick porch. "Let's go in and get tea."

Chakranna slid her key into the front door and they walked into the house. Michael smelled something like patchouli incense and an all-too-familiar Irish aroma: steamed cabbage.

"That you, Bridget darlin'?" a gruff male voice asked from somewhere in the back of the house. "And your bud?"

Michael mouthed 'Bridget?' Chakranna nodded and dropped her chin.

"Aye!" she hollered.

A heavy oak door swung from a wall covered with dingy yellow wallpaper. Out came a refrigerator of a man. A dark patch of military-cut hair sat atop a face that bulged from fat and dripping sweat. He wiped his thick hand against an apron that read 'Kitchen Dick' and held it out to Michael.

"Name's Liam," he said.

He squeezed Michael's hand firmly but dropped it immediately. He reached his massive arm around Chakranna's waist and pulled him to her. They exchanged a loud kiss.

"There's my little witch, so. She been doin' that spooky stuff and so on ya?"

"Not a toad quite yet," Michael replied. "I'm Michael, by the way."

"Well you have a sit, Mike bud. Bridget, why don't you get our guest a whiskey—or a Guinness if he prefers?"

"Guinness sounds great," Michael said. Chakranna pointed toward an overstuffed, dingy brown sofa.

Chakranna left the room briefly and returned with an open can of Guinness. She poured the brown stream into a large tin tumbler and handed it to Michael just as the foamy head reached the tumbler's rim. She placed the can on a glass coffee table next to a ruffled copy of the Limerick Post. Just as she reached for a glass ashtray with cigar butts, she noticed the edge of a magazine under the newspaper. She gasped and grabbed up both. Michael was sure he saw the edge and graphic 'P' of a Playboy magazine. Chakranna tossed both periodicals into a sliding wooden TV cabinet. The flat screen television wobbled a bit as she slammed it shut. Michael sipped the bitter roasted barley flavor of the Guinness that always reminded him of weak coffee. Chakranna took a seat in a high-backed, narrow, soiled orange velvet chair opposite him. She folded her legs into a yoga position and closed her eyes. She brought her open palms together in front of her chest.

"Are you meditating?" Michael asked.

"No. Opening my vibration to my spirit guides."

"Hope you like loin of bacon!" Liam hollered from the kitchen.

'As long as it's not pork chops,' Michael thought. He took another sip of the Guinness and let the foam cool his lips.

"Anything with bacon is good by me!" Michael hollered back.

"He wanted to make lamb stew, but I didn't think that was good enough for a guest tea," Chakranna said. She inhaled deeply, held the breath a few seconds, and then released it.

Liam stepped through the swinging door. He carried a pink frosted cake on a glass cake pedestal in one hand and a can of Guinness in the other. He presented the cake to Michael.

"And a strawberry cake for after tea, bud," Liam said. He set the cake plate on the coffee table and sat on the rolled arm of Chakranna's chair.

"Looks good," Michael replied.

"Liam is a great cook *and* baker," Chakranna said. She opened her eyes and stretched her arms over her head.

"Learned it all from those Yank cooking shows on cable, so," Liam said.

"He makes cakes for all the neighbors—birthdays, anniversaries, even a funeral once."

"Cake baking, too?" Michael asked. Liam nodded.

"Old lady O'Dowd three doors down—she's a helluva good sort," Liam said "Lost her husband last year after sixty-three years wed. Made her a bitter chocolate layer cake for her mourning."

"Wow. Sixty-three years. Stephanie—that's my wife—and I will celebrate thirty-one years in August."

"Well cheers to that!" Liam said. He tapped his Guinness can against Michael's. "My little witch and I are just seven years on."

"Cheers to that!" Michael raised his tumbler toward Liam and Chakranna.

Chakranna slapped Liam's thigh and prodded him to stand.

"Let's get our tea on, so," she said.

Chakranna led Michael to a small wooden table set for three. The Irish linen napkins were an odd contrast to the plain ceramic plates adorned only with a blue stripe on their rims. Michael waited for Chakranna to sit, and then slid into his chair. The wooden chair pushed hard against his back. Liam snatched up his plate.

"Bridget, would you pour our bud a nice glass of that pinot grigio while I plate the din?"

Michael almost declined since he had only sipped his tumbler of Guinness. But Chakranna poured the white wine into a cut-glass highball tumbler on his right before he had the chance to speak. He nodded in thanks and noticed a small glass dish of mustard sitting next to a golden slab of Irish butter and thick slices of bread. He wondered how the mustard and bacon were going to come together in the meal. Liam clanked serving tools against the plates in the kitchen. Chakranna filled her and Liam's tumblers.

"Like I said before, no stew tonight, so," Chakranna said. "Just the good cut of meat."

"Here's to that!" Michael raised his wine glass. They clinked. The wine was dry and crisp on Michael's palate.

"Okay, so I got to ask. Since your first name is 'Bridget', where does 'Chakranna' come from?"

"That's her witchin' name," Liam said as he entered with the plates. Michael was hungry and the idea of bacon made his mouth almost water. He could even put up with more steamed cabbage if only—

"There's your loin of bacon, bud."

Michael looked down in surprise at the boneless pork chop covered in--he barely could believe it--cream sauce. He smiled at Liam and Chakranna.

"Looks delicious, chef—thank you."

Liam placed a plate in front of Chakranna. He walked out briefly and returned with his own plate. As he sat, Michael noticed the glistening sweat at Liam's temples. His chunky cheeks showed pink from the heat and effort of the kitchen. Liam grabbed his fork and dug into the meat.

"Always can cut his loin of bacon with a fork—don't know how he does it," Chakranna said.

"It's the long simmer, does it. So my Little Witch, you going to tell our bud here where your name comes from?"

Michael noticed Chakranna's eyes flare at Liam. She pursed her lips in anger and chewed, making her lips flex from a black-violet oval into black-violet circle. Michael looked down at his plate and scraped some cabbage onto his fork.

"The cabbage is tender and sweet, too," he said.

"My name comes from—"

"It's not important. Don't worry about it," Michael said.

"No. She is going to tell you, right my sweet?" Liam said. His tone rumbled with a threatening irritation and all humor had drained from it. "Do try a spot of mustard with your loin, bud."

Liam slid the container of mustard toward Michael. He placed a small dab on his plate with the ancient silver spoon stained with what looked like decades of tarnish. Michael dipped a morsel of pork into the mustard. The soft burn of mustard really did make the tender pork somehow richer. He nodded and Liam slapped his shoulder.

"Told you. Now, my pet?" Liam said to Chakranna.

Chakranna took a deep breath. Michael thought he could see her face blush through the edges of her pale face powder. He so wanted to leave at that moment.

"When I joined the local Wicca group, I named myself and my aura 'Chakranna'. Before I was Wiccan, I had been taking yoga classes and learned a lot about the sacred chakras. I added my middle name 'Ann' to 'Chakra' and that was that."

"I think it was the Hindus who originated the idea of the chakras—the energy of creation located in spots along the spine and brain," Michael said.

"Aye! Kundalini energy! So you are a believer, then?" she asked.

"No," Michael said.

"There's a good bud. You and I will be with the good Lord and Virgin Mary while my Little Witch here, well, will be burnin' like all witches should. "

Liam took a bite of bread smeared with the golden Irish butter. He let out a groan of satisfaction.

"Butter is in good way this time. Damn good," Liam said.

"To be fair, I'm not a believer in anything."

"Not even in the church and pope?" Liam asked.

"No."

"Hmm," Liam said. After a moment, he added: "You the one going to hell, bud, not me. So that's fine."

"See that's where everybody is wrong," Chakranna said. "The spirits tell us that all great religions and philosophies are a part of the Great Truth."

"Ah, here she goes on her witchy thing, then," Liam said.

Chakranna's eyes screwed up with irritation.

"They all are correct," she continued. "There is nothing but the great energy after death that we reunify with."

"Sounds just like any other religion. How do you know you're right?" Michael asked.

"I know from intuition, and I have faith in my intuition."

"Faith is the other problem. As soon as people believe and have faith, it blinds them to other facts and ideas."

"What else is there but faith?" Liam asked. "Ain't no real proof 'cept for what the Lord puts in your heart."

"No one seems to doubt what they believe or have faith in. Doubt is humbling but it also fuels the search for truth based on facts and reality."

"But Jesus said 'I am the Truth, the Light, the Way,'" Liam countered. "Said nothing about doubt."

"So does the old Testament, and the Hindu gospels, and on and on. They can't all be right."

"And what makes *you* right?" Chakranna asked.

"I believe in the search for truth based on evidence and reality. That's it. Science is the best tool man has come up with to pursue the facts."

"What if science and all that other wanker stuff is wrong, bud? You ready to face St. Peter?" Liam asked.

"I stick with reasoning based on proof and probability. There's plenty of room for doubt in that and for revising my reasoning when new facts mess with it."

"Without the Lord and faith, there's just no point to any of it, so," Liam said.

"Yes, there is still a point. To make life better for myself and everyone I come into contact with."

"But what about all the confusing things in life? Prayer surely helps with that," Liam said.

"Or meditation and yoga," Chakranna added.

"My life is the sum total of all my choices and actions no matter what motivates me. I fail and I pick myself back up—no praying needed. I take full responsibility for my life."

"And when you're taking your last breaths? You think you'll be so sure?" Chakranna asked.

"Hopefully I'll be able to look back when I'm dying and say the life I chose and made was a good one for me and everyone around me. What happens after I die is none of my concern."

"As long as it gives people comfort and doesn't harm anyone, you okay with that?" Chakranna asked.

"I guess but it depends on what you mean by 'harm'. As soon as I see proof that people keep their faith and beliefs private and stop using the voting booth and legislatures, or worse, guns and bombs, to attack others who don't believe like them, I can go along with that."

"Cheers to that, bud!" Liam raised his Guinness. "We had The Troubles here because of such nonsense."

"In the U.S. for example, our system is based on liberty. If liberty is anything it must be about freedom to choose your life—we choose our leaders, we choose what faith to believe, or not to believe, we choose to have guns or not. That's all great. But even though people of faith can choose what to believe, they still try to stop women or gay people from freely exercising their choices."

"But why be good at all, then?" Chakranna asked.

"Because every living thing shares the same elements and molecules. We all sprang from the planet and exploding stars before that and so every living thing is a part of every other living thing. Why would you intentionally harm a part of yourself?"

"And we are all ultimately energy from the same source," Chakranna added.

"It's as simple as Lao Tzu, or the clever monk who probably made him up, put it: 'A man who sees all others as part of himself is a sound man to guard them.' Why would you lie, steal, or murder yourself?"

"That's like what Jesus said: love others as you love yourself. Aye?" Liam added.

"Not exactly: that was also about getting into Heaven. But I absolutely agree with the compassion and empathy of that idea."

"Oh, bud. Seems you will be burnin' in Hell with my little witch here. But you okay with Jesus' Golden Rule?"

"Yes—absolutely. He didn't coin the Golden Rule. It comes from India and pre-dates him by hundreds of years."

"Second time you mentioned India. Like they all know so much," Liam said.

"It's an old culture. They have a lot of good ideas about how people can get along. Lots of centuries to work on those ideas. Same with Buddhists."

"We Wiccans acknowledge Buddha as a great wise one!" Chakranna said.

"It boils down to two things that give me trouble with 'faith': there is some sort of magic God or universe in control of all this, and there's only one 'Truth'. Those two beliefs keep people tribal and at each other's throats."

Michael picked up a piece of pork, dipped in mustard and popped it in his mouth. He buttered a piece of bread and took a bite. He washed both down with some wine.

Liam's elbow was up on the table. He leaned on his left fist and just looked at Michael. Chakranna's eyes were downcast as she picked at her plate of pork. Michael felt a flash of embarrassment and some shame.

"Sorry you guys. I seem to get off on these tangents lately. You're right, Liam, the butter is really good."

The Uber drive honked for Michael just after he finished his slice of strawberry cake a bit later. His mouth was thick with sugar and shortening and it weighed heavy on the pork and wine already distending his stomach. He stood and Chakranna jumped up and led him to the door. Liam tagged behind.

"Thank you both. It was a real delicious home-cooked meal. I needed it."

Chakranna stood on tiptoe and kissed his cheek. Liam nudged her aside and extended his hand.

"Do come by the pub, bud, since it's pretty close to the Pery's so. 'The Frog's Hole'."

"Sorry?" Michael said.

" 'Frog's Hole'—that's the pub."

"Colorful name," Michael said. Chakranna screwed up her face and nodded.

"Some limey who hated the French opened it up back in the thirties or thereabouts." Liam chuckled. "All drinks on me!"

"Great," Michael replied.

The Uber drive honked again and Michael saw a white Ford Focus with its passenger door open. He climbed in and they pulled away. What Michael didn't notice was a black Ford Crown Victoria that crept from the parked curb a few doors down and began to follow them.

8.

"Oh, tell me you didn't go off on one of your tangents with them," Stephanie said over Facetime on Michael's phone a couple hours later. Michael lay under the blankets in the bed in a white T-shirt and his jockey shorts. He had his phone balanced on his chest using its small stand. His hands were woven behind his head, forming triangles out of his arms.

"Well she got into some of that new-agey, witch stuff and I just couldn't help myself. Hey, does my neck look like a pancake in this position?"

"Why don't you reverse the camera image and see?"

Michael tapped his phone screen. He winced and tapped it again quickly.

"You should have told me. I look like a croissant with whiskers."

"I just love that I can tuck you into bed each night and still finish the rest of my workday," Stephanie said.

"What time is it there?"

"Three-thirty. So you really have three more weeks there?"

"Yup. I'm just going to enjoy the next few days."

"What are you going to do?"

"I never got the chance to trace Uncle Terrence's footsteps here in Limerick—just his possible burial site. Plus, I think I want to hit the castle ruins in Cashel. Maybe even the cathedral in Emly where Terrence was bishop."

"Are you talking about the Rock of Cashel?"

"Yep."

"You probably don't remember the Waterford vase you gave me for our twentieth anniversary."

"Am I in trouble if I don't?"

"You remembered the anniversary—you're off the hook. But the vase is called 'The Rock of Cashel Vase'. I wonder if it's the same."

"No idea. But I am looking forward to checking all this out. Not exactly Indiana Jones stuff. But I'm genetically connected to it all so that's something."

"I wish I could fly out and join you. But all that time with that crappy Wi-Fi put me too far behind. You tired? You look like you're fading."

"I am. Big day walking around Limerick tomorrow. If I could just sleep straight through the night."

"Shit. You're not sleeping again?"

"Damn insomnia."

"Just remember: don't stress yourself if you wake up. Get up and read or watch TV. Try to get back to sleep after that. No fretting. And for crying out loud, no philosophical obsessing."

"I won't make any guarantees."

"Good night, love."

As Michael went to kiss the phone, Stephanie flashed her breasts. He dropped the phone and laughed.

"You just sexted me! You just went all nasty!" he hollered toward the phone.

He picked it up and her face appeared once again. She laughed so explosively that she snorted.

"I thought my saggy girls might help you sleep better! Good night!"

Michael stretched out on the bed. What he didn't tell Stephanie was that his insomnia revolved around the gnawing emptiness that had returned. The same feeling that caused him to almost ruin his marriage with that young teacher was surfacing again. The sense of losing his interest in everything about himself, the apathetic malaise that had abated during the dig had roared back. Boredom was the most potent reminder of his sense of purposelessness. He almost redialed Stephanie but instead decided to just allow the shadow of depression to creep over him. How privileged and self-indulgent he now considered himself. Seven and a quarter billion other people on the planet were too busy struggling to survive and had no time for depression. Poor little Michael and his unsatisfying life choices. He almost wanted to slap himself. After an hour, he dozed and a fitful sleep full of dreams began.

Groggy and feeling heavy from his lack of sleep, he stepped out the front door of Pery's and walked to catch the bus to central Limerick the next morning. He didn't need to arrange an Uber since the bus to central Limerick stopped near the hotel. His plan was to Uber to the areas of old Irish Town and approximate Bishop Terrence Flynn's footsteps the last few days of his life, from the end of the Siege to the gallows. He used an app that allowed him to overlay a map of 1650 Limerick he found on UC Berkeley's history department website over present-day Limerick. The historical summary notes from the dig along with a couple of archives he had googled gave him added confidence he could come close to some of the sites, even if parking lots or pubs now stood on them. As the bus chugged along, he reviewed the dig notes and glanced at his phone app.

"St. John's Square and Hospital coming up," the bus driver announced over a crackling p.a. speaker.

Michael reached up and pulled the bus stop alert. A woman in a thick sweater with silver, matted hair glanced at him over her narrow glasses. Michael smiled but she looked away. Two other men in work clothes slid out of the black, worn vinyl seats ahead of him and he stood and followed. When he stepped off the bus, he noticed the sky-blue, Georgian entrance gate to St. John's Hospital grounds. According to the notes and app, the remains of the Limerick Irish Town Citadel stood on the hospital grounds.

As he passed through the entrance, a mid-century, multi-story building, also painted sky-blue, rose up to his left. Asphalt, worn by time and Limerick's humid climate, crunched under his feet. The app gps led him to the right around the main hospital building and past a red brick wing. Just past rows of parked cars, he saw an ancient wing of a damaged building oddly contrasting the red brick and sky-blue walls of the hospital. He glanced down at the app and saw this must be the Citadel guard house. Stepping closer, around a couple of old Triumph sedans, he noticed cobblestones that met the asphalt in an uneven border. He also noticed random holes in the ancient wing that could have been from cannon blasts. He quickly googled and confirmed what he was seeing: the cannon ball strikes of the Cromwell forces. A chill went through him.

From the dig notes and his google research, he knew that during the last few days of the Siege of 1651, his ancestor attended the wounded men and Irish officers who fought against the English here in the Citadel officer's quarters. He had run across a few quotes of Bishop Flynn's where he not only offered blessings and final rites but also encouragement to the Irish fighters. That political support was in part why Bishop Flynn was one of the few singled out for immediate trial and execution. He felt a deep, almost spiritual sense of connection to his ancestor. For the moments he stood regarding the structure, imagining the violence of each cannonball strike and the fear each hit must have aroused, he considered his own depressing, midlife crisis as almost laughable. On the genetic shoulders of brave Terrence and his ancestors before and those he followed, he stood. Didn't he owe them better than malaise and self-pity?

One cannonball strike up to the right of the entry looked particularly deep. He wondered if that was the one that caused the breach that convinced the leaders of the starving and plague-ridden Irish to make the truce. He placed his hand on the ancient stones that were moist from the omnipresent humidity and overcast sky.

"Did you leave some of that courage for me, Great Uncs Terrence?" he said quietly.

He then chuckled at the irony of his ancestor, a bishop of great faith, reaching over the centuries to leave his atheist descendant a bit of bravery. Michael stepped back and took a couple of shots with his phone. His phone alerted him that his Uber was now waiting to take him to the rest of his stops since they were all off the Limerick bus routes. He turned and walked back across the parking lot and out of the hospital grounds entrance and saw the white VW Golf.

"Six stops then a drop back at the Pery's. You some kind of detective or something?" the driver asked as Michael clicked his seatbelt a few moments later.

"No. Just a tourist."

"I'm Kevin O'Bannon, by the way."

"Nice to meet you, Kevin," Michael said. He reached out his hand and shook Kevin's thin, pale hand. He sported a bracelet tattoo with a skull and crossbones at its center. Kevin smiled and nodded as Michael noticed his frazzled black Irish hair and narrow chin. He looked younger than either of his sons.

"Name's Michael. I'm a princi—an archaeologist and historian. At least for now," Michael said.

"Aye, are you then? Anyting you want to know about our history here, just ask. I might know seein' as I'm a descendant of old Hugh O'Neill, chief defender of the city against the feckin' English."

"I thought you said your last name is 'O'Bannon'."

"On me maw's side, 'tis the relation to clan O'Neill."

"I'm on the trail today of Bishop Terrence Flynn," Michael said.

"So, the old holy man who got the—" Kevin swept his fingertips across this throat.

"Yes. He's an ancestor on *my* mother's side. Checking out a few places where he lived his last days, and died."

"I might know a ghost story about him. Told to all of us lil' Limerickans. So, where's your first stop then? Need to get the buggy moving here."

Michael glanced down at his phone and scrolled.

"St. Leila Street."

"Feckin' really? It's right up the way there. You could have walked."

"I realize that. I just thought that St. John's here was a good landmark for us to connect up."

"Nothing much there except a few pieces of old Irish Town wall."

"That's *exactly* what I want to see."

A minute later, they pulled up in front of the ruins, kitty corner from Griffins Funeral Home. Michael's car door was now only a few feet away from the ruins.

"You can let me out here. I'll be just a few minutes."

Michael clicked open his seat belt and threw open the door. Michael eyed the ruins and felt a pump of adrenaline. He pointed off left toward the black and brown stones smoothed by centuries and thick with ivy and weeds. Kevin glanced at Griffins and raised his shoulders with a slight shiver.

"Cheery spot here. Right where me granny was taken after she died last year at St. John's."

"Sorry, Kevin. I wish I would have known. Why don't you swing a u-turn and park near the hospital wall so you don't have to look at it?"

Kevin nodded. He put the car in gear and made a wide right turn. Michael stood in front of the ruins, glancing between his phone, notes, and the wall, nodding the whole time. He looked back toward Kevin who had just finished parking. Michael caught Kevin's eye and pointed.

"These are definitely the remains of the ramparts," he hollered.

Kevin nodded, smiled, then looked down at this own phone. Michael turned back toward the ruins. As he did at the Citadel, he imagined Bishop Terrence pacing these fortifications and encouraging the Irish fighters that God and the Irish people were on their side.

From what he was able to find in the archives, Bishop Terrence spent most of the many months of the Siege standing alongside and supporting the Irish defenders. The ramparts surrounded the Irish Town on all sides—deep and thick piles of stone topped by the thick city walls. Musket fire and cannon strikes were unable to penetrate the defenses in 1651, but time had succeeded where the cannon had failed and done its inevitable damage. Michael glanced around to see if there was any way he could climb to the top of the ruins. That would insure he would stand where his brave ancestor once did. He thought about his rock-climbing, dig partner Yor. Michael wished once again that he were twenty years younger. And more coordinated. He kicked the base of one of the stones and saw dust fall from three or four feet above his head. That settled the matter. He sighed and set his phone to camera mode and shot a couple of photos.

When he walked back to the car, he noticed Kevin's thumbs flying over his phone, obliviously playing some sort of game. He tapped on the window and gave an 'ok' sign to let Kevin know he was ready for a ride to the next stop. Michael opened the passenger door and slid into the seat.

"Zombies suck!" Kevin said. "Take that, you bloody tosser!"

"I thought zombies eat brains," Michael said. "Vampires suck."

Kevin tapped his phone one last time and looked at Michael.

"What, bud?"

"Forget it."

"Where to now?"

Michael glanced down at his phone. He opened the 1651 map and using the overlay app, he was able to approximate the location of the next stop. This time there would be no ruins or plaques to guide him.

"Mungret Street. Near the Milk Market."

Kevin nodded and started the car.

"Gonna take a bit since it's all lefts to get there. If not for the one-ways we'd be there in a minute."

Michael kept an eye out for any other possible seventeenth century ruins as they made their way up St. John Street. The humid climate tended to weather any stone or brick to an ashy gray, making Victorian or later structures appear as old as the rampart ruins. His recently trained eye discerned the symmetric and even stone work of later periods from the random stone work that signaled seventeenth century or earlier. No seventeenth century roadway remained so he imagined the slapping sound of his ancestor's Dominican sandals against long-ago overbuilt cobble stones. Bishop Flynn most surely walked in and around these streets and alleys of old Irish Town Limerick. There was a depressing air about Limerick with its grayed brick structures beneath the omnipresent gray skies and Michael was not immune to the mood. This tour of his ancestor's last days must have weighed on his darkening mood as well. It reminded him of Stephanie's and his trip to Boston some years back and the initial excitement of visiting iconic Salem that gave way to a deep sadness later that day as they read the inscriptions of the Salem victims' last words on their memorial. The shallow silliness of Halloween witches was quickly eclipsed by the cruel historical realities scattered around the foot tour.

Michael's ruminations ended as Kevin made the final left turn onto Mungret Street.

"So the Milk Market's coming up shortly, bud. We'll need to take Ellen Street to Mungret, just pass Carr."

For this stop, Michael relied on the biography of Bishop Flynn in the dig notes. As Kevin began the turn onto Mungret at Carr, the Milk Market with its white big top roof stood on the corner. He knew the open market stalls lay under the big top. His gaze followed the curve of the big top and naturally moved left.

"Wait!" he hollered. Kevin hit the brakes.

"The bloody hell?"

Michael glanced down at his phone. He pointed toward Carr Street.

"It's down there! Can you make a u-turn anywhere?"

Michael opened the map of 1651 and overlaid it onto the street view satellite shot from the gps. From what he could tell, there was no Carr Street back then and Mungret was almost as wide as a highway. That would have meant that the rear of the structure he wanted to locate would most likely be the wall ruin he just spotted. Kevin had already managed the u-turn in front of the Milk Market to a chorus of irritated car horns.

"Down on Carr here, on the right?" he asked Michael.

"Yes, yes!"

Michael's heart raced once again with anticipation. This was more and more feeling like an Indiana Jones artifact hunt. They drove across Mungret toward red brick and faux stone apartment buildings. The wall ruins stood on the right, supported by a modern brown brick wall. Kevin had barely stopped the car on the street, partially blocking one of the apartment buildings, before Michael threw open his car door and hustled down a few feet of driveway, brandishing his phone like a gun. He paused at the ruin and his face lit up as he regarded it. The modern brick wall that separated the driveway between two apartment buildings had been cemented to the ruins, incorporating antiquity with dull modernism. But that very odd construction choice is most likely what preserved this section of wall, Michael conjectured. Glancing down at his phone and back up at the structure, he turned and looked down Carr Street. He began to walk away from the wall, pacing and counting as he went. When he arrived at a point about forty feet away, he turned back toward the wall and hollered with joy. He began clicking photos of the ruin with his phone.

Kevin watched until Michael began taking photos. At that point, he shrugged and looked down at his phone and resumed his zombie game app. After a few minutes, he looked up and saw Michael standing before the ruin and running his left hand around a stone arch that had long ago been filled in. He went back to his game.

Michael looked back down Carr Street where he had ended his pacing measurement and nodded. Michael glanced at Kevin and saw that he was occupied by his phone. He pulled out the dig notes and saw only the vague reference to the Pest House—a building that functioned similarly to a modern hospice for the Limerick citizens who were dying of the plague at the end of The Siege. Scant reports from that time indicated that victims were brought into the Pest House to suffer and die, only to be carted to an arched exit and out to a mass grave near the Irish Town wall. Michael was sure the brick arch in the structure he stood before was the departure point of the victims' bodies. More personally, it was within the structure long lost to time and progress where his ancestor was found and arrested by Ireton's troops as he ministered to the dying citizens. It was most probable to Michael that Bishop Flynn passed through this arch praying last rites for victims. Unexpectedly, a lump rose in his throat when he considered that his ancestor presumably didn't fear catching plague since he probably knew his own days at the hands of the English would be numbered. It was an act of bravery but more so, one of deep compassion, or so Michael would like to believe. Was any of that character woven into the DNA from his mother? He had always thought he got his guts from his dad, along with his humor. Compassion, empathy, and bravery were traits he struggled with but his mother, in addition to her zealotry, possessed those things. At least for people other than him. His eyes welled for a moment, making the last couple of photos blurry to his vision.

"You catch an allergy over there, bud?" Kevin asked him as he slid back into the passenger seat. "Your eyes look a little red and wet."

Michael shook his head as he reviewed the photos one more time. He pulled up the map.

"St. Mary's Cathedral," he said over a lump in his throat. "That should be easy."

"No directions needed," Kevin concurred and started the car.

A few minutes later, Michael stepped up the worn, stone stairs toward the imposing doors stained by centuries of grime from human contact. The façade of the church was no warm Mission style parish church to which his childhood Catholicism in Southern California had accustomed him, nor any sort of great European gothic edifice. Gray stone walls that resembled battlements with jagged stone teeth meeting a barbican with a four-cornered steeple made the twelfth-century structure feel like a castle ready for battle rather than a place to honor God. The dig literature had indicated that another ancestor of his and Bishop Flynn's, Donal Flynn, the last King of Munster, established the church in 1168. A remnant of his palace was incorporated into the façade. As Michael looked over the imposing and massive narrow windows above the entrance, they did remind him more of medieval arrow windows than sacred openings. The church remained Roman Catholic until Cromwell's attacks converted the cathedral to Anglican, but the feel of a medieval castle seemed to remain to Michael. And once again, as he touched the iron handle on the door, Bishop Flynn came to mind.

When Bishop Flynn stepped into the church for the last time, he wore shackles rather than the vestments worn when he celebrated masses at the church. While Michael could only approximate the Bishop's paths in the previous sites, it was well established that Bishop Flynn was led up these stairs and into the cathedral for his sham trial. Michael pulled open the massive oak door and traced the steps of his ancestor.

The gray stone nave lined with arches ended at a plain altar above which three glorious stained-glass windows in Gothic form brought in rainbows of light. But the oppressive pall from the dark wood ceiling absorbed most of the sunlight. Michael stepped forward and his sneakers made a soft suction sound against the slate floor. Just like the dour exterior, the interior of this church was bare of adornment except for memorial tableaus on the walls. Absent, too, he soon realized as he stood near the altar, was the ubiquitous oversized crucifix of a Catholic Church. There wouldn't be one since this was now an Irish Anglican church, he recalled. He stood transfixed as he imagined Bishop Flynn sitting near this same spot during his short trial. Several sections of the slate floor showed ancient chips and fractures and Michael recalled that those are alleged to have been caused by horses when the church was used as a stable for Ireton's troops. Bishop Flynn most probably heard the neighs and clomps of those horses while his trial transpired, Michael thought. But since he never offered a defense nor accepted counsel, maybe the horses were a comfort during the travesty of a trial. In the stillness, Michael heard his breaths echo in his ears. He pulled out his phone and took shots of the floor and the altar. He made his way back toward the entrance and took one more shot of the nave looking toward the altar. Sadness gripped him.

"Looking more and more down as we go along, bud," Kevin said as Michael slid back into the passenger seat. Kevin tossed his phone into the car console and started the engine.

154

"I guess you have a lot of practice reading people, huh?" Michael asked.

"Aye. Also, puttin' my way through university and studyin' psychology. Lots of people in Limerick can be using a few pokes around the gray matter."

"That goes for Americans, too," Michael said.

"Aye. Yanks!"

A few minutes later, as they drove Pennywell Road past the Good Shepherd Convent toward the corner of Old Clare Street, Kevin stopped the car and pointed at a bright blue store front.

"You mind if we stop there at A and R Supplies, bud? Need a plunger for the toilet and a stopper for a sink, too."

Michael glanced at the store front then further up the street. He checked his phone.

"Of course. My stop is right up at the next corner--Old Clare Street. Looks like a good place to park."

Kevin pulled the car up into a makeshift parking spot right in front of the store. They both hopped out.

"Meet you back here in a few," Michael said.

"Aye."

Michael walked toward the corner and heard the store keeper and Kevin exchange jovial Irish greetings. Just past the store, a white building with boarded up windows and door gave way to a chain link fence. Michael would have ignored it except for what lay about in the paved yard: headstones. They gave him the creeps, but especially the one whose inscription was only partially chiseled with the letters: 'S-t-e'. He had abandoned superstition along with his religion long ago, but he cringed to see the first three letters of his lovely Stephanie's name carved into the gray granite. He hustled past the gates and noticed the large purple print of the business front: 'Spirit Memorials.' How fitting this would be across the street from the execution site of his ancestor, if the dig notes source material was correct along with the app on his phone. At the corner

155

of Old Clare Street and Pennywell, he glanced around to see if there was any sort of memorial marker or plaque. Just the flat, large brown wall of some sort of mid 19ᵗʰ century factory lay before his eyes.

He crossed the street, thinking he would have to approximate the location once again. His eyes followed the brown, pocked wall of the factory on his right. Some graffiti in orange paint marked a section of the factory wall. Opposite on Old Clare Street, along the side wall of Spirit Memorials, graffiti stood out in bold neon green. He glanced down at his phone and started to walk toward the verdigris dome jutting from the factory roof. As he walked, he appeared to move further away from the point that marked the execution site. He turned around and walked back toward the corner, surveying the two-story houses on one side, the spire of St. John's, and a corner lot of another pleasant looking house. He turned left to walk down Pennywell Road away from Old Clare Street, and again, the app showed that he was walking away from the site. So he was going to have to approximate the location. But his disappointment was short-lived: he glanced up and saw a small, green plaque right at the corner of the factory building, about nine feet above the sidewalk.

'Farrancroghy. The site of public executions in the 16ᵗʰ and 17ᵗʰ Centuries,' it read. He felt a jolt: this was it—the spot, below the pavement, where his ancestor drew his final breath. Right here, he had removed a pectoral cross and handed it to his mother, Michael's great-times-five grandmother, and mounted the steps to be hung. For reasons Michael could not yet grasp, thinking about his ancestor handing the cross to his mother stirred up the odd feelings of emptiness he struggled with since his teens. Was it that his ancestor had a mother that had shown him love and devotion? Clearly, if the record was accurate, his ancestor loved his mother. Apparently, that didn't get passed down the gene cascade. How strange it was for Michael that he always *assumed* he loved his mother as was expected of him, but yet, could not identify a deep, true affection.

But even worse, he couldn't recall affection or a sense of love from *her*. Early on in his marriage, this brought grave problems to him and Stephanie. Stephanie's deep ability to love and support rescued their marriage and taught him what his mother never could or cared to try. Once again, tears welled in the corners of his eyes as the emptiness fought with his sense of loving Stephanie and the kids. He wiped his eyes and pulled out the dig notes.

Modern buildings blocked whatever the Bishop would have seen in his final moments, except for the sky. Michael raised his eyes to the soft gray overcast, knowing this would have been the last piece of sky his ancestor would have regarded. Left hanging for days so the English soldiers and occupiers could taunt, jeer, or tear at his corpse, he was then removed from the gibbet and beheaded. His body's final indignity was to be buried in an unmarked, shared grave after his head was placed on a spike above St. John's gate for weeks before it was tossed into the river.

All of the awful imagery played through Michael's mind, distracting him from his maternal emptiness, as he continued to regard this ancestral spot. If he had a jackhammer and a shovel, he would have excavated the spot to see if any of Bishop Flynn's ancient blood remained in the sad soil. He heard a car horn and looked and saw Kevin waving at him and shrugging his shoulders, holding his palms upward. Michael was glad to be brought back to the present and to finish up this morose tour. And if his DNA indeed matched one of the unearthed skeletons from a few weeks back, it would be some sort of avenging moment for Bishop Flynn, since his DNA would have survived the grave in a way he never could have foreseen.

When he slid back into the car, his ears were met by the warm and pleasant tones of an Irish singer.

'...*Just a bed for the night...somewhere warm till the morning light...*' she lilted.

Kevin muted his iPod.

"No, it's okay," Michael said. "Who is she?"

157

"Aye, bud. So she's Maura O'Connell. One of my favorite singing ladies. Just thought you were looking a wee bit more down after this stop and might prefer the quiet."

"Her voice is great. Go ahead, play more."

What Michael didn't bother to say is that he had a deep affinity for any good female voice. He often felt, never said, female singers somehow made him feel soothed. Making up for his distant mother again? He distracted himself from his Freudian rumination to glance down at his phone app.

"Last stop is St. Saviours Dominican Church. Time to look at my ancestor face-to-face."

Kevin started the car. The skin between his eyebrows wrinkled a bit.

"You're not going to see one of those glass caskets, so?"

"Do they have those in the church?"

"Wouldn't know, bud. Not my parish. I'm a Saint Augustine's lad."

"No matter. I'm curious about a painting and a stained-glass window there, anyway."

A few minutes later, as they approached the front of St. Saviours, Michael inhaled sharply and pointed. A gray tower accented with filigree columns at each of its four corners was topped by a clock face as large as Big Ben's. Above the clock face, the fascia, surrounded by sculptured finials and ending in an almost medieval castle keep pyramid roof, amazed Michael. This clock could have stood on Main Street in Disneyland, it was just that fanciful.

"Oh, so, you see the Tait clock there, then. Isn't she a beauty?"

"Really something."

"Funny enough, kind of connects to the wee war you had there in the states with Lincoln and all."

"The Civil War?"

"Aye. This fellow Tait was big in textiles and used to provide the weaves to the soldiers."

"Which side?"

"Let's see—what were they again?"

"Union and Confederate."

"Aye—the Confederate side."

"That's disappointing. They weren't the good guys."

Kevin shrugged and pulled the car into a space near the front of St. Saviours. As Michael unfastened his seat belt and started to open the door, Kevin tapped his shoulder.

"Seeing as though I'm a good Catholic—occasionally—might I join you to finally see this old bugger you been chasing? Won't hurt me to sprinkle a dash of the holy water on myself, either."

Michael chuckled. "Okay, whatever floats your boat."

He looked away from the tower toward the church. Sitting above and dwarfing the front entrance, four soaring stained-glass windows within seemed to point toward a sunburst of a stained-glass window. The sharp pitch and peak of the imposing gray and weathered stone reminded Michael more of photos of cathedrals in Spain or England he had seen rather than churches here in Ireland. Except for the ubiquitous overcast, Michael assumed that the light playing through the stained glass probably made the interior sparkle with rainbow light. Since Kevin had declared his faith, Michael thought better of not mentioning an observation he made years ago as his faith dissolved: the overwhelming beauty of such a cathedral, the ornate altar objects, the priest's silks, and a choir in perfect pitch certainly created a sense of awe and beauty, but not of God. Just wondrous, evolved human creativity. He pulled the wrought iron handle and the door's weight caused him to lean back. He nodded to Kevin to step ahead of him.

As they stepped through the foyer into the main nave, both he and Kevin inhaled sharply: stained glass windows over the altar did let in the rainbow of light despite the outside gloom and gray. Kevin tapped Michael's arm and nodded toward a white marble holy water font to the right of the door. He stepped over, dipped his fingertips, crossed himself and walked toward one of the rich wood pews on the right. Kevin's sneakers squeaked against the polished gray and black granite floor that sparkled as it reflected the altar light. The altar seemed to explode with gold and silver. Michael wondered why such objects didn't get stolen regularly but then he recalled how he had been taught somewhere along the way that God, Jesus, Mary, the saints, and all dead family members looked down on every moment of your life. That troubled him in his early adolescence especially after he discovered masturbation and enjoyed many an impure thought during his sins of emission. He figured it was one of the reasons the holy objects remained safe: a Catholic thief might possess the same dose of afterlife paranoia.

As Kevin began to murmur a Hail Mary behind him, Michael continued to make his way toward the altar. From the dig notes, he understood that there was a small wing or niche to the right side of the altar with a stained-glass window depicting Bishop Flynn and an oil painting by Thomas Ryan. Michael stepped to the last gray marble pillar and paused to view the fresco of what must have been the twelve apostles in miters with Christ ascending upward. The figures set against a light blue background filled in the arch above the altar. The work appeared to be as fine as Rubens but Michael would have to grab a guide on his way out to determine who painted the fresco. As he turned toward the wing, he noticed the life-size statue of Mary, labeled Our Lady of Limerick, set in a golden niche. Like all the other artistic beauty around him, the statue was a fine work of delicately carved wood.

But as his gaze moved away from the statue, his eyes met a true rainbow of color: a side anteroom with walls of stained-glass windows. A black stone floor and low, dark ceiling gave the room an ambience of the shadow boxes he used to make in grammar school. Austere wooden pews in a simple shaker style reflected the barrage of colors from their lacquer finishes. The windows seemed to be flowing panels of Limerick's history as they started on the left with an image of a man standing next to a hanging scaffold and ended with modern images of smokestacks and a depiction of Pope Jon Paul. Chills went through Michael as he stepped toward the window depicting the hanging scaffold image. That must be his ancestor. And on approaching that image, a perpendicular wall painted in dark brown displayed an oil portrait. Not just any: it was the Thomas Ryan painting he had known up to this point only from the faded photocopy in the dig notes.

Michael stood transfixed as his eyes darted between the stained-glass image and the painting. They couldn't have been more different. The stained-glass image of a cherubic, placid face with an arm extending from beneath a sapphire blue robe pointing toward the image of the sun in its chest almost mocked the austere burnt sienna and raw umber tones of the painting. The gaunt face in the painting contorted in pain above a gray beard. The figure in the painting also clutched a pectoral cross between tan, strong hands. As he considered the two images, Michael felt drawn to the portrait since it exuded not a placid saintliness but a tortured man most probably facing the gallows with strength and courage. Yes, for Michael, the Thomas Ryan painting most certainly must have been the better likeness between the two, though he would need to google the source of Ryan's depiction of his ancestor.

But no matter, he was in awe of his ancestor. He let himself sit on the pew nearest the painting. If he had any remnant of his long-dead faith, he might even have prayed to and for the suffering man.

"I might have seen your bones, Uncle," he said quietly. He rubbed the back of his neck as he leaned back against the hard pew. The sounds of muffled footsteps interrupted his reverie. He wondered if a mass were starting but for the moment, wanted to remain to contemplate his ancestor. He studied the suffering eyes of the painting and found no similarity to himself. Glancing at the stained-glass face, he saw only a flat, placid expression, too peaceful to be believed. But what if his ancestor had found some peace before his death? Might not that be more accurate than the oil painting?

"*Laaaa—crimosa diiiesss iiilaaa...*

Michael was startled out of his rumination by a choir of male and female voices. The music echoed through the nave and made his chest vibrate with the sound.

"*...qua resurrrgett eexxx faaaavillaaa...*

He was not familiar with the chorale piece, but there was such a haunting, sad quality to the music. Considering his ancestor's oil painting with the choir reverberating caused his eyes to well up. A tap on his shoulder startled him.

"You found your old pappy, so," Kevin said quietly. "I don't see any family resemblance. He's a wee tired and hungry I'd say."

"The music?" Michael said as he choked back his tears.

"Aye, the choir is practicing so we best make ourselves scarce."

"*...judicandus home reus...*"

"Do you have any idea what this piece is?" Michael asked.

"I suspect it's from Mozart's 'Requiem'. They drag that out around Easter and such. That Mozart was a good Catholic, after all."

Kevin led Michael out the side door of the church and back toward the car. The choir dissolved into a muffled echo with only the high notes making it through the thick, stone walls. Once they got to the car, the choir fell silent. Michael slid into the car and clicked his seat belt while Kevin checked his phone.

"Back to the Pery, then," he said. "I got another pick-up near there so we'll be saying our goodbyes in just a few."

As Kevin pulled the car down the lane, the black Ford Crown Victoria that had followed Michael's ride a couple nights before tailed them once again from a distance.

"From a distance, the world looks blue and green..." a gentle American female voice strummed and sang with her Texas twang over the music system as Michael walked into the Frog's Mouth. The lyric struck him two ways: first, that a Texas country singer would be playing here in this cave of an Irish bar and second, if only everyone could see the planet that way. Fucktards all around with their stringent beliefs and insular cultures. Michael sighed and surveyed the bar. Benches with high tables crowded with men and women lined the walls. Glasses of Guinness stood on every table like brown devotional candles. He made his way past several standing patrons and noticed a small, parquet dance floor and four empty chairs with music stands in front of each.

"Over here, bud!" he heard Liam's voice over the din. When the patrons parted to let him through, Michael paused with a start: Liam stood behind the bar with his arm around a young woman with spiky short, dark hair. Her perky, large breasts jutted through her jade green blouse, making the buttons strain to contain them. Liam kissed the woman on the neck and Michael turned quickly to go.

"I'm right here, bud!" Liam hollered to Michael's back.

Michael turned back toward Liam, glad that the dim gold and silver lights hopefully hid his face that felt hot with embarrassment. Liam kissed the woman's neck once more and extended his thick hand over the bar toward Michael. Michael shook his head.

"Oh, come, on, bud. Ya' think my little witch doesn't know about this? I'm quite sure she's glad I get some on the side rather than poking at her constantly. Let me pour you a Guinness so. Piss off, then, Maggie."

The woman sighed. She lifted a section of the bar on the right and stepped past Michael and into the crowd.

163

"Maggie's got some friends here tonight in case you got an itch to scratch," Liam said. He grabbed up a tall glass and began to pull a draught of Guinness. Michael could only think about Chakranna and her odd sweetness. He took the glass of Guinness and hoped the crispy chill on his fingertips would make its way up to his face still hot with embarrassment.

"Thanks. And no thanks—I'm good," he said.

"Suit yourself. The Guinness—or anything else you might want—is on me tonight," Liam said. "Cheers!"

Liam raised a shot glass of whisky and clinked Michael's glass. He slammed the shot back and wiped his mouth with the back of his hand.

"Enjoy yourself. The live music, too, bud. Got some of the best Irish talent around these parts playing tonight."

Liam waved his arm toward the crowd and another woman—this time a freckly redhead with curvy hips and a perfect pear of a bottom--skittered up to the bar. Michael had a hard time ignoring her melon buns jiggling lightly under her tight, pink skirt. Liam leaned over and whispered something into her ear. She turned toward Michael and he had just enough time to avert his eyes from her ass.

"Liam says you're one lonely Yank, so," she said. Her voice lilted with a soft accent. She placed her right hand gently on his shoulder. "Aye, you do be having some muscle there."

Michael cleared his throat and stepped back. He bumped into a man just behind him and turned his head.

"Sorry, sorry," he said.

"Is that meant for him or me?" she asked.

"Both. 'Scuse me."

He raised his glass toward Liam and nodded. The crowd parted as the musicians began to set up. He found an empty corner halfway between the musicians and the door and made his way quickly to it. After plucking up an empty stool near three male patrons

164

who nodded 'okay' for him to take it, he sat. The pressure of the hard wood put him at ease for some reason. He took a large gulp from the glass of Guinness and watched as the four musicians pulled their instruments from various cases. The squeak of an accordion caught his ear and he winced. If an accordion was involved, he figured he was in for some sort of tacky folk tunes. But when the other musician pulled out her violin, he questioned his snap music judgment. The other member of the quartet pulled out a piccolo-sized pipe and a guitar that resembled a lute. After a few moments, the player with the accordion nodded and began to slowly play. Within a few bars, the violinist joined in. The guitarist followed, strumming away such that he created the percussion as the cadence increased. When the piccolo joined at last, the music sped on with a joyful pace.

"What do you do with a drunkin' sailor?" someone from the crowd began. Another voice joined in, repeating the verse and now the bar erupted with clapping in unison. The music pounded in Michael's chest and he couldn't help but join in the clapping.

"...Shave his belly with a rusty razor..." the song continued.

Michael clapped, sang along, and drank a few more pints. All the time, he avoided looking toward Liam and his wandering flirtations. When the group wrapped up the music with a Chieftains song an hour later, Michael felt tired but content. He hadn't expected to enjoy a folk music night and it lightened his heart. He grabbed his phone and arranged an Uber.

"So you enjoyed the pub and music, aye?" Chakranna asked him as he stepped into the hotel lobby.

Michael noticed that Chakranna wore less of her goth make-up and her hair was soft on her shoulders. She was cute, no question, but no competition for the pink skirt and boobs back at the Frog's Mouth. He wondered if that's why she sought

165

out all hocus pocus crap—obviously something missing from her marriage. While he didn't consider himself very perceptive when it came to people, Michael sensed a plaintive quality in her question.

"Music was great. The place was crowded," he said.

"And you saw Liam, so?"

Oh shit, he thought. *She's checking on Liam.* He considered mentioning the two ladies because he felt so bad for her. But would that really help? And it wasn't like Liam was hiding anything, so she probably knew about all of it. Worse, she must have felt bad enough about herself that she allowed it. This was the best she was going to do with marriage maybe. Wasn't it up to the both of them to work it out? He wrestled with telling her then decided to keep his mouth shut.

"Yep. Just a quick chat and then four Guinnesses. It probably would have been more if I had stuck around."

"Oh."

Chakranna went back to the check-in computer and began to type. Michael stood at the counter and began to feel awkward.

"No messages for me?" he asked.

"You mean from the lab and all? Nothing."

"It's been over three weeks. Jesus."

"They did pay your bill again this morning. That count for anything?"

"Sure does. More free vacation."

As Michael walked to the elevator, feeling in part responsible for Liam's infidelities, he didn't notice the black Ford Crown Victoria's driver eyeing him from just out front of the Pery's. But that ignorance would prove to be short-lived.

9.

His pasty mouth and slight headache reminded Michael of something he hadn't felt since college: a hangover. He eased his eyes open slowly but even the anemic light of Limerick burned. His back creaked stiffly as he sat up and cleared his throat. The red digits of the old Timex alarm clock showed nine-forty AM. He rubbed his eyes and scraped his whiskers with his fingertips. He reached over for the bottle of Ballygowen water but felt the empty bottle collapse under his grip. He sighed. Rolling onto his left side, he let his legs heavy and stiff fall to the wood floor. The cold stung his bare feet as he stood and moved toward the bathroom. It felt as though he was swimming in molasses. At the basin, he splashed cold water in his face and took a deep drink of water from a small glass on the edge of the sink. He reached for the hand towel to dab at his face and was once again frustrated by the moist towel. Nothing ever seemed to dry here, and he found himself missing the Santa Ana wind that seasonally roared down the Verdugo Hills near his home. He glanced at the mirror and tugged at the sides of his eyes—were there more lines than yesterday? He laughed and noticed his Gabby-Hayes-white whiskers vibrate on his ever-loosening jowls. The sharp clanging of the room phone interrupted his ravages-of-age reverie.

"Yeah, yeah, I'm awake," he said thickly. A pang of guilt shot through him as he heard Chakranna's soft brogue. Liam's dalliances at The Frog's Mouth replayed through his mind.

"Are you watching the news?" Chakranna asked.

He looked around and found the television remote. He clicked it on and a "Lord of the Rings" movie played.

"What channel?"

Michael flipped through the channels until he recognized the face: Dr. Reilly who took his DNA swabs at the institute weeks back.

"It may not be as big as the Brits finding and confirming Richard the Third's remains," the doctor said into the microphone being held just off screen. "But it's quite the special moment for us here in Limerick and Ireland. Bishop Terrence Flynn was and is a hero of a holy man."

"And 'twas a yank who provided the DNA so?" a female reporter asked.

"Aye," Dr. Reilly replied.

"Can we talk to him?" the reporter asked.

"That'll have to wait a wee bit till we get his permission. 'Tis legal confidentiality and such."

The camera cut away to the reporter. As she began to speak, Michael switched off the TV and grabbed up the phone receiver.

"Thanks, Chakranna! Gotta call my wife. "

He hung up the room phone and grabbed up his. Stephanie's phone rang several times.

"Come on, Steph. Pick up. It's me—Facetime."

Michael's phone screen lit up and Stephanie's face emerged from the technoplasm. Stephanie's hair shot out in different directions and her eyelids puffed so much that her eyes were slits.

"What the hell?" she struggled with her voice filled with sleep. "Michael?"

"Oh, shit. I forgot the time difference."

"Uhhh…What? You okay?" she asked.

"It's a match! They found my ancestor's bones!"

Stephanie cleared her throat and sniffled. She flipped her hair out of her face.

"You did it, Indiana Jones junior."

"I know, I know. I have goose bumps about the whole thing."

"What happens next?"

"They want to get me on TV and I guess that will be about it."

Stephanie sensed the disappointment in his voice. She snorted again.

"Well you'll come home with a little adventure. If you end up going back to teaching history, this will be quite a great thing to share with students."

Michael sighed. "I guess."

"Just be sure to get some video so that you can maybe post some of this on Youtube. As an educational supplement for your students, of course."

"Just what kids want to see on Youtube. Their grandfather talking about some dead Irish guy."

"The mind boggles with the 'likes' and the ad income."

They both laughed at the whole idea. The room phone interrupted them.

"I wonder what she wants now."

"Who?" Stephanie asked.

"The witch."

"Oh. Go grab it. I need to get back to sleep. Hopefully."

"Love you!"

"Love you more."

"Bye."

Michael answered the room phone.

"Are you decent at this point?" Chakranna asked.

"I'm still in my sleeping duds. Why?"

"I see an RTE news van pulling up at the curb in front. I'm guessing they come to see you, so."

"Jeez. I wouldn't think the news about some old bones is that urgent."

"Not a lot happens around Limerick. This is big news."

"Stall them for me a bit, would you? Gotta at least brush my teeth and comb my hair."

"'Tis my pleasure, sir."

Chakranna hung up and greeted the news team in the lobby. She let them know Michael would be delayed a few minutes.

When he made his way down to the lobby, a news reporter and camera woman greeted him. As he answered questions about how he felt to be part of the historic find, Michael wondered if he would hear from Monsignor Leahy about a plane ticket home. He didn't have to wonder for long. After the news interview broke up, two men in black suits stepped into the hotel lobby.

"Mr. Dunphy?" one of the men said with a thick Italian accent. Michael noticed the man's square jaw and olive-green eyes. He looked like a model.

"Yep."

"Can you come with us outside a moment?"

Michael glanced at Chakranna. She shrugged and nodded, pointing at the handsome one and mouthing 'Wow'. The other man took Michael's elbow and Michael recoiled.

"But I answered all your reporter questions already. Nothing left to add."

Michael noticed the other man's sunken and pock-marked cheeks as he reached into his pocket and pulled out his identification. He held it out. Michael read it aloud:

" 'Corpo dello Gendameria'? An Italian newspaper?"

"No. Vatican police. We have been sent by the Holy See," the man said with a thick Italian accent.

"Vatican? I haven't been to confession in decades, guys. You don't mess around."

Chakranna chuckled along with Michael. Both men glared at Michael, their black eyebrows knitted with disapproval. The gaunt man reached out for his elbow again.

"This is about your ancestor, Bishop Flynn. May we step outside?"

It was Michael's turn to shrug at Chakranna. He nodded to the men and the three of them walked out to the curb in front of Pery's. The black Ford Crown Victoria that had tailed him before sat parked nearby. The handsome one leaned against the side of the car and pulled out an ornate gold and rosewood cigarette case. He clicked it open and offered a cigarette to Michael. Michael shook his head and the man lit up a cigarette. Something like burning hair and cow dung hit Michael's nostrils and he stepped back from the smoke.

"You like to see the Vatican maybe some special parts no one else gets to see?" the gaunt man asked.

Michael felt as if he were in a scene from 'Wise Guys'. He wasn't sure exactly how to answer. He shrugged. The handsome one pinched the butt of his cigarette between his thick lips and leaned forward with a scowl.

"Who don't want to see the most blessed of all places and get special treatment?" he said.

Michael gulped. His heart pounded a bit faster.

"I gotta get home, guys. I gotta find a job and get back to work."

The gaunt man stepped closer. He reached into his coat pocket. Boxed in by the two men, Michael closed his eyes and braced for the bullet. But the gaunt man pulled out a white envelope.

"Here's a business class ticket on Alitalia flight twenty tonight at seven. You fly with us and we take you to the Vatican."

These were odd guides. Michael shook his head, still uneasy.

"All expenses paid, two nights in Rome," the handsome one said as he blew a breath of smoke over his head. "Enough time even to find a nice signora."

He smiled and exposed a fence of perfect white teeth. Michael, still unsure, took the envelope from the gaunt man. He flipped the envelope open and glanced over the ticket and saw his first and last name and a roundtrip ticket from Shannon to Rome. Considering the ticket, the Vatican identifications the men presented, and their general openness, Michael concluded this was for real.

"Okay, gentlemen. At least I hope you are."

Both men laughed. The gaunt man slapped Michael on the back several times.

"You fly with us, then. Me, I'm Vincenzo. That ugly face there, he is Marko."

"I'm in," Michael said. "To Roma with love!"

"Rome! I'm so jealous!" Stephanie said a couple hours later. Michael's overnight bag was packed and the Alitalia ticket sat inside his passport.

"I wish you were coming with me. But it is just two nights."

"What the hell could the Vatican want?"

Michael shrugged.

"Maybe they just want to see me since my DNA confirmed the bones. But maybe I really will be able to sneak in a *'signora,'*" he said, mimicking the handsome Italian's deep voice and accent.

"Ha," Stephanie said. "You just watch your Indiana *Jones*-ing there."

"I'm ready to come home *after* I see what this is all about. Hopefully the Vatican doesn't burst into flames when I walk through its gates."

"That would require two troubling things."

"What would those be?"

"That you still believe in God *and* the church."

"Worry not, my love."

The room phone rang and Michael raised his hand for Stephanie to wait while he answered. A few seconds later he thanked Chakranna for the call and continued the Facetime with Stephanie.

"Michael, you do have your Tegretol with you, right?"

"Yep. Inside my carry-on."

"I don't need a call from some Italian hospital that you seized at the Vatican."

Michael held up his laptop case and pointed toward the side zipper pouch.

"Right here ready to be checked at Shannon. Okay, gotta go catch my ride."

"The thugs again?"

"I have no idea. But this may be our last chance to see each other."

"Oh shut up and get out the door. Call me when you get to the Vatican."

"If they have Wi-Fi, of course. Otherwise, roaming charges. No thanks."

"It's okay if you call me when you're back in Limerick. It's only the day after tomorrow."

"I love you, Steph!" Michael held his phone up to his lips and kissed the screen.

"I love you." She kissed her screen.

Michael went to hang up.

"Wait!"

"What?"

"I will kick your ass if you go near any signoras!!!"

"Okay, no signoras. Only if you stay away from Sergio."

"Our gardener?"

"He's kind'a cute."

They laughed as he pressed the disconnect symbol. A few minutes later, Michael slid into the back seat of the Crown Victoria. Vincenzo slammed the trunk shut and then hopped into the front seat next to Marko who put the car in gear.

"Whoa, guys. I don't even have my seatbelt latched yet," Michael said.

"Seatbelt?" Vincenzo said. "You make us laugh."

Vincenzo and Marko laughed at another joke as the Crown Victoria made the right-hand turn just past the Pery's.

10.

Michael awoke to the sound of muffled Gregorian chants. He stretched and looked around, recognizing he was in an apartment at the Vatican. When he had arrived last night, Cardinal Adamanto and he had a chat about a cross that belonged to Bishop Flynn. It had whetted Michael's scholar appetite. To think that this morning, he was about to meet the Vatican's chief history scholar, Emilio Aponte, who had more degrees after his name than any PH d or medical doctor he ever met, almost sent shivers down his spine. He had utilized and cited several of Aponte's treatises in his undergrad term papers and senior thesis as well. Like all other areas in academia, the Catholic clergy so often excelled and were permitted to stretch their scholarship beyond the church doctrine provided it did not contradict it. It was a Catholic physicist who first proposed the Big Bang, he recalled, and the Pope used the theory to support creationism—God set the spark of the Big Bang. What would this great scholar of international repute have to share? What would he, with his limited and comparably puny academic achievement, learn from this giant? He yawned and rolled out of bed. As he made his way to a small bathroom, he noticed a tray with a silver pot and a teacup. He popped the lid of the pot and the aroma of a strong coffee enticed him.

The heavy doors to the chamber opened. Cardinal Adamanto stepped through and held the door. Following him was a hunched over figure in the brown, hooded robe of the Franciscan order. His diminutive stature was underscored by the huge leather folio he carried, like a wizard with his incantation book. Yoda popped into Michael's mind. He stood as Adamanto and Emilio Aponte approached him.

"Esteemed Brother Aponte, this is Michael Dunphy."

Aponte handed the folio to Adamanto. His wrists and hands wore their years in sharp, boney edges ending with fingers crooked from arthritis. He slowly reached for his hood and Michael winced in sympathy at his pain. But as he pulled the hood back to reveal his face, Michael was surprised to see crystal blue eyes peeking out from valleys of lines and creases under wild, snow white eyebrows. Aponte smiled and held both hands out to Michael. Michael held them gently, feeling no weight or pressure from them.

"How long it has been that I hoped to meet a child from the line of Blessed Terrence," he said. His English was thick with southern Italian, but his voice was clear and strong.

"Sir, I am honored to meet such a great scholar. Thank you," Michael said.

"Cardinal Adamanto tells me that he wishes you to know the history of the cross, no?"

"Yes, yes I would like that very much."

Aponte nodded and smiled broadly. He patted Michael's back.

"Let's sit at this table and I will tell you all I know. Cardinal Adamanto, will you please also bring the dossier folio?"

Adamanto paused to consider how he would manage the folio and guide Aponte. Michael interceded.

"May I please?" Michael said. Adamanto nodded and stepped over to the blond, marble table.

When Aponte and Michael reached the table, he paused. He pointed a quivering finger toward the large, red velvet bag with a tie of gold tassels ending in crucifixes.

"Is that our Blessed Terrence's bones as you told me?" he asked.

"Yes, Brother," Adamanto replied.

Aponte crossed himself slowly, brought his hands together and nodded in reverence toward the bag. His gaze moved slowly toward the box containing the cross.

"That, my young friend, is the box containing Blessed Terrence's cross. Cardinal Adamanto, would you mind placing the folio in front of this chair?"

Adamanto placed the folio on the table. Michael pulled out the heavy, carved oak chair and helped Aponte onto the faded green leather cushion. He then took the chair opposite Aponte. Adamanto pulled out the other chair but only leaned against its back.

"Sit, Cardinal. Please," Aponte said.

"Brother, my lower back vexes me again. For now, I prefer to stand."

Aponte tapped the cover of the folio and looked up toward Adamanto

"I trust you recall how detailed my research is on the cross. This is going to take some time."

"I'll take leave if needed for my pain, Brother. This is all for Mr. Dunphy here."

"As you wish."

With that, Aponte cracked open the aged folio. Michael could see the typed pages of a dissertation presented by Brother Aponte to Notre Dame University and his heart skipped a beat to be in the presence of a great scholar's thesis pages. And in English, no less. Aponte held up his hand.

"Has our young friend seen the cross as of yet?"

"No," Adamanto and Michael said in unison.

"Well?" Aponte said to Adamanto. Cardinal Adamanto nodded. He picked up a small box gingerly and placed it in front of Michael. He unclasped it and opened the box. Michael smelled the faintest aroma of spice and decayed wood. As with any time he was within physical proximity of an historical relic, his head grew light for a moment. Adamanto tipped the box toward Michael, and he could now see a crude cross. The diffuse light from the stained-glass window behind them made the tarnished silver cross sparkle on its edges. Michael touched the edge with its ridged surface. Softened by time, it was smooth and cool. It resembled a plus sign topped by an exaggerated, cursive 'p'. The ancient tau rho style of the cross

177

excited his archaeological historian mind. There was something so much more intimate about the delicate pectoral cross than the human bones of his ancestor that lay in the red velvet bag on the table near them.

"You recognize the Hellene tau rho, then?" Aponte said.

"Archaic early Essene?" Michael replied.

"You clearly are a good student, but no. This cross predates the Essenes."

Michael picked up the small box. He noticed the four faded small tiles and opened the lid fully to see the Arabic script under the lid.

"Pomegranate motif on the tiles?" he asked.

Aponte nodded approvingly.

"And Arabic script under the lid?"

Aponte nodded again.

"What's the translation?"

"'He who betrays shall be revealed'," Aponte said.

"But why the Arabic motif and curse if the cross predates the Essenes? What's that all about?"

"You shall learn shortly, my son," Aponte answered.

Michael regarded the cross once more

"Have you had the cross itself dated?" Michael asked.

"We trust the word of witness to determine provenance of such things," Aponte replied. "What do you make of the tau rho symbol?"

"You got me there."

"It was the symbol for crucifixion. A very early one, indeed."

"I only lightly studied the Greek classical period I'm afraid."

"Do you recall the silver of Judas from the Bible?" Aponte asked.

"Of course."

"Since you are a learned scholar in history such as I, I'm going to refer to this area of my thesis for your great American university, Notre Dame. They had an early interest in Blessed Terrence and of this cross, long before Georgetown."

Aponte pointed toward the first page of the thesis that looked to have been typed on an ancient Underwood typewriter.

"This is a summary of the words in a Latin text from three hundred fifty-one Anno Domini. An early monk, Benedict of Napoli, tells us in his text that Simon Iscariot had discovered his dead son, Judas. Sarah Magdalene, sister of the legendary Mary of Magdalene, had gone with him on the search for Judas. My voice is weak, young man. Would you mind reading the text here?"

Michael didn't have to be asked twice. He turned the folio and began to read:

"Simon, the father of Judas Iscariot, trudged deeper into the olive grove, shouting for Judas. Sarah Magdalene, sister of Mary and a friend to Judas, accompanied Simon. As Simon turned left and shouted Judas's name once again, a glint of something caught Sarah's eye. She turned her head and noticed one olive tree standing away from the rest. The tree appeared to be larger and older, a crooked trunk and gnarled arms twisting and reaching in all directions. Many more glinting objects lie below the tree. It was as if it had dropped fruits of precious jewels. Her eyes followed the gnarled trunk and she noticed a single, thin branch hanging from one of the larger branches.

"Sir! Simon!" she shouted.

Simon emerged from a thicket of trees. Sarah pointed toward the lone tree. Simon rushed past her, his thick, robed frame pounding the soil as he ran to the tree.

"Judas! This is father! Judas!!" Simon hollered.

Sarah quickened her pace. Tears streamed down her face as she raced behind Simon. He had fallen to his knees below the tree. All around them now were the strange glinting objects. Horrible gasps of sadness erupted from Simon.

"My son...my son..."

Sarah stepped toward the tree and beheld the terrible sight: a rope tight around Judas's crooked neck slithered away to a frayed end that had snapped under his weight. His dark eyes were glazed with death like the fish in the marketplace. Judas's ephemera spilled from his gut. Sarah turned toward the tree, braced herself against the trunk, and wept.

"Your blasphemous Nazarene!" Simon growled. "He has killed my son!"

Sarah uttered a quiet prayer as He had taught them. Around Simon and Judas lay the glinting objects. Sarah realized that they were silver coins. Simon looked around and noticed them.

"Coins?" he asked.

Sarah leaned over and plucked one up. As her fingertips contacted the coin, she felt a chill as if a rare winter frost had descended. She turned the coin over and saw the insignia of a staff and read the inscription: 'Of Tiberius, Emperor'.

"Yes, Sir. These are silver coins."

Simon choked back a sob. He turned his head and looked toward Sarah. His eyes were swollen carnelians. He jutted his right arm toward the coins. Sarah's eyes followed the billowing beige of his sleeve and saw Judas's blood where Simon had clutched his son. She looked away and bent to retrieve the coins. Each one chilled her and she dropped them into a cradle she had folded into her robe with her left hand. Once all the coins were gathered, she announced the tally:

"Thirty, Sir."

Simon did not respond. He caressed Judas's hair and gently adjusted his head to remove the awful twist. After carefully loosening the noose, he tossed it toward the tree with an angry grunt. He held his hand out to Sarah. She held her hand out toward his. He batted it away and thrust out his open palm.

"Two of the coins."

Icy sparks shot through her fingers as she dropped them into Simon's hands. He flipped his hand, dropping the coins to the ground. He looked up at her puzzled.

"What is this bewitchment?"

Sarah shook her head. Simon picked up one coin at a time, wincing from the iciness. He softly closed Judas's eyelid and placed the coin over his right eye. The second coin gave him a start but he placed that one over Judas's left eye. With a swirling gesture, he removed his woven purple and gold shawl and spread it over Judas's face and upper body. Quietly, he whispered the El Malei Rachamim. Sarah noticed the tears spill from Simon's eyes and disappear into his thick beard. Simon stood and pulled a satchel from his robe and drew it open.

"Please, the silver pieces."

Sarah opened the cradle in her robe and poured them one-by-one into the satchel. When only five remained, Simon held up his hand. He pulled the satchel shut and tucked it back into his robe.

"I will use these coins to bury my son. The five that remain in your possession are yours with my deepest appreciation."

Aponte clutched Michael's arm weakly. Michael stopped reading. He cleared his throat. He could look neither at Aponte nor Adamanto, he was so disappointed. Where was the scholarly tome with citations he expected? If this was all penned by Benedict, then what sources did he rely on writing this account three hundred years after the alleged betrayal and suicide of Judas? Did Aponte even research the sources, or did he accept this on faith?

"Cardinal Adamanto, might you bring us some water? Our young friend must be parched."

When Adamanto left the room, Aponte clutched Michael's arm again.

"I am as skeptical as you of this myth," Aponte said. "However, two facts supporting the story are interesting: one, I certified the text of Benedict myself so he very much wrote this within a decade or two of 351; two, Benedict is the first to mention the peculiar aspect of the cold silver. We will come back to that."

"What about Benedict's sources? What did he rely on? How does he know what these people thought?"

Aponte smiled and nodded in an almost condescending way. He patted Michael's arm.

"He made no references or citations of any kind."

"Odd. So should I continue reading?"

"Let's move past this time period. I will tell you that the myth goes on to say that Sarah eventually took her pieces to a renowned silversmith of the time, an apprentice of Demetrius of Ephesus. She had the silversmith fashion this cross before us. The folio, please?"

Michael turned the folio back toward Aponte. Aponte scanned each page with his right index finger that resembled a dehydrated turnip, pausing occasionally to enjoy words from his early university days. He then flipped to the next page, continuing through the folio. Cardinal Adamanto returned with a crystal pitcher of ice water with lemon slices floating atop. He poured a glass for each of them. Aponte paused.

"Now, here. The cross has an ancient Arabian story and then one from the Holy crusaders as the cross makes its way

181

across history. Brother Paul Jerome of my own order was the source for both sections back in twelve fifty-seven."

He turned the folio back to Michael. Michael swallowed a second drink of the lemon water, and then began to read aloud once again:

> *This, my brothers in Christ, is the last testimony of Tariq Al-Sid as was recorded at the time of his death by a Persian scribe and translated here at the Vatican by our own Cardinal Poliglotti: The great horse snorted, shaking the acrid dust from its flowing white mane. I clutched the leather reins tightly, making the creature rear on its hind legs. A short, mud brick wall separated me from the graveyard of the Infidel. The graveyard stood untouched over the centuries, spared by the Roman sack and pillage of Jerusalem since it laid a day's journey north of the city. Lying between Kerioth and Bethany, it was the last of its kind having not been plundered. The field of mounds ended at the base of a massive cliff. A narrow cave rose above the graves. I knew from my scholarship that Sarah and her sister of legend, Mary Magdalene, had been buried in a tomb cave adjacent to a Hebrew burying field. They had been buried in the honor befitting princesses of Magdolon Castle, confirmed by the Tigris scholars. They had also confirmed that the Essene scrolls had corrected the myth: Mary was not a woman of the night but a princess of high bearing and status. I ordered my battle-weary soldiers to sack all the tombs except the cave.*
>
> *'The cave, I will examine myself.'*
>
> *I had learned of the silver cross during my tutelage under the Tigris scholars who had studied the ancient scrolls of the Essenes. I could think of no greater treasure than to possess the earliest symbol of the prophet, Jesus. More personally, I wished to place the cross around the neck of my beloved and only wife, Sanaz. I had longed for her these many months away from Thaj and could think of no greater symbol of my undying love and fidelity for her. I would chant Hafitz's "You Don't Know How Beautiful You Are" and place it around her neck before a passionate night. The Persian poet's songs had inspired my heart as much as the histories of the Greeks and Assyrians I had mastered at Tigris. I laughed quietly to imagine this symbol of the Infidel blasphemy lying limp and useless between our heaving bosoms.*

182

The soldiers dismounted and descended on the tombs. Their boots and shovels sent whirling dervishes of dust into the sky. Shattered stone and wood filled the air as I rode toward the cave. I dismounted my horse at the mouth of the gaping stone wound. From the pack on the horse's saddle, I withdrew a torch of wrapped goat skin and olive oil. I struck a flint against a boulder at the cave's opening. After several strikes, a spark ignited the torch. Touching the hilt of my scimitar for luck, I stepped into the cave. Sand gritted beneath my boots.

Within ten steps, the orange torchlight revealed the writing of the Infidel Hebrews. I read the words I recognized as blessings from the Hebrew God. I dared not read the words aloud for fear of Allah's wrath. Just past the walls of blessings, the cave narrowed and revealed eight niches. Hebrew names appeared near each niche along with more blessings. I held the torch near two of the niches and saw dust, skulls, and human bones. I proceeded to search each one for the silver cross, but it was not among them. Disappointed, I began to turn back toward the cave opening when the torchlight revealed an opening to another chamber. My heart quickened.

I stepped between two narrow walls, each pressing against my chest and buttocks. At one moment, I felt as if I were going to become trapped. As I dislodged myself from the stricture, I noticed the torchlight spill into a large chamber. Pressing forward, my eyes beheld wonder. Before me lay two oval sarcophagi. Two shelves on either side contained jars and dusty remains of offerings. When I stepped nearer to the sarcophagi, I saw on the cave wall the name 'Magdolon' in Hebrew, followed by a blessing. Below the words was the symbol of a fish.

A fissure separated the top of one of the sarcophagi into two sections. The symbol of the fish was also carved into the top of the sarcophagi. This tomb contained the remains of two of the most beautiful women ever to have lived, if the Infidel legends were to be believed: Mary Magdalene along with her sister, Sarah. As an avid devotee of feminine beauty, this thought saddened me for a moment. As I passed to the left of the damaged sarcophagus, I noticed a ray of torchlight strike something within it. My heart skipped a beat.

'The Betrayer's Cross" I said quietly as if the Princesses Magdalene might hear through their eternal slumbers.

The legend as was recorded in the Essene scrolls described the ability of the cross to reveal to Sarah Magdalene a non-believer in the prophet, Jesus of Nazareth. I found the idea to be nonsense. But the fact that this cross was fashioned and worn by Sarah Magdalene was not a trifle.

I reached under the fracture in the lid. The sarcophagus was of an odd, soft stone and it broke under my pressure. I tore into the lid and within moments, revealed the contents. In disbelief, I stared: the face of Sarah Magdalene, uncorrupted by time and decay, slept peacefully. The shroud that once covered her lay strewn across her body in stringy filaments. The robe in which she must have been buried spread across her body in dusty, gossamer threads. Her feet, legs, hips, and torso lay fully intact. I waved away the dust of centuries and revealed some of the skin of her face and bosom. I found myself transfixed by her alabaster skin and voluptuous form. And there, lying between her lovely breasts, was the Betrayer's Cross. The silver tau rho soiled by the filth of the ages still shone through the dust. My mind raced through passages of the Qur'an. Was it evil to behold with lust a corpse? Would I be cast out in fire for desecrating a tomb? The second question was less perplexing: of course, no punishment for desecrating the tomb of an Infidel. The first question clung to my mind like an unripe fig and I would explore it more fully on my return to Thaj.

I considered her fine cheek bones, narrow, elegant nose and full lips. What miracle of Allah had allowed her to be unscathed by time? After deciding that I could not allow any of the soldiers with me to be aware of this possible blasphemy, let alone anywhere near this ancient treasure, I reached for the cross hesitantly. I grimaced as my fingertips reached around the cross and brushed the hardened flesh beneath. With a snap of something behind Sarah Magdalene's neck, the Betrayer's Cross and remnants of a chain now lay in my grasp. I rubbed the cross against my thawb. Silver now reflected the warm light of my torch. I nervously regarded the cross, looking over my shoulder for signs of soldiers. I looked over my head for some wrath of Allah. My palm began to tingle with cold. A chill seemed to breathe from the cross, and in fear, I dropped it into the pocket of my thawb.

As I made my way past the tight cave walls of the chamber and back out toward the sunlight and the entrance of the

184

cave, with my torch warming my face, I wondered if this strange chill from the cross was the sign of betrayal. If so, I realized that having plucked the artifact from Sarah Magdalene's corpse, I had in fact betrayed her. But what of it? Allah saw me through to exit the cave with no wrath rained upon me. I mounted my horse, feeling the cross tap my right side as I began my ride toward the soldiers. The image of my own beautiful Sanaz began to soothe my mind. In only half a day's journey, I would be back in Thaj to surprise my bride.

Michael paused and cleared his throat. He took a sip of lemon water and glanced at Adamanto who now rested his right cheek against his right fist, eyes closed. He looked over toward Aponte whose eyes had grown impossibly younger and almost anxious.

"Again, I too am skeptical of much of what you have read, but the puzzle of the coldness of the cross intrigues me," he said.

"I suppose, like the previous entry, I would want to review the text, the translation notes, and all other supporting information," Michael said.

"Yes, later my young friend. But this time, would you mind continuing a bit longer on Tariq's confession?" Aponte asked.

"Sure."

"Not for the history of the cross. His story is so moving to me each time I hear it," Aponte said. He patted Michael's back for encouragement. Michael began again:

When I reached the front patio of my home in Thaj two nights hence, I thought I saw a figure run out the side door and toward the mountain. I quickly racked up my horse and made haste to my beloved. The heady and welcoming scent of burning olive oil from the lamps beckoned me as I rushed to my bedroom.

"Sanaz, my adored. Are you safe?"

Sanaz lay across the thick cushions of tafta and satin. Her onyx-black hair lay across her bare shoulders, uncharacteristically tousled. She held a goatskin blanket across her heaving breasts. I fell to my knees with exhaustion, adoration, and worry.

'I was attacked,' she told me.

185

'My beloved,' I said.

Filled with the fury of revenge, I reached for her but she pulled away. Unsure of how to soothe her, and with the rage of Allah in my heart, I ran to my horse and leapt onto the saddle. We galloped with speed in the direction of the black figure. For over half an hour, I searched the rocks and slopes of the mountain and the bushes that grew in all directions. My battle scimitar lay in its scabbard, ready to lop off the head of the attacker. A metallic taste filled my mouth as I realized I had bitten into my lip in anger. Wherever the attacker had hidden, I was not going to find him. With rage still coursing through me, I rode back to my beloved.

Sanaz greeted me at the door. Her hair was now back in place as was her amethyst-colored veil. Her round, brown eyes looked fearful. She greeted me tentatively and bowed.

'My husband and sayyid,' she said. She raised her face toward me but seemed to look over my shoulder and past me.

'My beloved,' I replied.

'Did you avenge me?' she asked. Her tone was nervous and odd.

'I was not able to find the swine. He maintains his head for another day.'

Sanaz's face softened and she smiled. I was confused by this.

'Do you feel ill, my beloved?' I asked.

'No, I am well.'

Sanaz turned and walked into the house. I followed, leaving my scimitar in its scabbard by the door. I also removed my ghutra and waist sash. Sanaz placed cushions about the floor. She filled a cup with wine. I began to relax. I sat and raised my right leg. Sanaz set down the copper wine vessel and began to loosen the straps of my boot. Once she removed the boot, I raised my left leg and she continued. She placed my boots against the wall near the door, brought over the cup of wine, presented it to me, and then sat. I nodded and she removed the veil.

I withdrew the silver cross from my thawb pocket. I turned away from Sanaz and rubbed the cross vigorously with my sleeve. She looked on curiously. The cross now sparkled as if the last seven centuries had not elapsed. I turned and held it up to her.

'My beloved, I have brought this ancient symbol to adorn your most beautiful bosom. I have not yet had time to have a proper chain made, but I hope this will please you. Once worn by one of the most beautiful women in history, I offer it to you, my most beloved.'

Sanaz was transfixed by the silver. The cross was odd to her.

'Is that the cross of the Infidel?' she asked.

I smiled.

'Yes. A most holy symbol for the Infidel, but simply an object of beauty to adorn you.'

Sanaz held out her hand. I placed the cross into her palm and held my palm on top of hers. As I was about to recite the love poem, both of us cried out. The cross dropped to the floor.

'It burns with cold!' she cried. 'What is this strange object?'

I picked up the cross. It began to warm in my hand. I grabbed Sanaz's hand and placed the cross in it. In seconds, it chilled again. She pulled her hand away. My mind began to reel as I recalled the myth of this Betrayer's Cross. Could it be real, I wondered. A dark emptiness boiled up within me. I turned my back on my beloved and tucked the cross back into my thawb.

'Did you recognize your attacker?' I asked. I felt tears filling my eyes.

'Why do you ask that?'

'It would help me in finding him if he is someone from here in Thaj. Maybe someone you have seen before."

Sanaz leaned into an upright position. I could hear her breath quicken.

'I would send you out after him immediately if that were true.'

'My beloved, I was away these many days to liberate the great city from the Infidel. My heart aches to wonder that someone took over my marriage bed in my absence.'

Sanaz began to tremble. My heart shattered. The law of Allah required me to turn her over to the elders for a lashing and rajm. I could not bring myself to allow my beloved to suffer the onslaught of stones until her death. I stood. Sanaz cowered and kneeled before me, weeping. I stepped over and withdrew my scimitar from its hilt. Whatever violation of the Sacred Book I

187

was about to commit, I knew I would not let my beloved suffer a worse fate. I walked toward Sanaz, raised the scimitar, and began to weep.

Thus, I broke the laws of Allah, and murdered my beloved to spare her a worse fate. I am as damned as the wretched silver cross of the Infidel I place in your keeping.

"Stop, you may stop, young friend," Aponte said. His weak voice was choked by emotion and his crystal-clear eyes flowed like springs. Michael reached for his lemon water and Brother Aponte wept into his sleeve for a moment.

"To imagine such love and such agony," Aponte said. "Every time, it is the sad and mysterious workings of love and God in that one."

Adamanto handed Aponte a handkerchief. Aponte dabbed his eyes and blew his nose. He folded the handkerchief back up and handed it to Adamanto.

"Please, Brother. Keep it with my blessing," Adamanto said.

Aponte regarded the handkerchief and its fine linen for a moment. He nodded and tucked it under his cassock. Michael grinned.

"Sorry, my young friend. Crying like that. I guess you Americans might say it's an Italian thing?" Aponte said.

"Something like that," Michael chuckled.

Aponte gestured for the folio once again. He flipped several pages, making subtle noises of approval or grunts of dissatisfaction as he skimmed the thesis. He paused and tapped the open page.

"Now the Holy crusader who recovered the cross and brought it into your family tree, young friend. You can read again for us, yes?"

"No problem."

Michael was about to start reading when he paused, his brow furrowing. He pointed to the text.

"Mure-che-tack? Is that how you say that Gaelic name?" Michael asked.

Adamanto shrugged and shook his head. Aponte waved away the minor concern.

"Just read as best you can," Brother Aponte said.

"Okay. I thought 'Tar-ique' was tough enough in the last section."

"Call him 'Smith', if it's easier, young friend," Aponte said. "Just go ahead and read. I want us to get to Blessed Terrence before my last rites."

Michael laughed. He began to read:

Muirchertach Au Briain, high king of Ireland, and holy crusader, had within his possession at the time of his death a strange Saracen box containing a tau rho cross. In his last will and testament, he bequeathed the cross to his son, Donal. The text of his will wherein this cross is described is as follows:

'...in the holy city of Jerusalem, near the shrine of the Holy Sepulcher, I did obtain this holy relic from a Saracen woman with an infant and two small babes. As homage she did offer the relic to me for sparing her and her babes the sword. Upon receiving and examining the strange cross, in my distraction did but another holy crusader from Gaul mortally wound her with an accursed arrow. With grief and the gravity of my sin of distraction, I did soon offer the babes safe protection and passage to the Tower of David where many of their people did remain imprisoned by order of Count Raymond of Aguilar. The great and honorable count did allow that the babes could join the captives who laid down their arms on promised deliverance to Ascolon. Those babes and their fellow captives were delivered as the honorable Count had promised. I did then return to Briton from Gaul with this holy relic on comfortable passage, as if blessed by it. On passage from Briton to Eire, the sea leapt with fury and Charybdis' evil hand and did nearly drown us all in the Viking knarr which held true and fast. Kissing the land of my birth when landing from that wretched misery, I did remove from my tunic this holy relic and returned with God speed to my palace at Cashel. Here and now, my son, I grant thee possession of this strange relic that when held by some, grows cold with the revelation of betrayal. Hold it dear and guard it well, perhaps it will aid you in time of need if treachery of knight or chieftain is afoot...'

Aponte tapped Michael's hand. Michael was glad to pause and take another sip of lemon water. Brother Aponte slid the folio over and once again began to leaf through its pages.

"I didn't realize crusaders had come from Ireland as well," Michael said.

"Oh yes, yes," Aponte said. His eyes remained trained on the pages he skimmed. Aponte paused. He took a deep breath and passed the folio back toward Michael.

"Now we come to the very most important section. This will tell us the last part of the cross story, and some of the story of our Blessed Terrence here, too."

Aponte reached out and gently patted the red velvet bag of bones. He pushed the box with the cross next to the bag.

"This part contains elements of the bit of biography of the last days of Blessed Terrence written by our Dominican abbot of Limerick in eighteen forty-three, Brother Maurice O'Brien. His research was quite thorough."

"Might I just read this section? My throat is becoming raw."

Aponte waved away Michael's concern.

"You're still young. Let us all enjoy the words together, shall we?"

Michael found it impossible to not accept the challenge. He took one more sip of lemon water, and began.

'*Bishop Terrence Albert Flynn had a light voice which was known to soothe many almost in the way a mother's might. But he had no need of a stronger voice since he did not deliver the liturgy of the word nor ever celebrate the Eucharist at Emly cathedral. He only occasionally visited the village for which his bishopric was named. His was a different calling.*

Until he found himself on the ramparts of Limerick, he had busied himself with the duties of his calling by re-establishing Dominican monasteries and schools repressed by the invading English Parliament heretics. To have beheaded their own anointed king, Charles I, a unifier with a Catholic wife, made the invaders an enemy to God and faith. But when the heretics under Cromwell and his wretched son-in-law Henry Ireton turned their eyes back on his beloved homeland, Bishop Flynn appeared as minister to Irish defenders wherever resistance was being fought. Ireton and his troops lay only paces outside the city walls but the clan chiefs and defenders within had been holding it steady for nearly six months. He left the ministering to the twenty thousand citizens, many of them plague-infected and near starving, to the capable and faithful hands of the other abbots and priests. Here on the ramparts, he continued to minister to the dying and wounded soldiers. But many soldiers later reported that Bishop Flynn often rallied troops and spoke out in support of the garrisons. Less than two thousand strong at the beginning of this hellish siege, outnumbered two-to-one by Ireton's forces, their numbers had dwindled to twelve hundred or so. Bishop Flynn's faith in them never seemed to have wavered. And the Bishop had one other force behind it: his pectoral cross. Rather than a crucifix as would befit his stature, he wore a cross in the form of an ancient tau rho from a silver chain. The cross had been in his family for centuries and held a strange power.

The most miraculous demonstration of the Bishop's cross came just before the end of the Siege of Limerick. It is said that the Bishop, standing in his usual position on the ramparts, removed the cross from his neck and placed it in Colonel Fennell's palm. When he placed his hand over it to begin a blessing, the cross flared with icy cold. Colonel Fennell reportedly jerked his hand away. Colonel Fennell joined Captain Kelly and they shortly marched toward the Thomond Bridge.

A soldier reported that Bishop Flynn said toward the two officers' backs: "You are fighting on the side of righteousness and the true faith. The Lord keep and be with you."

Later that night, under a canopy that stretched and formed a small, private space on the rampart, a soldier on watch found Bishop Flynn sitting quietly eating a bit of stale soda bread and sipping weak tea. The soldier thought he heard Bishop Flynn weeping but it was difficult to be sure over the moans of the sick and starving citizens below in Limerick. The soldier placed his hand on Bishop Flynn's shoulder and the Bishop, startled from his sadness, nodded and blessed the soldier.

191

The next morning, Bishop Flynn woke with a start. A garrison troop clutched his shoulder and was shaking him.

"Come, quick, your eminence," the soldier said. "Captain Kelly and Colonel Fennell abandoned the Thomond bridge defense and now have captured cannons at St. John's Gate and aimed them at Commander O'Neill and other defenders."

When they arrived, numerous soldiers leaned over the rampart, many with their muskets drawn and aimed toward the inner walls of the city. Four cannons were aimed toward Commander Hugh O'Neill, the leader of the Limerick defenders. Soldiers stood with Captain Kelly and Colonel Fennell, muskets drawn and also aimed toward Commander O'Neill. A large cadre of soldiers stood behind Commander O'Neill, their muskets drawn and aimed at their former comrades. Many soldiers and citizens reported the following exchange between the former comrades:

"Stand down, Captain and Colonel," Commander O'Neill demanded. "You are mutinying and will be subject to full discipline."

"You have led us and the rest of the citizens into a wretched condition," Captain Kelly hollered back. "It is you who must stand down and begin surrender negotiations with the enemy. We demand this now!"

Behind O'Neill dirty, angry citizens formed a mob. They screamed in unison:

"Aye! We are with Captain Kelly!"

Cannon and musket rounds continued to explode and bombard the outer rampart. Soldiers were hopping between returning rounds toward Ireton's forces and witnessing the mutiny within. More and more citizens gathered behind O'Neill. Faces drawn by hunger and dirty from lack of bathing. And those were the citizens who had not been stricken with dysentery or worse, plague. The mob behind O'Neill began to chant:

"Surrender, surrender, surrender!" Soon the city walls echoed the words again and again. Commander O'Neill lowered the saber he had been rattling and dropped his head for a moment. The chants grew louder than the salvos from Ireton's forces. O'Neill raised his head.

"HUSH!!! ALL HUSH!!!" he roared. The chanting stopped and the crowd now muttered. Captain Kelly and Colonel

Flannell nodded for the cannon brigade to stand down. The soldiers with muskets also lowered their guns.

"It is with a heavy heart that I agree to negotiate surrender terms. May God have mercy on us all."

The crowd let out a cheer. Captain Kelly and Colonel Flannell both smiled and dismissed the soldiers from the cannons. Commander O'Neill replaced his saber and turned toward the crowd. It parted to let him through, with many people touching his shoulders and waving as he passed.

Two days later, having agreed to the terms of surrender, all gates to the city were thrown open. The Parliamentary army flooded in and began to usher citizens into their homes to gather their belongings or stay if they repudiated their Catholic faith. A garrison of Parliamentary soldiers brought forth O'Neill from his quarters, in shackles. Following a list drawn by Ireton himself, they arrested troop leaders, the mayor and aldermen.

Bishop Flynn had abandoned the ramparts at the moment O'Neill agreed to discuss surrender terms and joined the other clergy who attended to the ill in the pest house. He kneeled before the bed of a woman whose body was riddled with the pocks of plague. Her fingertips, swollen black, clutched at the gray stones of the wall above her bed. Her daughter stood near, wearing a robe and hood to guard her from the plague that wracked her mother. Bishop Flynn placed his hand on her forehead and made the sign of the cross with his thumb upon her forehead, left and right cheeks, and then her chin. As he began the last rites, the woman heaved her final breath.

As Bishop Flynn closed a small vial of holy oil, the battered door behind burst open on its rusty hinges. The daughter let out a shriek. Bishop Flynn stood and turned.

Four English soldiers stood before him, three brandishing swords and one a scroll he opened. He began to read:

"The citizenry of Limerick did surrender and settle terms with the Parliament of England, Ireland, Scotland, and Wales. Such terms hath included arrest of all leaders of the defenders, Royalists, and the mayor of Limerick. Since you are included in such list, you are hereby under arrest for war and conspiracy against the Parliament. By order of Sir Henry Ireton."

Bishop Flynn was then placed in shackles and surrounded by a phalanx of English soldiers. The phalanx joined up with other groups of prisoners as they made their way across Thomond Bridge to Englishtown. Once the prisoners made their way over Thomond Bridge and down Mary Street to the Tholsel, they were led through the jail's massive oak gates.

Bishop Flynn was made with the other prisoners to strip to their loincloths and remove their shoes. Bishop Flynn was allowed to keep his pectoral cross. He was then separated from the others and placed into a cell with planks for a bed.

Bishop Flynn's trial and execution was duly recorded by an English clerk as was the custom and requirement of parliamentary law of the time. The clerk thus recorded:

When offered a defense counsel the next morning for his trial, Bishop Flynn declined. He wished only to have a confessor and the wish was granted. High treason with the penalty of hanging was the verdict late in the day at the short trial held in the knave of St. Mary's.

A phalanx of soldiers appeared at his cell two days later on October 31st. Only two days after his arrest, Bishop Flynn could barely stand for lack of food and water. They marched him barefoot down Bishop Street toward Clare Street and the gallows, still clad only in his loin cloth and pectoral cross.

Bishop Flynn's mother, Catherine, stood with the crowd near the gallows. The phalanx escorting Bishop Flynn moved past the crowd and opened at the foot of the gallows. Before he mounted the gallows, Bishop Flynn paused and lowered his head. The guard reacted in surprise.

"Be at peace, my son. I wish to give my cross to my maw. Would ye mind removing it and handing to my maw?"

The guard nodded. Catherine Flynn approached. The guard held the chain and cross out to his mother. She took it gently and kissed it.

"Thank you, my lamb. I love you dearly and you'll be with our Lord soon."

Aponte suddenly clapped his hands. Michael gasped and stopped reading.

"What's wrong?" Adamanto asked.

Aponte waved weakly at both of them. He then brought his hands together as if he were going to pray. His blue eyes looked like tiny blue fames.

"These, our young friend, are the true and final words recorded by the English clerk at Blessed Terrence's execution. This was my direct research and I had confirmed the veracity of the report through multiple sources. So now, your ancestor speaks to you, to all of us."

Michael found Aponte's solemnity somewhat silly. But he also trusted that the words he was about to read were as authentic as any other historical document he had ever read. And once again, sitting next to Aponte, he felt a different sort of reverence: the reverence for knowledge and the authority of that knowledge. He began to read:

The guard turned the Bishop's mother away. He guided the Bishop to the wooden steps and followed the Bishop as he mounted the steps. The Bishop paused at the top and it appeared as though he was about to faint. But instead, he drew in a deep breath, pulled his shoulders back, and began to speak:

"Good people, this is a very uncomfortable place, for me to deliver my self unto you; but I beseech you pardon my failings... For men can have no more power over me, than that which is given them from above; and although I am denied mercy here on earth, yet I believe I shall receive it in heaven. For myself I am (and I acknowledge it in all humility), a most grievous sinner, and therefore I cannot doubt but that God hath mercy in store for me a poor penitent, as well as for other sinners; I have upon this sad occasion ransack'd every corner of my heart, and yet I thank God, I have not found any of my sins that are there deserving of death by any known Law. And I thank God, though the weight of the sentence lie very hard upon me, yet I am as quiet within, (I thank Christ for it) as I ever was in my life; I, I was born and baptized in the bosom of the Church of Rome (the ancient and true Church) and in that Profession I have ever since lived, and in the same I now die. As in regard to my engagement in arms, I did it in two respects. First, for the preservation of my principles and Tenents. And secondly, for the establishing of the King, and the rest of the Royal issue in their just Rights and Priviledges. I forgive all the world, all and every of these bitter Enemies, or others whatsoever they have been, which have any ways prosecuted me in this kind; I humbly desire to be forgiven first of God, and

195

then of every man, whether I have offended him of if he do believe I have; Lord do thou forgive me, and I beg forgiveness of him, and so I heartily desire you to join with me in prayer."

Bishop Flynn's mother, the mob of witnesses, and the guards all lowered their heads in a silent prayer. The clop of horse hoof beats interrupted the silence. Lord Henry Ireton sat astride his horse at the edge of the crowd. Wearing the regalia of his rank and class, he looked around at the praying mob. The executioner, on noticing Lord Ireton, spoke:

"Terence Albert Flynn. You have been found guilty of inciting war against the Parliament and the People. I deliver to you just and deserved punishment as has been found right by the court and judges."

The executioner placed the noose around Bishop Flynn's neck. The crowd hushed and only the whispering of Bishop Flynn's prayer could be heard. Bishop Flynn's mother erupted in a wail as the hanging proceeded.

Some month's later, Catherine Flynn left the family castle in Kilcor and made a pilgrimage to Rome. In a private audience with Pope Alexander II, the Pope proclaimed that Bishop Terrence Albert Flynn had died a martyr. Catherine Flynn presented the box containing Bishop Flynn's cross as a tribute to her son.

Michael turned the page of the manuscript and saw a section labeled 'Analysis of the Determinations and Findings'. He paused. Aponte slid the folio back over. He skimmed a page or two more, nodding and smiling. He closed the folio.

"I always enjoy this particular thesis, especially because I was much younger when I researched and wrote it. My young friend, do you have any questions for me?"

"Any possibility I might get a copy of the thesis? For family purposes you understand."

What Michael didn't say is that he would be cross-checking the research, particularly the broader claims and histories that he still doubted were accurate. Not to doubt this genius, but he remained skeptical of Brother Aponte's faith-bias that must have weakened some of the foundation of his study of Bishop Flynn.

196

"You have aided us to reunite our Blessed Terrence with his cross. I think you deserve the reward of a copy. Do you agree, Cardinal?"

"Yes, Brother Aponte. I think that is quite appropriate. We'll arrange for that."

Adamanto stepped around the table. He picked up the folio.

"Brother Aponte, thank you for indulging this request. I'll escort you back to your chamber. Mr. Dunphy and I have a bit of business still to discuss."

Aponte looked toward both of them. He smiled and nodded with resignation. Michael stood and helped Aponte to his feet. Aponte grabbed Michael's forearm as he reached his feet.

"Thank you again, young friend. May the Lord bless you with a long and good life."

Aponte released Michael's arm and reached back with his hands. He raised his hood back over his head. Adamanto led him to the door, he paused, turned back toward Michael, and made the sign of the cross and blessed him.

Michael sipped more lemon water and glanced once again at the velvet bag of bones. It was intriguing to see how the Vatican treated what they called 'holy relics'—physical remains of saints and other beatified persons like Bishop Terrence.

"Feel at home, old boy?" he said to the bag. Though he was still appreciative that Adamanto had arranged the time with Aponte, and despite his dry throat from reading out loud the last hour, he continued to wonder what the purpose of all this really was. His eyes landed on the box containing the cross. That artifact certainly compelled his interest and curiosity. What he wouldn't give to take it to a lab somewhere and have it analyzed, and perhaps to Cal or Princeton to have its provenance and Aponte's thesis confirmed. He stood and stretched. The door creaked open and Adamanto joined him once again.

"He is a treasure to us all," he said.

"Agreed," Michael said.

"Let's sit again and talk," Adamanto said.

Adamanto walked behind and supported himself against the opposite chair. He glanced back to toward the door and cleared his throat. Michael sensed that he was nervous about something.

"What do you think of the history of the Flynn cross?"

"That was an intriguing myth," he said.

Adamanto tapped the box.

"You doubt the proof of witness?" Adamanto asked.

"Witness is the lowest form of evidence. Clearly, a bit more research could be done to confirm Brother Aponte's thesis. It's dated. And discounting the biblical characters and imagery, of course."

"Discounting?" Adamanto said. His tone grew irritated.

"*If* any of the people in the Bible lived, and that's a big '*if*', in their time, dreams would have been mistaken for reality. A bump on the head like Saul supposedly got could have caused his brain and eyes to act like a projector rather than a camera," Michael said.

"I see. You demand more evidence."

"Of course. In the modern world, witness, observation, must be supported by experimental evidence. Even proof of the existence of Jesus boils down to only two passing references in Roman and Jewish texts written decades after his supposed crucifixion. Not much to go on other than witness."

"And faith," Adamanto said between clenched teeth. "But that's not why I brought you here. And I find it quite insolent that you would doubt the Word in this most resplendent house of God."

"I meant no disrespect, sir. I'm a social scientist and believe only in the word of facts and the search for them."

Adamanto shook his head. He reached behind and rubbed the small of his back, the titian-red robe fluttering at the sleeve.

"You're sure you don't want to sit, Cardinal?"

Adamanto shook his head and instead leaned against the blonde marble table. He slid his rear end partially onto it to take the weight off his left leg.

"Sciatica," he said quietly. "I should not have sat so long with you and Brother Aponte."

"Maybe also from all that kneeling and standing in mass?" Michael said with a weak attempt at humor.

Adamanto winced as much from the joke as from his back pain. He reached over and opened the box. He plucked up the cross. He pointed it toward Michael like a laser pointer.

"Mr. Dunphy, were you ever faithful?"

"I was raised Catholic. With a mother like mine, I certainly did my best to show I was faithful."

"Acts are not the same as the faith in heart. But I am relieved that you were baptized. I have recovered many a fallen Catholic."

Michael shrugged. "I'm sure you have."

"When that young man threatened your high school students with the gun, did you have any stirring of faith?"

"Wow. You know about that?"

"We know much about you, Mr. Dunphy."

"Aside from the creepy level of that statement, I can assure you that there was no 'faith in the foxhole' sort of thing, if that's what you're implying."

"Not even the stirring of a 'God help me' thought?"

"No. I acted on the pure human animal traits of survival and protection. God did not enter my thoughts."

Adamanto glanced back at the door once more. Michael wanted to ask him what he was so anxious about but kept his mouth shut. Adamanto leaned closer and now spoke in a hushed, deeper tone.

"You may find your lack of faith challenged with this relic. While I am passing this relic on to you, since you are a rightful heir, it also could be that I'm cursing you with an evil thing. It has hurt as many as it has helped. And I don't just refer to its history in that 'myth' of Brother Aponte's.''

"How's that?''

Adamanto raised his thin, hairy-knuckled index finger to his lips and shook his head. Michael felt a pang of anxiety shoot through him. Adamanto held the cross out to Michael. Michael's eyebrows knitted and he paused for a moment.

"So you may have some doubt?'' Adamanto asked.

Michael shook his head.

"Not that at all,'' he said. "It's just as once-aspiring archaeologist and historian, I have reverence for this cross that meant so much to my ancestor. I mean, if the history is to be believed in that regard, he handed it to my ancestral grandmother just before he was executed. It's very personal.''

He took the cross from Adamanto. The cross chilled his fingertips and he dropped it back into Adamanto's hand.

"It's cold,'' he said. "Like an ice cube.''

"Ah-ha,'' Adamanto said. "There's a little more proof for your skeptical mind.''

"Alright,'' Michael said flatly.

Adamanto sighed and shook his head. He handed the cross to Michael once again. Michael took it with his fingertips. He went to slip it into his pants pocket. Adamanto fluttered his hands in protest. He handed Michael the ancient box as well.

"You may do well to store it in this—for your and its protection.''

"Sure,'' Michael said. He pulled the cross from his pocket and placed it in the box.

"You will also need these papers to clear Vatican customs and Italy's, too.''

He handed Michael a manila envelope inscribed with the Vatican Insignia. Michael accepted the envelope and nodded, understanding he could otherwise be charged with smuggling antiquities without the papers.

Adamanto slid his rear end off the table and his robe made a whooshing sound. Michael reached for his elbow to help him to his feet. Adamanto winced and groaned a bit. Adamanto turned toward Michael, and his milky-blue eyes seemed to bore into Michael's eyes. After an awkward moment, Michael spoke.

"Thank you for deciding to return this to my family after all these years," he said. "No matter what, it's an amazing artifact, so personal, too."

"Of course," Adamanto said. "My son, better to not discuss that you have the cross until you're safely out of Italy."

"Why?"

"And you leave us tonight, si?" Adamanto asked.

"Yes. It's a red-eye at eleven-fifty."

Adamanto only smiled. "Just do as I suggest."

Michael could not sense the relief Adamanto now felt knowing the cross would be out of Italy and away from the hands of murderers. Adamanto turned and gestured toward the door. Michael followed behind as Adamanto crept painfully toward the door, rubbing the small of his back with each step. Adamanto stopped and slowly turned.

"Go in peace with the Lord's protection, my son." Adamanto blessed Michael. "Enjoy the rest of your stay here with us."

A few minutes later, Adamanto returned to his office and slid into his chair behind his desk. He dialed the Vatican travel department and confirmed Michael's flight and time. He was also assured that there were no anticipated delays. This, then, was the last step in his plan to rid the Vatican of the unholy relic: to alert the Palermo family that the cross was no longer at the Vatican. He would no longer have to wait, nor dread, a face-to-face confrontation. He dialed the Vatican press office.

"Hello, Allesandro. Cardinal Adamanto. Please arrange for me tonight at midnight an important press conference regarding Blessed Terrence Flynn and a holy relic. Yes. Midnight. I assume the Holy Father and no one else will need that time for any urgent matters? Good. Thank you, Allesandro."

Adamanto hung up. He pulled out a pad and began to make some notes for his press conference.

Michael sat on the bed of the Vatican apartment. The louvered doors of a small balcony let in moonlight and the faint voices of a Gregorian chant performing Vespers. Two small lamps with emerald-green lamp shades cast soft light against the dappled, faded yellow stucco walls of the room. Michael's face was illuminated by his phone screen.

"Wish we had stayed here," he said. "The Wi-Fi is great."

"It's all that old money. Why wouldn't they have the best?" Stephanie said.

"Good one!"

"So he gave you an antique silver cross," she said.

"Antique, hell. More like an antiquity."

"Probably worth a fortune."

"But you're not going to believe this: they think it comes from the silver pieces Judas got for betraying Christ."

"Twilight Zone!"

"I know. I know. They had a collection of ancient documents they had me read with Emilio Aponte."

"And he would be…"

"Just one of the greatest living historians."

"Uh. Okay. Then what?"

"I was in awe. He really is a world-class scholar. But he and this cardinal both believe this cross can actually reveal someone who betrays."

"Oh, please. But why give it to you if they think it's so magical?"

"No idea. Other than the cardinal wants my family to have it."

"Family, hell. The thing must be priceless."

"We'll decide what to do with the cross. But the myth and the mumbo-jumbo crap. I want to have it examined and tested to determine what it is, how old it is, and what it does, if anything."

"What about your mom? Since it's from her side, are you going to give her any say in all this?"

"I'll decide after I get the thing looked at. She doesn't need anything else to support her whacked beliefs."

"I guess you can figure all that out when you get home."

"Since I already have access to the DNA guy at Trinity, I'm going to see if they can exam it there."

"Don't tell me you're staying longer?"

"No. I'm sure they can take filings or something."

"I still think it's odd they gave it to you."

"You mean as in 'suspicious'?"

"Yes."

"The cardinal said it might be 'cursed'. Would be great to prove him wrong. And then, let mom know about it after it's debunked."

"So your new career path isn't Indiana Jones—it's iconoclast?"

"I don't see a chapter two career hunting artifacts. But maybe one where I apply science and research to disproving 'holy' relics."

"I'm not sure LinkedIn will have a category for that job search."

"What could it hurt to try?"

"When is your flight?"

"Eleven fifty. Red eye."

"How long?"

"I think it's five or six hours. Not sure."

"And you won't sleep a wink, I know. Just bring something to read if you get nervous."

"I'm thinking about downing a few glasses of prosecco before boarding."

"There you go!"

Antony Palermo rubbed his stomach that was on fire with indigestion. He did not recall recently having a bad reaction to veal piccata but maybe the house cook had played with his mama's recipe. He would deal with her in the morning. But right now, he needed to sit back against the burgundy satin easy chair and just let the bicarbonate of soda do its job. He lowered the volume on the television though it was quite doubtful that the sound would make it past the ornate walls covered in tapestries and awaken anyone else sleeping in the palazzo. He flipped past a few channels until Cardinal Adamanto appeared, with a chyron below that read: 'Vatican Office of Reliquaries.' A jolt of acid made the digesting picatta burn again as he recognized Cardinal Adamanto.

"So while we rejoice that the bones of our Blessed Terrence Flynn have been brought into our holy sanctuary, we also give thanks that his personal pectoral cross has been returned to his descendants."

A reporter shouted: "Can you disclose the name of the person?"

"Oh, yes. He is an American scholar named Michael Dunphy."

"May we talk to him?" another reporter asked.

"Oh, no. He flies as we speak to Ireland and then back home to the United States in the next few days."

"That pig!" Antony hollered at the TV set. He threw the remote at the television followed by a heavy crystal ashtray. The television screen shattered and popped off. His velvet slippers shuffled as he made his way across the marble floor and into a side room with a heavy, ornate cherry pocket door. He flipped a light switch and a crystal chandelier blazed into life. He took a seat behind a baroque-period desk. He picked up the phone.

"Antony here. The cross we use for the purges? It's on the way to Ireland. That Cardinal—I knew we couldn't trust him. Get in touch with that mick bunch we used in that heroin deal awhile back—yea, Pat. Yes I know what time it is. Just get that cross back here. By any means."

11.

Michael opened his carry-on bag and presented the box containing the cross to the customs inspector. He pulled out the Vatican envelope and handed it to the customs inspector as well. He yawned.

"So, what's this, then?" the inspector asked.

"It's a Vatican artifact I'm declaring. The paperwork inside this envelope should explain it all."

"Aye, and from the Vatican, no less. Pope Francis give you a souvenir, did he?" the inspector asked with a chuckle.

"Something like that."

"Your passport also, if you please. Stand over here a wee bit."

Michael stepped away from the customs counter and looked back at the long line of passengers. He pulled out his phone to check the signal.

"No, no phones there!" hollered a female customs agent. She waved a stern finger toward him and pointed to the huge sign over on the left wall.

"Just wanted to check the signal, that's all," Michael said. He was able to see a fair signal as he slipped his phone back into his front pants pocket. A baby let out a loud wail and Michael noticed a toddler, with copper red ringlets of hair, turning pink with anger in his mother's arms. She patted him as she stepped up to the counter Michael had just left. The baby's thick arms and tirade made him think of his oldest son, Phillip, when he was around that age. The child wore pajamas that looked like a Batman costume. He felt the pang of missing his own boy and the Halloween when he was six and sick with a stomach bug but still insisted on wearing his Batman costume to bed. That pang morphed into the mean clutch of awareness of the passage of time. Once again, a feeling bordering on mourning swept over him and only the strident wail of the Batman baby snapped him out of it.

"Mr. Dunphy, then?" the inspector who had taken the box and papers stood back at the counter said. He gestured for Michael.

"That wasn't too long," Michael said.

"Aye, and you're also good to go. The papers check out."

The inspector handed Michael the papers, the box, and his passport. As Michael opened his carry-on and slipped the items back into the main pouch, the inspector lightly touched his arm.

"'Tis something quite special you have there. Don't go about being a greedy Yank and melting her down for the silver when you get back state side."

"I'll try not to," Michael said as he stepped away.

But Michael knew what he was going to do with the cross his last couple of remaining days in Ireland. The flight gave him time to decide on a metallurgic test to determine what alloys comprised the cross and how and why it turned cold. Oddly, he had felt it a couple times during the flight. It was room temperature the first time, nowhere near the chilliness it displayed at the Vatican. When he felt it the second time, holding it briefly, it did begin to turn cold. That was just after the plane had recovered from a couple of pockets of turbulence. His curiosity was stirred.

He made his way down the drab, gray corridor among the throng of people slapping their heels against the shiny linoleum floor all heading toward the exit of the terminal. Cell phones popped on all around him like little solar flares, but he waited till just before the sliding glass exit doors before turning on his own phone. The signal had increased one additional bar from the customs hall.

He opened the Uber app and arranged for his ride back to the Perys. He then pulled up Dr. Reilly's number at Trinity and left a voice mail that he needed to see him once more before leaving the country. A few minutes later, as Michael hopped into the burgundy Ford Fiesta, Dr. Reilly returned his call. Michael was surprised to hear from him so quickly and so early in the morning.

"Oh," Michael said into the phone. "I'm leaving Shannon now so I can be there late morning depending on trains. Hang on."

Michael turned toward the fresh-faced young woman driver.

"You mind taking me to Limerick-Colbert Station instead of Pery's?"

She rolled her round, gray eyes toward her creamy forehead dotted with brown freckles. After a pause, she nodded.

"Aye. Not a big change but you need to edit our route so as to allow it. Only an extra two Euros for the change."

"Thanks," Michael said to the driver. "Dr. Reilly. I'll text you when I'm on the train."

As the Uber driver pulled away from the terminal curb and onto the main road of the airport, a black Hyundai Tucson with four male passengers began to follow. Once again, Michael was unaware of being tailed.

"Damn it, aye, he's got himself into an Uber," the man in the passenger seat of the Hyundai said into his phone. He stroked the coal black whiskers on his chin, his dark brows knitting over crystal blue eyes that should have made his face handsome. Instead, they shone cold and mean over the dagger sharpness of his features.

"We can't bloody grab an innocent Uber driver, too. We'll tail him till we get our chance. Aye, arrivederci, so."

He dropped the phone into his orange-checked flannel shirt front pocket. He put his right black cowboy boot with its sharp tip that ended in a chrome arrow up on the dashboard and rubbed his forehead.

"Pat, the dashboard, so," the driver said. He nodded toward Pat's boot. Pat smirked and dropped his leg.

"So, Pat, then," the driver said. He chewed his bottom lip that was surrounded by an orange, wiry goatee. "We really gotta kidnap the yank?"

The two men in the back seat, one wearing a baseball cap with the image of Tupac Shakur, and both with lumbersexual dirty blond beards, groaned. Pat turned toward them, his blue eyes flaring out of his head.

"You want to piss off these Sicilians, then? Bullet through your head and tossed down some old well sound like a good time, so?"

"Me dadai wouldn't 'a' been pushed around by no Sicilians, so," the man in the baseball cap said. "He'd blow 'em up like he did in Londonderry. I got gangsta' blood in me veins, so."

"Oh calm all of you down, then," the driver said. "We're all good Catholics—the Sicilians, too-- and rescuing our ancestor's cross is what we're here for."

Pat turned back around and shrugged. The other man in the back seat chimed in: "Even if it takes killing the yank, I'm ready for that."

"I don't care much for that idea," the driver said. "I just wish after all this that we could keep the cross here in Limerick where it belongs. He's our feckin' bishop."

"The Sicilians are paying us big, so," Pat said. "We need to deliver. Not too much blood if we can help it."

"Aye," said the man in the baseball cap. He pulled a black rosary from his shirt pocket and kissed the cross. "It is for the good of the Lord."

"Looks to be they're headed back to Limerick," Pat said. "Sit back and enjoy the ride, mates. Let's see where she drops him."

The man in the back seat with the baseball cap shrugged. He slid his ear buds into his ears. Hip hop could be heard faintly. The other man next to him shook his head.

"What?" the man in the baseball cap said. "You might learn some real gangsta' if you listen to some hip-hop."

"Oh, for cripes sake, so," the driver said a half hour later. "Looks to be that she's dropping his arse off at Colbert Station. Now what?"

They all watched as Michael pulled his bag from the trunk of the Ford Fiesta. Michael nodded toward the driver who had hopped out to help him. She slammed the trunk and smiled.

"Nice bum she has there," the driver said.

"You two will follow him onto the train," Pat said over his shoulder to the men in the back seat. "Haggerty, once you buy the ticket, text me so we know where you're headed. Red and I will follow and catch up with you there."

"You'll take good care of my piece, then?" The man in the back pulled out his pistol and handed it to Pat.

"Aye, don't you worry about a thing, O'Neill!" Pat said.

Pat pointed the pistol toward O'Neill. His thick brows arched as he narrowed his eyes.

"Shite, let's go," Haggerty tugged the shoulder of O'Neill's navy-blue jacket. O'Neill nodded and glared at Pat. They threw open their doors and made their way into the crowd, following Michael as he stepped up the stone stairs toward the arched entrance doors of the imposing gray stone building.

"Place reminds me of a feckin' prison," O'Neill said. Haggerty nodded.

Pat and Red watched as the two men entered the train station. Red looked in the rearview mirror and smoothed his hair.

"Should'a' run them off the road earlier and grabbed that Uber driver along with this guy. She was quite a lass."

Pat's text tone sounded.

"Oh feck," Pat said. "They're heading to Dublin/Trinity."

Red groaned and slapped the wheel with his palms.

"Two feckin' hours?" he said.

"Let's just get our arses out to Parnell Street and get going," Pat said.

Michael glanced out the window and saw the patchwork of low green hills divided by hedges of black green as the train whirled past the Irish landscape. A large sign read 'Birr Castle' off a side road and he knew that there was just another hour to go. The idea that had percolated into his mind months back re-emerged: 'Evolutionary Mind Construct'. In his briefcase, sitting on the floor at his feet, the cross lay tucked away in a side pocket. Like a talisman that pointed toward fact and evidence instead of superstition, it stirred his thoughts. Soon through the lenses and machines of science, the secret to its elements and reactive properties would be revealed. This thing that had inspired his ancestor to action, if that mish-mosh of history and myth he read were to be believed, would doubtless prove itself to be powerless. That his ancestor invested his faith in it was the only real power it had. Soon Dr. Reilly's colleagues would provide the evidence he needed to support his 'Evolutionary Mind Constructs': the human capacity to believe in order to inspire action to survive, informed by genetic and evolutionary imperative. But all endogenous to the structure of the developing brain—no exogenous magic.

This was now a bigger quest as he and Stephanie had agreed than coming to Ireland to find his ancestor's bones. If this cross proves to be a chunk of tarnished silver as he assumes, though, what then? If another piece of the foundation of the archaic and passé human need to believe is removed, what ethic replaces it? He paused and considered his father-in-law's words some years back: 'Religion is the only thing that has kept human beings from completely massacring each other.' '*Completely*' was the word in that statement of which he most vehemently disagreed; religion was nothing but tribalism that fostered massacres in the name of the given god so one group could annihilate another with righteousness. He glanced up to see the husk of a ruined church, its steeple a shriveled finger covered in black moss overlooking a nave of nothing but arched windows sprouting moss and ferns. But these faiths, these myths, these stories with violent and gory histories of their own over millennia now mostly just provide comfort against fear. Who was he to take that away? 'If you come to me with a problem, please also stretch your mind and offer me some solutions,' he heard the words of his supervisor from the talent agency accounting department where he worked part-time during his undergrad years. Just now as the train rumbled and vibrated underneath him, he didn't have a solution.

While Michael ruminated, O'Neill and Haggerty sat four rows behind. Haggerty sported his ear buds and slapped his right knee to the rhythm only he could hear. With a big chomp he bit two sections from a Cadbury Dairy Milk Bar. O'Neill kept an eye on the back of Michael's head as he crinkled a bag of Keogh's Crisps. When the digital train sign showed Trinity/Pearse Station as the next stop, he pulled out his phone and texted Pat.

There in 15 or so. Yank still in sight.

A moment later, Pat replied:

Here now. Near gate to left of front exit, just off road. Follow and get him to car.

O'Neill texted back a thumb up emoji then tucked his phone away. He elbowed Haggerty whose mouth was dappled with chocolate.

"Clean off your feckin' mouth," O'Neill said.

Haggerty dragged his sleeve across his face.

"You ain't me ma. Kiss me arse."

"They're waiting for us in front of the station. We got to figure how to get the yank to the car."

"No problem" Haggerty said. He patted his side and recalled that he didn't have his pistol with him. "Shite."

"We'll just have to man handle him," O'Neill said. "He ain't a bruiser of a yank so I think we'll manage."

A few minutes later, the train slowed as it approached Pearse Station. Michael glanced up to see the gaping mouth of a tunnel at the front of the red brick and brown Victorian façade with gold accents and what looked like medallions. It was his turn to text, and he pulled out his phone.

Train pulling into station in moments.

Dr. Reilly replied within seconds:

Dark sedan to right of Pearse Street exit near green kiosks. Sign will have your name on it. 5 to 10 minute ride dep traffic.

Michael replied with a thumb-up emoji. He tucked his phone away as the train entered the station. A myriad of glass panes spread across a soaring arch greeted his eyes. He did not expect the station to have such a modern feel. The train slowed as the overhead sign spelled out 'Welcome to Trinity' in green digital letters. One sharp tone sounded as the train stopped. Michael grabbed up his briefcase as the passengers on the train immediately filled the aisle. He was able to nod toward a passenger just behind who let him into the line. O'Neill and Haggerty stood three rows of people behind.

As Michael stepped through the deep green doors of the silver train that was accented with yellow, he was struck by the expanse of natural light that shined through the arched roof of glass and steel. He noticed the Southbound Café and a strong cup of coffee sounded good. He glanced around and saw clusters of people walking briskly toward a wide stairway above which read 'Pearse Street' and dismissed the idea of a coffee break. He made his way toward the stairs as O'Neill and Haggerty followed close behind. When the crowd pushed open the main doors, the sounds of street traffic carried along by a crisp breeze jolted him. He began to turn right toward the green kiosks and thought he felt someone tug him toward the left. Surrounded by various passengers and unaware of O'Neill's grasp, he shook free.

Urged on by the cold air, he spotted the driver and a sign with his name a few steps away and hustled toward it. O'Neill and Haggerty were caught in the surge of exiting passengers walking left and were swept away in the crowd. When the crowd finally thinned, they stood helpless watching as Michael hopped into the back seat of a sedan. The shrill tones of a horn blaring at them made them turn just as the sedan carrying Michael drove past. Pat waved his hands toward them from the passenger side of the Hyundai and they jumped in just as Red pulled away to follow the sedan.

"Oh, good work ye gobshites!" Pat snarled at them. "We lose him it's bullets in your brains--not mine!"

A few minutes later, the sedan carrying Michael pulled up to the front of Trinity Institute of Genetics. As Michael slid out of the rear passenger door, he didn't notice the Hyundai Tucson carrying Pat and the others roll past. Michael nodded a 'thank you' to the driver as he threw the strap of his briefcase over his shoulder and pulled his overnight bag from the rear of the sedan. He headed toward the glass doors of the atrium. Before he reached the reception desk, he heard his name and turned.

"Hello Michael!"

He saw Dr. Reilly waving as he walked toward him escorted by another man with thinning hair and horned rim glasses. Dr. Reilly reached out his hand. Michael set down his overnight bag and shook it.

"Good to see you," Dr. Reilly said. "This is Doctor McDonald, distinguished professor of inorganic chemistry."

"Hi," Michael said. Dr. McDonald shook his hand firmly.

"That's a good Yankee handshake there," he said. "You can call me Aidan."

"Dr. McDonald is going to take over from here, Michael. He and his staff will be analyzing that cross of yours."

"So we got some sketchy history of that legendary trinket," Aidan said. "I and my materials staff will be honored to unlock its molecular secrets."

"Dr. McDonald's lab is in the next building over so you'll take a little walk. You want to leave your bags there?' Dr. Reilly said.

"There's not much in them. I'm fine."

"We'll spend about an hour taking filings and what not," Aidan said.

"I'll get you set up with a car out front of the institute once again when you're all through," Dr. Reilly said. "You'll make the four-thirty back to Limerick from Pearse, no problem," he added.

"Let's make our way, then," Aidan said. "Thank you, Doctor Reilly."

Michael reached his hand out to Dr. Reilly.

"Yes, thank you once again, Doctor Reilly."

Aidan took Michael's elbow and led him across the atrium to the rear exit. They stepped out the doors near a parking guard arm. Aidan tipped his head toward an alley off to the right and began to walk briskly ahead of Michael. He paused and looked back.

215

"Sorry, bud. It's the Trinity Sprint I'm afraid. Forget that you yanks don't always walk as much as we Irish do."

Michael caught up with Aidan. He noticed a small guard booth to the left and bicycles lined up along a modern, two-story building on the right.

"Student dorms."

"Pretty quiet for dorms," Michael said.

"Day and night, it's quiet like this. Our science majors aren't quite 'Animal House' types. Virgins one and all, I suspect."

Michael laughed.

"I met my wife before my graduate studies, so I'd sowed my wild oats before that," he said.

"Did ya' then? What was your field?"

"Undergraduate and master's in history. PhD in education."

Aidan nodded.

"Good schools in the states, lot of them," Aidan said.

Michael noticed a row of air conditioners along the base of the next building.

"Air conditioning—here?"

"Ha. Only for lab equipment and such. You know I did postdoctoral work at the University of Minnesota for several years. Now there's a place that is in no need of air conditioning."

"University of Minnesota? Wow."

"Yah, yah, you betcha!" Aidan said through a chuckle. "Picked up the native tongue, you see."

At the end of the alley, the arches and filigree of another ancient gray stone building arose. Once again, Michael was struck by the serious and imposing baroque architecture of Trinity College. Aidan and Michael turned down the path and walked toward the front façade.

"Our department is in this leaky old relic. As if chemistry takes some sort of backseat to genetics. It's the feckin' start of it all. But no soaring glass and steel

216

here to be sure. And don't let me begin about the toilets."

Michael chuckled but detected a slight bit of resentment in Aidan's tone. Aidan and Michael made their way up a dimly lit, dark oak staircase lined by a wall smeared with the grunge of time. Aidan paused midway up the stairs when he noticed Michael looking at the wall.

"That grime probably reaches back to James Apjohn or Robert Kane I'm quite sure. Wouldn't be surprised if we found some remnant of manganese alum from Apjohn's hands or even ink from Kane's first drafts on chemistry," Aidan said.

Once they reached the second floor, natural light flooded in from a wall of windows surrounded by ornate stone casements. Michael began to understand Aidan' resentment since this hall appeared more like a defunct library rather than gleaming with modern angles and bright light like the genetics institute building. At the end of the hall, ornate tarnished bronze letters indicated the Materials Testing Lab. Aidan paused before grabbing the dirty brass knob that had been cast to resemble a clover.

"'Tis our stop. Let's get to work."

Michael left the lab a half hour later on assurance that Aidan would only need the cross over the weekend. With the fatigue of his early flight from Rome and facing a return train ride to Limerick, he was glad to leave behind Aidan and his colleagues as they nattered on about alloys and molecular bonds that they were confident would reveal the cross's reactive properties. Michael's stomach grumbled as the last remnants of the orange and parmigiano reggiano snack on board the flight had long ago been digested. Michael's briefcase and overnight bag began to feel heavier as he made his way down the front steps of the chemistry building. Aidan's assistant had let Dr. Reilly know he was on his way to the genetics institute to catch the ride back to Limerick.

When Michael reached the front of the genetics institute building, he noticed a black, compact SUV pull up to the curb. The driver waved him over.

Michael glanced at him curiously as Red let down the passenger window.

"Uber!" Red said.

"I thought they were sending around the sedan again," Michael said.

"Ah, feckin' no. They called you an Uber. Jump on in around the other side, bud," Red said.

"I got my bag here," he replied. "I'll hang on to my briefcase."

"I'll grab it for you," Red said. He threw open his door and took the overnight bag from Michael. He nodded and smiled for Michael to head to the other side of the car. Red opened the rear door and threw the overnight bag into the back seat, causing someone to say "ouch".

The rear passenger door flew open as Michael approached it. O'Neill jumped out and before Michael could react, he was forced in and onto the floor of the suv. Michael's vision went black as Haggerty pulled a burlap bag emblazoned with Flynn Patrick Potato Farmers over his head. He could smell what he thought was musty potatoes as he heard the murmuring Irish voices of his captors over the sound of the Hyundai Tucson's speeding engine. He felt the pressure of someone holding him down. The snap of something like cable ties binding his wrists from behind made his heart pound out of his chest.

"I'm nobody. I'm just an American school principal," he cried through the folds of the sack as it abraded his lips.

"Shut up!" He felt the tip of the barrel of a gun push against the back of his head. Surges of adrenaline made his heart pound and his breathing sped up almost as fast. Even the kid whose shooting spree he stopped didn't jar him as much as the muzzle against his head. Each bump in the road or sound of a car honking jolted his nerves. Michael was five years old again in the dark under the covers but this time, it wasn't Dracula; it was real. And just like then, as a child in a full fit of terror, his bladder let go.

"Bloody, feck, he pissed himself!" O'Neill said.

"Shut your arse up—no more bloody jawing!" Pat said through clenched teeth.

"The damn thing ain't here!" Haggerty said.

"Hand me the bags, then," Pat said.

"I bloody emptied them. Nothing left but here you go."

In his dark, now wet state of fear, Michael had one thought: The cross. That must be what they want.

"Nothing in these," Pat said. "Let him up a bit, then."

Michael felt the pressure on his back ease up. O'Neill pulled him from the floor by his collar, almost choking him.

"Talk," O'Neill said.

"What are you looking for?" Michael asked. The pounding of his heart seemed to choke his voice to a near whisper.

"The feckin' cross. Flynn's cross." Pat said.

"I don't have it."

"Then this is a bloody bad day for you, yank," Pat said.

"Wait, wait. I know where it is."

"Where?"

"Back at the chemistry lab. Trinity—where we just left."

"Bloody feck!" Pat said. "Well, then, all of us are going to have a bloody bad day." Pat said.

O'Neill pushed Michael back down to the floor. He felt the pressure on his back return. Before the blackness of fear took hold again, he heard his phone ring: it was Stephanie's ringtone, 'Babe I Love You' from Styx. It was like a soothing caress to know she was just there on his phone.

"I thought I told you to silence them for now?" Pat said.

219

"Ain't us," Haggerty and O'Neill said. "Bloody bad eighties shite," Haggerty added for emphasis.

Michael felt his shoulders being tugged vertical as his phone rang again. A hand yanked the phone from his shirt pocket, and what felt like some hair and flesh from his left pec along with it.

"He won't be needing this," Haggerty said. He let down his window and tossed the phone out.

Michael was sure he heard Stephanie's ring tone once more as the phone flew out the window. An emptiness he had not known overwhelmed him.

"We got some work to do tonight," Pat said. "Taking suggestions on where we take this bloody yank."

"The bogs," Red said with a chuckle.

"Gotta get the cross first and check in with the Sicilians," Pat answered.

"The basement at—" Haggerty cut himself off. "Wait, I'll show you on me phone."

"Right in the feckin' middle of town. By the square no less?" Pat said.

"The basement there is isolated and quiet," Haggerty said. "I do me some part-time work there sweeping, and such, so have the key and all. Closes up at four-thirty so we can get in after sundown when I start me shift."

After taking one more look at Haggerty's phone and at Haggerty, Pat nodded.

"That'll do as good as any place. No one going to be around in the wee hours when we take care of our business here. For now, head to the bay."

Some minutes later, the car stopped. Michael's inner thighs began to burn and itch with a developing rash from the moisture of his urine. But when his captors opened the car doors, he could smell the fresh sea air. It was a strange relief.

"You can go ahead and sit up," O'Neill said. He released his legs from Michael's back.

"But you're my boy right now so don't even think of trying something stupid."

220

Michael shifted his legs that were deeply asleep. That gave him just enough leverage to slowly raise his shoulders from the floor of the car, creaking his lower back and waist into a weak side bend. When he was upright, with his knees pushing against his chest, he leaned back against the seat bottom. His bound hands pushed into his lower back, but it didn't matter. He also realized that sunlight made its way through the burlap, making bits of sparkling light dance before his eyes. His adrenaline pumped.

"My Tegretol. I'm going to need my medicine!" he cried.

"The bloody feck?" O'Neill said.

"I'm epileptic. I have seizures. I gotta take my dose soon."

O'Neill shook his head and sighed. He looked over his shoulder at Michael's bags that were like deflated crisps bags in the cargo area. Scattered all around them were Michael's clothes, papers, maps and other personal detritus.

"Hold on," O'Neill said. He placed the barrel against Michael's temple.

"This better not be a load of bull, yank. And try anything and I'll blow yer feckin' head off."

He hopped out of the car, careful to close the door behind him. Michael heard the rear hatch open. O'Neill muttered as he tossed Michael's belongings about. The rattle of the medicine bottle made Michael heave with relief. O'Neill slammed the back hatch and climbed back into the back seat. He read the bottle.

"This says 'T-E-G-REE-TL.' That your shit?"

"Yes, yes."

"When the other lads get back with our fish 'n' chips, we'll be sure to let you take one of these. Sure you're thirsty, too."

"Thanks. Yes."

"You ain't smellin' too pretty with the piss and all but can't help you there."

Moments later, Michael felt the whoosh of fresh air passing over his arms as the other three opened the doors and joined them. The smell of fried fish and potatoes made his stomach rumble with hunger.

"So the priest says 'Well then, I'll take the Arab!' " Red said bursting out in laughter. Pat and Haggerty laughed, too.

"So how's your girlfriend, there?" Pat asked O'Neill. "Let him up for a breather, did ya?" He passed a Styrofoam container of fish 'n' chips to O'Neill along with a tall, capped soda with a red and white straw extending from its top.

"Yank's got some sort of disease and needs his pill," O'Neill said. Michael nodded and held up the pill bottle. "Sure he could use some water or something, too."

Pat grabbed hold of Michael's hand and read the pill bottle. He let his hand go and nodded.

"You got your soda, there. Give it on over to him and let him take his pill."

"So the bag on his head?" O'Neill said.

"No one's around this road at all. We'll keep an eye," Red said.

O'Neill removed the sack and Michael felt the fresh air sting his face as the sunlight burned his eyes. Michael also felt the relief of believing that maybe they would let him live if they were willing to let him have his pill. Before his eyes could adjust, O'Neill blindfolded him. O'Neill fumbled with the cap of the Tegretol bottle.

"How many you take?" he asked.

"Just one."

Michael heard the rattle of the bottle as O'Neill shook out the tablet.

"Open up," O'Neill said. Michael obliged. O'Neill flicked the tablet onto his tongue. He raised the soda straw to Michael's lips.

"Take a sip," he said.

Michael drank the soda heartily, hardly noticing the burn of the Coca Cola. His thirst was quickly quenched by the cool fizz and sweet flavor.

"So, all right," O'Neill said. "You can have it."

Michael drank again from the straw. This time, the soda made his stomach growl loudly.

"Shite, he's hungry, then?" Haggerty asked. "Here." He handed a fried fillet to O'Neill.

"Here comes some lunch," O'Neill said. Michael took a huge bite and the salty crunch and tender fish tasted as if he had never eaten before.

"Go slow there, yank," O'Neill said. "May be your last meal ever."

O'Neill and Haggerty laughed. Michael finished the rest of the fillet. The car was filled with the sound of the men eating, nothing more.

"He's like that Sir Thomas Moore the feckin' English tossed into the dungeon before cutting off his head," Red said a couple hours later.

"Oh, he's just upstairs you—" Haggerty stopped himself. Pat glared at him.

Michael sat blindfolded in a hard-backed wooden chair. His hands were now woven around the back of the chair and bound. Dingy work lights lit the dirty gray walls but he couldn't see it though the blindfold. A dank smell filled his nose. Pat pulled a twisted mess of a gag from Michael's mouth. Michael let out a deep breath of relief and licked his lips as his saliva began to flow freely again. He smacked his lips together several times.

"So you can scream the top of yer lungs here and no one's 'bout to hear you," Haggerty said. "Everybody's long gone."

"All right already," Pat said. "You need to tell us again where the cross is if you want to make it till morning."

Pat's phone dinged with a text. He looked down.

"Them Sicilians is getting a might bit impatient," Pat said.

Red, O'Neill, and Haggerty let out a collective grunt.

223

"I don't care if Pope Francis himself is involved long as we get paid," O'Neill said.

"So you're going to want to tell us exactly where again at Trinity," Pat said.

Michael sighed with fatigue, hunger, and thirst. For the last hour, all he could think about was Stephanie and the kids. Though he wondered why the hell these thugs wanted it so badly, the cross had become an albatross he was happy to rid himself of if he could get out of this mess alive.

"Second floor of the chemistry building, Materials Science Lab. You'll find it there, probably in its fancy old box."

"O'Neill, Haggerty, and I will head out there, Red. You can stay and keep the yank company."

Red shrugged and nodded.

"And you better hope we find the thing," Pat said.

O'Neill and Haggerty headed to the rusted steel door but paused when they noticed Pat texting. His phone dinged with the reply.

"They want to hear as soon as we got it," he said. "Let's go."

12.

The black Tucson pulled into a parking spot on Lincoln Lane, across from Kennedy's Pub. Pat checked to be sure there were no parking limit signs. He checked his phone map one more time to confirm they were within short walking distance of the chemistry building.

"Here?" Haggerty said.

"It's just a short walk around that big genetics building," O'Neill said. "But is that anywhere near the chemistry building?"

Pat nodded and held up his phone. Haggerty glanced at it, and then looked up to see the side and roof of the genetics institute.

"Oh, I got it then, O'Neill. But why not park a bit closer?"

"Don't want to arouse suspicion," Pat said. "You two get the cross then join me in there."

"The pub?" O'Neill said. "It's full of people—the doors keep popping open with drunks."

"Aye. Irish sots. Nobody's going to be noticing us. We'll then just stroll on back to the car here and be done."

O'Neill sighed. He patted his gun, Clint.

"I was hoping for a 'Bonnie & Clyde' kind of thing."

225

"This ain't a big bank job, you wanker," Haggerty said. "Just some little trinket. By the way, what the hell does the thing look like?"

"Shite if I know," Pat said. "The Sicilians didn't send no pretty pictures. I 'spose you'll know it when you see it. A cross, for Christ's sake."

Haggerty and O'Neill slipped on black ski masks, keeping them rolled up like beanies. Pat pointed toward Haggerty's and he rolled it down over his face for a second.

"We'll use these only if we have to," he said.

"The building and campus should be quiet right now—it's near eight-thirty," Pat said.

"And if we run into any trouble, I got me pistol," O'Neill said.

"You'll want to be making that a last resort, aye?" Pat asked.

O'Neill nodded. They slid out of the SUV and started up the street toward the genetics institute and the cobblestone alley that led to the chemistry building. Pat checked his hair in the mirror, and then stepped out and headed to the pub.

Just at the corner of the genetics institute building, Haggerty noticed two men with briefcases chatting. He nudged O'Neill and they paused until the two men separated and walked off. Haggerty and O'Neill dropped their chins into their coat collars and made their way down the alley toward the chemistry building. Laughter, a young woman hollering: 'You're a shit tard!', and Elton John's 'Benny and the Jets' assaulted their ears as they walked past the lighted dormitory windows. But as Pat suggested, they encountered no one in the alley.

The chemistry building loomed up on the right, its windows looking like dark angry eyes in the partial moonlight. Weak, golden light shone from the windows just above the main door as they walked to the front of the building. They paused at the formidable dark entrance doors.

"Feeling a bit nervous at all?" Haggerty asked O'Neill.

"I don't get nervous."

"Well I do and I'm hoping it don't hit me bowels," Haggerty said.

"I'm sure there'll be a loo."

Haggerty reached for the front door and felt the wrought iron handle seize under his thumb. He was about to ask if O'Neill could pick a lock but didn't need to since O'Neill already had the opposite door opened.

"You're fast," Haggerty said.

O'Neill held up a jeweler's screwdriver.

"All in the technique."

O'Neill held the door for Haggerty and let it click softly shut after he stepped through. Their shoes squeaked on the hard granite floor as they began to search the hall. Haggerty pulled out a pen flashlight and shone it on a large staircase. As they approached, they noticed the heavily carved banister pocked by centuries of studious hands. Just as they stepped on to the first stair, they heard the sound of a vacuum cleaner roaring to life somewhere in the distance.

"Poor lad must have the night shift," Haggerty whispered. "And if he's like me, he'll be down at that end of the building for half the night."

O'Neill nodded and they continued up the stairs to the second floor as Michael had instructed. Haggerty began to feel faint as the dusty smell of books and scholarship assaulted his nose. How he hated school. He paused. O'Neill glanced back at him.

"The bloody hell?"

"Just haven't been in a school in cripes knows how long. I don't care a wee bit at all for it."

O'Neill shook his head and shoved him on. When they reached the hall at the top of the stairs, they saw the imposing doors at the opposite end. They paused to see if there was any other direction to turn but nodded silently in agreement that those were probably the doors to the Materials Testing Lab. When they stood a few feet away, O'Neill swept the sign

227

above the door with the beam of his flashlight and the ancient brass letters confirmed they had found the lab.

O'Neill reached for the knob on the right-hand door and was pleasantly startled that it turned with ease. No need to pick this lock. He shrugged toward Haggerty and pulled the door open. A gallery of glass offices opened before them. Pinpoints of blue fluorescent light shone like dull stars, reflecting off the dark glass cubicles and stone floor. But then they noticed, some thirty feet or so down the hall on the right, the last glass cubicle glowed with full light.

They paused and glanced at each other. Silently nodding again, they pulled the ski masks over their faces. O'Neill withdrew his pistol from his pocket. The pinpoints of fluorescent light played across its stainless-steel barrel as O'Neill led them toward the lighted office.

When they reached the cubicle, they saw a young woman with dark hair seated with her back to them. Her white lab coat pushed against the nylon netting of the lab chair and rolled over her shoulders as she examined something closely. Haggerty noticed the wires of two ear buds protruding from her ears and pointed to his own ears while shaking his head. 'She can't hear us,' he mouthed.

O'Neill held up his left index and nodded toward Haggerty to let him know he would count down to three with his fingers. Haggerty nodded.

O'Neill held up the thumb of his left hand. Pause. Then his index finger. Pause. Just as O'Neill went to extend his middle finger, the woman turned and looked over her shoulder. Haggerty noticed she was a pretty Asian.

She screamed. They burst through the door. O'Neill thrust the gun at her face.

"Shut up!"

She nodded, pinching her lips together in fear. She dropped her hands to her sides.

"The cross!" Haggerty yelled.

"Cross?" she whimpered.

"Yes. Where is it?"

She covered her face with trembling hands. She pointed to a work surface a few feet away. O'Neill kept the gun trained on her and nodded for Haggerty to go get the cross. O'Neill reached out and removed her hands from her face. A strand of her raven hair lay across her left eye and he placed it gently back in place.

"You're quite a beautiful lass for a brainy sort."

The young woman's eyes flashed with terror. O'Neill shook his head.

"No time for any of that so you needn't be worryin'."

"Aye!" Haggerty hollered.

The cross sat upright, pinched between the clamps of a small, padded bench vise. Just to the right of a rat tail file Haggerty noticed an ancient box.

"Looks to be the cross and the box like the yank said."

Haggerty loosened the clamps and removed the cross.

"And no bigger than your wank—maybe three inches! All that over this little shite?"

He shrugged. He opened the box and placed the cross into it, and then stepped over and joined O'Neill once again. The student continued to cower and look down. Haggerty now noticed her face.

"She is a beauty, so," he said. "But we got things to do."

"Hate to do this but we need some escape time, lass," O'Neill said. He motioned for her to sit. He looked around for something to bind her hands and saw a telephone cord. He pointed to it. Haggerty ripped it from the wall and plucked it from the phone. In a moment, O'Neill had the student's arms wrapped around the back of the chair and wrists bound.

"Pardon me once again," he said. He tore the left pocket from the lab coat then stuffed it into her mouth.

"Slan agat!" O'Neill said.

"Aye. Ta!" Haggerty said over his shoulder.

The student trembled. She took a few deep breaths through her nose and focused on the petri dish of metal shavings she had been examining. She began to struggle against the cords.

Red withdrew the rim of the plastic water bottle after Michael had his fill. He paused to look at the pattern Michael's disheveled hair made against his lined and sweaty forehead just above the blindfold. He glanced at his watch.

"You know, yank, nobody's asked me yet what I think should be done with you."

Michael shrugged. He just had no energy or fight left him in at this point to care what Red had to say.

"I'm big on peat bog burials and such. 'Course, after you cut the head off and leave it in another bog somewhere off a distance."

"I guess it's the Celt in you," Michael managed.

Red chuckled. Of his four captors, Red was the least fearsome. O'Neill he could tell was a petit tyrant with that gun. Pat, though, that's the one who scared him.

"The good news is you'd look just like yourself a thousand years from now, 'cept for that tea-black stained skin you'd be sportin'."

Rumbling sounds from the staircase leading to the basement door startled Red. He shoved the gag in Michael's mouth and went to the door and listened. The soft tap and muted "Red, it's us," relieved him. He pulled open the door. Pat hustled in followed by the other two. Pat placed the box on the table and smiled widely.

"The yank was right!" he said.

"Then let's take care of the yank once and for all and claim our Sicilian reward," O'Neill said.

"Hold on. Plenty of time for all that," Pat said. "Need to check in with them."

Pat tapped his phone keypad, jittery with anticipation. It wasn't just about the reward he expected for the cross, and it had nothing to do with disposing with Michael. He had wanted to connect his local thugs with a bigger Italian syndicate for some time and he was sure this was going to be the heist that would insure that.

"Ciao," Pat said into the phone. "We got the cross and the yank, too."

Michael's neck and hands began to sweat as he listened to Pat's side of the conversation. He suddenly thought of Thomas Moore hearing his execution order from Henry the VIII's chancellor of justice. Susannah Martin of the Salem witch trials being condemned now flashed across his mind. Was this *his* last moment? Images of Stephanie's and the kids' faces made his eyes well up. Here he was at his moment of becoming pointless; life was full of meaning with love of his family and friends as the guiding purpose, but death marked the end of his life's meaning. Remembered for only so long until those who remember also die, he paraphrased Marcus Aurelius in his mind. He shuddered.

"Aye, ciao, then," Pat interrupted his reverie by grabbing Michael's shoulder. "Looks like I get a free round trip to Sicily to drop off the cross. I'm going to be askin' for a tip before I turn this thing over."

"Careful with that, so," Red said.

"Bloody feck to that. But right now, they left this wanker to us to decide as to what to do with him." Pat said.

"I would just as soon dump him in the bay," Haggerty said.

Michael could smell the sea as he rode on the floor of the Tucson, once again blindfolded. Red stopped the car suddenly.

"Look good to you?" Red asked Pat.

"As good a place as any."

O'Neill and Haggerty pulled Michael from the Tucson. They pushed and prodded him. O'Neill kept his gun trained on the back of Michael's head. His

231

shoes sunk into wet sand and rocks. He felt the binds on his hands loosen but his hands felt like one mass of dead flesh as electric nerve shocks began to awaken them. He heard mushy footsteps as someone else joined them.

"Did you check him out for any identifying jewelry and such?" Pat asked.

O'Neill and Haggerty looked at each other and shook their heads. Michael's heart pounded as someone checked his hands, pockets, and then paused and pulled the metal from his neck.

"Well what the hell is that, then?" Red asked.

"Hold it-hold it!" Pat said. He regarded the medal.

"Where'd you get this?" Pat asked.

"My mother."

"She a follower of Mother Harriet, then?" Pat asked.

"What the bloody feck?" Red said. "Who gives a shite about all this right now?"

"Mother Harriet is *my* mother."

"I don't believe you," Pat said.

"She's Mother Harriet Flynn Dunphy. I'm Michael Dunphy. Check my driver's license."

Haggerty pulled Michael's wallet from his own pocket. He opened it and nodded.

"Wanker's name is 'Dunphy'," he said.

"Hang on," O'Neill said. "Checking google."

After a moment, O'Neill held up his phone to Pat. Pat enlarged he screen with his thumb and forefinger. Pat gasped. Red, O'Neill, and Haggerty looked at him, puzzled. He pulled a chain from under his shirt and revealed a Mother Harriet medal.

"So what?" Red asked.

"So everything. We are not going to kill the son of the one woman on earth who is in direct contact with the Virgin Mary."

"Are you feckin' on drugs?" Haggerty asked.

"The yank ain't seen our faces and don't know nothin' 'bout where he's been," O'Neill added.

Red folded his arms and considered the circumstances. He sure as hell wasn't planning on pulling the trigger. And if O'Neill was siding with Pat, he was done.

"Fine. We leave the wanker here. Good?"

"Just be sure he knows the blindfold stays on till we pull away," O'Neill said.

O'Neill glanced at Pat. Pat nodded. O'Neill withdrew his gun and tucked it away. He and Haggerty ran toward the idling car. Pat walked carefully backwards. He crossed himself and hopped into the front seat of the car. Red started to pull away but then made a loop around Michael and stopped the car for a moment.

"I still say you'd look better with that bog-stained skin!" He laughed as the car sped away.

As soon as Michael heard the Hyundai's engine fade, he dug into the blindfold and tore it off. Out directly in front of him lay Galway Bay, with a finger of land jutting into the ink blackness. Soft yellow lights reflected from the row houses played on the lapping waves. How close was he to being dead at the bottom of Galway Bay? And who was Pat bringing the cross to in Sicily? The mob? And strangest of all, the medal he wore, the only symbol of love from his mother so long ago, now saved him. His head swam with these thoughts. He turned back toward land and saw a church a quarter mile or so away. He walked toward it, taking deep breaths of the briny air.

13.

"So this Mick thinks he can raise the price of the cross on *us?*" Antony said. He pounded the edge of a greasy workshop table, making the tools vibrate.

"I know, I know, one of my boys paid him the extra lira yesterday," a young man who looked no more than eighteen said to Antony. "What the hell is so important about this thing, Antony?"

"Tell you what, Bido. I'll show you when this shithead Mick gets here. When is he supposed to show?"

Bido raised the left cuff of his lemon-yellow dress shirt and checked his watch. He nodded.

"Any minute. Eleven forty-five."

Antony clapped and laughed.

"Just in time for the noon bells."

Bido shook his head. Antony feigned a gun to Bido's temple with his fingertip.

"Ding. Dong. Pow!" Antony said.

"And dead Mick!" Bido added, laughing.

A moment later, Antony and Bido heard pounding on the workshop door. A silhouette shifted behind the yellowed window caked with grime. Antony nodded to Bido to let Pat into the workshop. Bido reached for his revolver but Antony shook his head. Bido hustled to the door, pulled open the rusted latch, and slid it open. Pat stepped in and paused, waiting for his eyes to adjust to the dim light. He saw Antony and walked toward him. Antony nodded toward Bido. Bido slammed the door shut behind him and pulled out his revolver. He stuck into Pat's back.

"What the bloody feck?" Pat said.

Bido patted Pat down and pulled out a switchblade, his wallet, and the small box with the cross.

"Just to be careful," Antony said. "Bido, basta abbastanza."

Bido handed the items to Antony. He placed his revolver back into the waist band of his brown dress slacks and folded his arms.

"My young friend here don't speak English like me. Sorry for any discomforts," Antony said.

"He bloody didn't need to take all my shite."

Antony tossed the switchblade onto the work bench. He pointed toward a stool.

"Have a seat. Gotta check things," Antony said.

Pat sat, his eyes darted like a pinball between Antony and Bido. Antony opened the box and smiled when he saw the cross. He held it up by its silver chain.

"Bido, vuoi vedere come funziona?"

Bido nodded. Antony waved him over and he paused just behind Pat's left shoulder.

"I asked Bido if he wants to know how this cross works," Antony said.

"Okay," Pat said nervously.

"Open your hand," Antony said.

Pat opened his hand. Antony lowered the cross into Pat's palm. Pat held it for a moment.

"Bloody feck!" he hollered. Antony plucked the cross from Pat's hand.

"Thing's cold as Dublin in winter. Shiite!"

Pat rubbed the inside of his palm. Antony placed the cross back into the box. Bido's eyes screwed up in confusion.

"Dice chi ci tradisce. Si?"

"Si," Bido replied, now understanding.

Pat stood. Bido stepped up and pushed him back onto the stool.

"Tradimento," Antony said. Bido nodded.

"What the feck is all this?" Pat asked.

"Tradimento. Betrayal. You have betrayed our deal and us." Antony said.

The cheese vendor rolled up the peacock blue, corrugated stall cover. His thick hands struggled a moment until the door rolled open with a rusty screech. The morning sun at the Fera o' Luni illuminated the rounds and bricks of white cheeses and made them glow like church candles. As the cheese vendor leaned over to open the large glass case, he paused.

"Oh, merda!"

He jumped back from the cheese case and looked around frantically, pointing. The vendor from next door ran to his friend and gasped and pointed.

"Polizia! Polizia!" both vendors screamed.

Several other vendors rushed to their aid, each one pausing to gasp and point. Sticking out from a mound of small rounds of parmigiano reggiano, blocks of asiago, and slabs of fontina were a pair of human legs in black cowboy boots. The chrome tips of the boots sparkled in the Palermo sunshine. It would take the police several days to identify Pat, the Irish thug.

Michael finished rolling up his last T-shirt and placed it inside his suitcase. He had already packed up his laptop bag and smaller carry-on. The gray light of the Limerick morning barely made it past the window sheers, making it necessary for the room to be lit by the soft yellow glow of the bedside lamps. He double-checked his air ticket and placed it inside his emergency replacement passport. He was anxious to get home. Someone tapped his door softly. He opened it and Chakranna smiled. She handed him a small glass vile with some dried wildflowers and powder. He held it up and arched his eyebrows. She smiled.

"I know you don't go in for the witchin' or much else magic. But 'tis a wee bit of Irish magic good luck. Be sure to pack it in your suitcase—not in your carry-on. Might look a bit odd. You know, drugs and such."

"Thank you, Chakranna. And thank you again for that lovely dinner and all the nice chats."

"Aye, that lovely dinner. So I'm separated now from Liam. He needs to sort out some things before we can go on."

Chakranna's voice wavered when she said 'go on.' Michael leaned over and kissed her on the cheek.

"You just insist that he put your needs, wants, and desires before his. That's all he really needs to know."

"And me?"

"You do the very same."

"Thank you. Ta!"

14.

Michael was relieved to have the aisle seat on the flight back to Los Angeles. As the plane rumbled and the engines roared down the runway, his heart sped up as usual. He kept his eyes closed and felt his body push into the seat as the plane lifted from the land. Clutching his knees, he opened his eyes moments later as the engines died back to climbing speed. The windows of the cabin let in the gray light he had grown so fond of as the plane sliced its way through the omnipresent Irish overcast. And while the anxiety from being on a plane gripped him, there was a deeper nervousness and melancholy that began to seep into him.

The adventure of his life had just ended. From the discovery of Bishop Flynn's bones, even through the sheer terror of his kidnapping, he felt absolute presence of self. The platitude of living his bliss in the moment had happened. And it was over. He peaked, he now knew. There would be nothing going forward except for grinding out a living until a meager retirement. That thought sent an adrenaline pump through him.

Applications, interviews, rejections—who the hell needed a fifty-two-year-old school principal? Did he even want to pursue education administration any longer? 'You'd be wasting that PhD that you worked so hard for, and you and Stephanie continue to pay for,' he chided himself. But Michael knew that he had fifteen years before he could retire and even then, social security and his 401k would only help him and Stephanie scrape by. In all of that, he knew that starting any kind of new career as an investigative archaeologist was not going to happen. Let alone the beating his muscles took over the days of the Limerick dig. The old gloom began to creep back into him, and despite each jolt of turbulence that startled him, his mind wrestled with these thoughts in a fitful sleep.

"Your sleep should improve somewhat as well," Dr. Berg said a week later.

Michael sat on the exam table while Dr. Berg waved his pen light past Michael's eyes. Dr. Berg raised his index finger and instructed Michael to track it with each eye, and then both. He nodded. He reached around Michael's head and felt the injury sites on his skull.

"No pain or tenderness?" he asked.

"Nope. All good."

"Great."

Dr. Berg leaned over and typed into his laptop sitting on an adjacent table. Michael looked around the barren room with its laminate cabinets and white Formica countertop. He glanced through the blinds and could see the Hollywood sign just barely through the haze.

"So here's where we are," Dr. Berg said. "Your last scan and EEG showed normal functioning. I'd say the epilepsy has resolved itself so we can forgo the Tegretol."

"That makes me a little nervous," Michael said.

"Keep the remainder you have on hand. If a seizure comes on, go ahead and take it once again and contact my office immediately. I just don't see that happening, though."

"I wouldn't mind seeing the particles and elements one last time," Michael chuckled.

"You and I both know that all you were seeing is what your brain was biased to see. Basically, it was all

239

the science textbooks you ever studied meeting your imagination. If you were religious, you'd probably be seeing people morph into Jesus or Buddha."

"Somehow I'm going to miss it."

"Watch 'The Fantastic Voyage' if you need a visual fix of scientific imagination. It's on Netflix."

"Thanks, Doctor Berg."

"Rachel Welch isn't hard on the eyes, either." Dr. Berg chuckled and patted Michael's shoulder. "Be seeing you."

"Hopefully not," Michael said.

Dr. Berg nodded and marked the air with a 'one for you' gesture and stepped out of the exam room.

As Michael drove east down Franklin Ave toward Highland after his appointment with Dr. Berg, he did feel a sense of relief. Neither he nor Stephanie took vitamins and rarely, an aspirin to manage aches and pains. It was good to know that he would be done with the Tegretol and for that matter, doctors for awhile. The traffic ahead of him stopped dead about three blocks back from Highland. He tapped his steering wheel and looked around to see a faded mansion with stone columns that reminded him of The Haunted Mansion at Disneyland. The house looked stained with soot, almost gray but hinting at a glorious white it must have been in its heyday. Dead shrubs and a withered California pepper tree gave the house a feeling of neglected despair. Judging by its proximity to the street, Michael figured it must have been a grand old Hollywood house from the teens or twenties, long before Franklin was a traffic-jammed thoroughfare. Old Hollywood history always piqued his curiosity and he wondered if Charlie Chaplin or Clara Bow ever crossed the house's threshold. He had the briefest thought that it would be a wonderful job to curate a Hollywood museum, but the strident honk of a Toyota interrupted his fantasy.

When he arrived home after a forty-five-minute traffic fest, Stephanie greeted him at the front door. She kissed him briefly and hugged him tightly. The love, warmth, and security of her hugs always made him melt a little; nowhere and with no one in the world was he so completely himself and whole.

"So tell me, tell me!" she said. She pulled him over to the chair and sat on his lap.

"You were right—no more doctor appointments, no more Tegretol."

Stephanie sighed with relief and smile. She wrapped her arms around his neck loosely.

"More good news—a junior high in Mission Hills and a high school in Van Nuys both emailed you. They want to interview you for vice-principal positions."

"Hmm. L.A. Unified, huh?" he said.

"I gotta say you sound a bit underwhelmed."

He nodded and kissed her cheek. He lifted her arms off his neck and nodded toward the sofa.

"You tell me I'm too heavy for your lap, you'll be sleeping in here tonight."

She slid off his lap and her knees cracked as she stood.

"Or getting too old," she added under her breath.

She waved a warning finger toward him not to say anything. Michael made a zipping motion across his mouth and shook his head. She sat on the sofa and folded her arms.

"It's just a lot of red tape and bureaucracy at L.A. Unified, that's all. That was sort of my last choice."

"You submitted twenty-four CV's and applications. No other replies," she said.

"I'll go, I'll go. I just want to keep shopping around a bit, that's all. Kind of hoping one of the junior colleges might be interested in a myth-busting archaeologist."

"Whatever makes you happy."

"I won't wait forever."

Three weeks later, Michael had been turned down on both positions. After another flurry of fifteen job application submissions, he failed to secure a single interview. None of the junior colleges had shown interest. He walked into the house behind Stephanie, lugging two armfuls of groceries in paper bags. Just as he placed them on the kitchen counter, his phone text signaled.

"God, I miss the plastic bag days," Stephanie said.

He glanced down at his phone. It was a text from Gregory. After a moment, he told Stephanie what it said.

"Looks like Louisville Private Prep School in Woodland Hills needs a history teacher. Gregory's ex is the principal there and he says I'm a shoe—sorry—a spiked heel-in, if I want to give it a shot."

Stephanie pulled open the refrigerator and placed an eighteen-count carton of eggs into it. She placed two packages of bacon, and one of breakfast sausages into the deli drawer. She said over her shoulder: "Teaching might not be all that bad."

Michael placed his phone back in his pocket. He pulled out a carton of cream and bottle of pure maple syrup. He handed them to Stephanie.

"It's not like I have a lot of options at this point."

Stephanie looked over the refrigerator then closed the door. She leaned against it.

"Why don't you ask Gregory to come for brunch tomorrow along with boys? We have enough for three batches of baked French toast. And since Antoine is actually going to be here, it would be great for him to see his gay auntie Gregory again."

"And the teaching position?"

"I can't imagine someone who could make history come more alive for kids than you. Set up an interview."

"Here to see my Fairy Gay nephew!" Gregory said the next day.

Michael stood at the opened front door. He glanced down at Gregory's arms. In the left, he cradled a paper bag with two bottles of champagne peeking their golden foil lids out from the top. In his right, he held a large bottle of orange juice. Michael reached for the bag, but Gregory thrust the orange juice toward him.

"Mimosas!" Michael smiled.

"No. Gay reunion juice. Step aside and let me see my handsome nephew!"

Michael stepped aside just as Antoine came up to join them. A handsome exact cross between Michael and Stephanie, his retro pompadour haircut bounced as he ran up and threw his arms around Gregory.

"There's my Fairy Gay Auntie!!!!"

They hugged each other. Michael was just able to grab the bag of champagne before it dropped to the floor. They separated and Gregory held Antoine's shoulders and looked him over.

"You're all grown up. Did you bring a date?"

"Not much time for that right now, Uncs. But I'm loving the screenwriting and finally have a project in pre-pro."

"Don't wait forever. Those good looks will fade."

He nodded toward Michael. Antoine laughed.

"I'm focusing on my work and career right now. That's enough."

"All those early drawing and painting lessons paid off. A true creative in the house," Michael said.

"Wait, wait, before we talk about all that. What do I smell? Homemade doughnuts or something?" Gregory asked.

"Not quite!" Stephanie stepped in from the kitchen to greet him. "Oven-baked French toast—plain or caramel pecan."

Gregory let out a breath of joy. He pointed to Antoine.

"Caramel pecan, of course," Antoine said.

"You got your mom's good taste, too!" Gregory said.

Gregory kissed Michael and Stephanie on the cheeks, and then snatched the bag of champagne back from Michael.

"Mimosas for my lovely Stephanie!" he said. It was Stephanie's turn to let out a joyful sound.

"I thought this was gay reunion juice," Michael said.

"Oh, keep up, will you?" Gregory said. Stephanie, Antoine, and Gregory all laughed. Michael just shook his head.

As they made their way into the living room, Phillip stood. Camryn sat on the couch, her hands resting on her eighth-month belly. Phillip held his hand out to Gregory.

"Hi Uncle Gregory," he said. They shook hands. Phillip gestured toward Camryn who waved.

"This is my wife, Camryn."

Gregory glanced down and smiled.

"You *are* pretty far along. And gorgeous, I might add," he said.

"Not feeling that so much these days," she said.

"Well you just make sure this smart husband of yours invents another line of software. You and your—"

"Girl," Camryn said proudly.

"Baby girl deserve the best," Gregory said.

Stephanie ran ahead of the group when she heard the oven timer. She glanced at the dining table and hollered over her shoulder: "Gregory, would you mind getting the mimosas for whoever wants them while I tend to the French toast? Tall glasses are in here to the left of the fridge. Everybody come on in and take a seat at the table."

Gregory glanced at Michael and Antoine.

"She's still the boss, isn't she?"

Michael and Antoine nodded enthusiastically.

"Coming. Madame!"

244

Stephanie and Antoine cleared the brunch dishes away. Camryn helped as best she could, scraping and stacking the plates though she remained seated. Antoine grabbed them up and handed them off to Stephanie. Moments later, Stephanie returned to her chair wiping her hands with a dish towel. Antoine leaned against the kitchen doorway, sipping his mimosa. Stephanie pulled out her phone.

"Sorry gang," she said. "I wanted Dad to hold off on stories from his adventures until I could get Marissa on Facetime. I was going to set up the phone here so we could all see it."

"I love the idea but I gotta get back on over to the couch. My back can't take much more of this Chippendale chair," Camryn said.

"Sweetheart, of course," Stephanie said. "But I don't know how I can set up the phone…"

"Mom, I can set up a Google chat on the Samsung in the den," Phillip said. "It will take like five minutes and then we'll have wide-screen Marissa."

"Would you, Phillip? I'll help Camryn to the den couch. The rest of you, head on in to the den. "

Everyone stood to go. Gregory grabbed up the remaining bottle of champagne, the orange juice, and his glass.

"Refills on the mimosas coming so don't forget your glasses."

Once everyone had settled on the playpen couch and side chairs in the den, Phillip had Google chat up on the large screen of the wall-mounted television. The Google dialing sounds began and in a moment, Marissa appeared on screen. She wore a white blouse that contrasted against the dark walls of her dorm room.

"Marzi-Marzi-Marzi!" Michael hollered.

Marissa spoke but no sound came through.

"Oh, crap," Phillip said. "Hold on."

He disconnected the Google chat. With a few quick keystrokes on his laptop, started the Google dialing once again. The screen went black.

"Are you there?" Marissa's voice said, but no image.

"Son-of-a!" Phillip said. "Something must be up with your internet, Mom."

Stephanie shrugged. Phillip disconnected the chat once more and pounded his laptop keyboard furiously.

"Okay, it should work this time," he said.

The Google dialing sounds began again. Marissa appeared once again.

"Marzi-Marzi-Marzi," Michael said with less enthusiasm.

"Daddy-Daddy-Daddy!" Marissa said.

"Yea!" the group hollered.

Marissa adjusted herself and then looked down and made some other adjustments at the bottom of her screen.

"There, now I can see everybody including my soon-to-be niece!"

"Hey, girlie!" Camryn said.

"Are those mimosas?" she asked.

"Oh, yeah, Wart!" Phillip said, raising his glass to taunt his sister.

"Blow me, Phillip," Marissa said. "Oh my god, Toiney!!! I haven't seen you in forever," Marissa said.

"Hi, Marzipan! You look great!" he said.

"You have to Facetime me privately soon. Gotta catch up!" she said.

"Busy with pre-pro on my script. Pretty intense stuff."

"Cut the crap. Political science classes here at Berkeley are intense, too. You can make some time for me," she said.

Everybody laughed.

"That's my girl!" Stephanie said.

"She is your daughter, no doubt about it," Gregory said. "Cheers, Marzipan!"

"You, too, Uncle Gregory! Mwwwaaaaahhh!" she said, blowing him a kiss.

"Okay, if we're all set, let's let your dad talk," Stephanie said. "Midee, start with the kidnapping, that's about as crazy as it got."

"Yeah, yeah!" the group hollered.

Michael related the kidnapping experience as well as the odd time spent at the Vatican. He spoke of the dig, of Chakranna and Liam, the cross and the lab test for his DNA, and of walking the streets of Limerick in search of their ancestor. As the afternoon wore down, and the questions from the family dwindled, with coffee having replaced mimosas, Antoine stood and stretched.

"This was so great, Mom and Dad. I gotta get going though so I can jot down some stuff before a dinner meeting with the producer."

"Dinner meeting, producer? I approve. Let's go pick a china pattern." Gregory said.

"Not that kind of dinner, Uncs. This really is just business."

Antoine leaned over and kissed Gregory on the cheek. Michael and Stephanie stood to walk him to the door.

"Catch you on the upswing, Antoine," Phillip said.

"WHHAAAATTTTHHEEFFFUUUUUUC CKKKKKK!!!" Camryn suddenly screamed.

She clutched her belly. Everyone but Stephanie froze. Camryn started breathing quickly.

"Oh, shit, it hurts, hurts!" she cried.

"Everybody, calm!" Stephanie roared. "I think our granddaughter is making an early entrance."

"I'm out. Love you all!!!" Marissa signed off.

Phillip stood but wasn't sure what to do. Gregory patted his back, stepped around and touched Michael and Stephanie lightly on the shoulders and made a quiet exit.

"Just call her doctor, Phillip," Stephanie said. "We'll get her to the hospital, no worries."

"Call mom, too, mom too," Camryn squeezed out between painful breaths.

"Anything I can do?" Antoine asked.

"You go do your meeting. We'll call you once your niece is here," Stephanie said.

Antoine kissed his parents and then left. Moments after Phillip had called the doctor and his mother-in-law, Michael drove Phillip's BMW suv toward the hospital. Phillip clutched the clothing hook over the passenger door, rotating his head like a nervous bird to check on Camryn in the back seat. Stephanie had her arm over Camryn's shoulder and guided her in counting her breaths.

Glory Adele Dunphy was born full of energy and wailing at three forty-five the next morning. Michael and Stephanie became grandparents for the first time.

15.

"Mr. Dunphy, I said with the execution of Charles the first, the monarchy had begun its fast decline to its current ceremonial status," a soft-spoken male teen voice said. "Mr. Dunphy, are you having a stroke?"

The classroom of teenagers erupted in laughter. Two girls pulled out their phones and snapped selfies, pointing over their shoulders toward Michael. He popped out of his daydream and stood up. He walked over to the two girls who both fumbled to put their phones away.

"Nope," Michael said. "Pull up the selfie you just took and show me it's deleted."

"But don't I have First Amendment rights here?" the blonde girl on the left asked.

"Amber, you do but those rights don't extend to my image. Plus, remember, this classroom is a dictatorship, not a democracy. What I say goes."

Amber's cocoa brown eyes that gave her teen face a gentle sweetness narrowed in anger. She held her phone up toward Michael and Michael could see his face clearly over her shoulder. She tapped the delete symbol and then showed Michael she had deleted the file from the temporary delete hold file as well. The other girl held up her phone, her pale, plain face looking at Michael for approval.

"Fine," he said as he turned.

"Whatever," Amber grumbled in that entitled, dismissive generational way.

"You are correct as usual, Fred," Michael said. Michael added 'as usual' in his reply to the awkward teen whose handsome face belied a nerd demeanor. Fred nodded and smiled, making his wavy chestnut hair fall in front of his face. Michael recognized himself in that young man: his intelligence masked the struggle to define himself in the same way Michael felt in his teens. This kid had so much potential but was lost in the confusion of achievement for achievement sake. Michael so wanted to reach out to him, as he had done with his own sons years ago, and tell him to focus on the subjects and things he loved, on his strengths, rather than straight A's and college admissions. That way might lead to a career in law or medicine, but middle-age boredom and angst would follow, too, he wanted to tell Fred. And Fred's gentle personality made Michael wonder if the teen were gay. That would be the most important thing Michael would tell him: be clear in your heart and express yourself honestly and everything else is secondary. A good life will follow a life lived honestly and true. You don't need to conquer the world; the American dreams of money, power, and fame are horseshit. But this was AP World History, not the counseling office. His days of guidance as a principal were over. Michael would not play the role of the caring, inspired teacher like so many he had experienced in his education. Fred had parents and came from a privileged life like most all students at this private college-prep high school. Fred would have to rely on his parents to help him, and Michael hoped they were aware of their son's unique needs and were enlightened enough to guide him.

"Mr. Dunphy, I didn't mean the stroke question to be funny," Fred said as Michael returned to his desk.

"I know you didn't Fred, thanks."

But Michael was concerned that he had slipped once again into daydreaming. And his daydreams were always centered on the same thing: searching for Bishop Flynn's bones and then the thrill of finding them and matching his DNA. The Limerick dig was six months ago this week and Michael felt a pang and yearning for it. He had hoped that by this point in the first school year he had started teaching again, he would have still felt fresh and energized. Instead, he found himself bored, listless and now prone to daydreaming in the middle of an AP History period. *Get your shit together. You have to help support your household and like it or not, this is all you know how to do. No college was interested in an over-the-hill religious artifact iconoclast.*

"By the way, class. Fred's concern is not unwarranted. I did suffer epilepsy for awhile. I was kicked in the head a year or so ago in the parking lot of the last high school where I was principal."

The classroom erupted into a collective gasp. Michael scanned their faces for reactions and saw rows of wide eyes and o-shaped mouths. No one uttered a word.

"Since there are just a couple minutes left in the period, we'll finish up with seventeenth century England tomorrow. Instead of that, let's talk about my being attacked a couple of weeks after I stopped a school shooter."

"So you can meet me at the conference and we can grab some lunch on campus? After all, I haven't seen you since that little fiasco in Ireland."

"'*Fiasco*', Mom?"

"You survived. Don't make it bigger than it was."

"Gangsters held me captive and then we're ready to bump me off until one of them saw my Mother Harriet medal."

"See, there you go, Michael."

"There I go what?"

"Obviously, those weren't all mobsters, Michael. At least one of them was devout. They spared your life thanks to the Blessed Mother."

251

"La Cosa Nostra AND Sinn Fein are just devout, Mom?"

"Of course they are, Michael. Why else would they have wanted that cross?"

"So they're just believers who sinned a little bit?"

"Why did you want the cross, Michael?"

"It belongs to me, our family. Your ancestor for Christ's sake."

"Knock that off."

"Oh Mother, please."

"Those men must have some faith to want the cross. You have no faith."

"What's your point?"

"Seems to me the cross ended up in better hands."

"The cross belongs to us. And for your information, I'm still waiting on lab results on it. "

"Why would you dare to subject an obviously holy relic with an examination?"

"To determine what the hell really is going on with it."

"And chip away at faith? You are so judgmental in your secular superiority."

"It's called being open-minded and curious, Mother."

"Be that as it may, even mobsters are made in the Lord's image and capable of redemption. I know you're not concerned about that."

"All children and adults, too, every damn body, deserves opportunities to make their lives better. I'm all in favor of that. It's called humanism, Mother."

"No humanism without God first, and the Blessed Mother protecting all her children."

"That's so infantilizing. Making people depend on a father or mother in the sky."

"Godless talk, sinful arrogance."

"No. Waking people up that they are in control of their lives--their internal grit-is not arrogant, it's empowering."

"And the power flows from the Lord."

"No. The power is from taking action and accepting the results of our actions and learning from them. Action and progress, not prayer."

"I really need to go, Michael. Am I going to see you?"

"I'll be there, Mom."

"This is the first multi-faith, multi-denominational conference on the internet. With the holiest of men and women from all faiths grappling with solutions to poverty and hunger. Even Pope Francis will join via satellite. It's going to be bigger than any of those TED Talk things you love so much. It is so very much not just about me and my flock."

"You may need the Hells Angels again—I'm just thinking a Sunni and Shia mixing it up, and then adding in a Jew and a Hindu."

"We of all faiths must shine the light of hope and God's love together. Mankind needs us now more than ever."

"Any atheists or humanists involved?"

"Those who deny God have no place at the table. There is nothing they can offer. We'll do quite well without your bunch."

"Or not. We'll see."

"Gotta take a call from Tibet now, Michael. See you at the conference Thursday."

"Oh. Well say 'hello Dalai' for me, would you?" but Michael said that into a dead phone. He hung up. He grabbed his phone and swiped open the calendar and added the conference that was set to be held at USC in the Mudd Hall School of Philosophy library. He heard Stephanie's footsteps on the hardwood floor just before she rubbed his neck and shoulders. She paused and slid onto the couch next to him.

"That was a short Sunday call," she said. "Any interest in some take-out Hogly Wogly's? It's too hot to cook anything."

"Yep. Ribs and that mac salad sound good. And by the way, I get the pleasure of having lunch with Mom this Thursday at USC."

Stephanie leaned over to pull on a pair of sandals. Michael noticed how her manicured toenails matched the pink daisies accenting the white sandals. Her impeccable style made him fall in love with her again for the umpteenth time.

" 'SC. For what?" Stephanie said as she straightened up. "Don't tell me—she's going to use some of that televangelist loot to pay off her grandson's film school student loan?"

Michael chortled. "Don't we wish. We still have to wait for our little Spielberg to pump out a screenplay that sells. No, she's put together some big confab with the heads of a bunch of the world religions to solve poverty and hunger."

"If they all just donated what they have from their collection plates, they could solve hunger right on the spot."

"She got me thinking, though."

"Uh-oh."

"Smartass."

"Okay, okay. What did she stir up this time?"

"I'm thinking *I might* stir something up at that meeting."

"What for example?"

"She's assembled all the major religious thinkers alive."

"What would you be 'stirring up'?"

"For one, she's not including any atheists or other free-thinkers."

"It's her meeting, Midee."

"It's just that you have all these people assembled and why not make the conference about something even bigger than hunger and poverty?"

"Where are you headed with this?"

"I don't know yet."

Stephanie gently slapped Michael's hairy knee that stuck out from his brown plaid walking shorts.

"Let's get going. I'm starved," she said.

When Michael popped awake early the next morning after only four hours of sleep, he could feel the heaviness of beef ribs and macaroni salad pushing against his stomach. As always, he couldn't resist finishing the half slab that always reminded him of the Flintstones' closing credits and the ribs that flip their car onto its side. And as always, the rich beef challenged his digestion and disturbed his sleep. After he took a capful of antacid and settled back into bed, he began to ruminate about the upcoming religious conference. He imagined his mom sitting at the center of a long dais, wearing one of her white, gauzy robes with her silver hair piled high above a white headband. There she would be pointing at the Orthodox Jew and asking him what he thought about what the Sikh just said. How in the world was this larger group of believers going to have anymore impact on poverty and hunger than any of them separately were already having? What really was the point? He smiled when he thought about Stephanie's comment again: if they just donated from their collection plates en-masse, world hunger would end immediately.

As the antacid cooled his harsh indigestion, his mind wandered to the unit on ancient Rome he'd be finishing with his first period AP class in a few hours. How much richer it would have been had he been able to volunteer at a few dig sites back in his undergrad days and been able to share a sense of awe in antiquity with his students. But he hadn't done that and most all of his students only cared about scoring fives so that they could get into Stanford or Cal. There was not a twinkle for classical history in a single pair of those adolescent eyes. The image of the black and silver dirt brushed away to reveal his ancestor's bones back at the Limerick dig played before his eyes. It thrilled him again: ancient human bones being uncovered, and bones that shared his family DNA. Irish history was barely a footnote in the AP curriculum so there was no point in sharing the moment with his students.

And then it occurred to him: this was all his life was going to be about. Teaching for work, loving his wife, helping with grandkids. Nothing great, nothing glorious, nothing more. But unlike before, the dark cloud of depression didn't descend. I guess in the end, he thought, most of us are never going to be Indiana Jones or Bill Gates. Maybe we play it safe because it's our only real choice: we're too lazy or not as smart or talented as we thought. We get to feel dissatisfied and think less of ourselves thanks to those hucksters with their 'live your bliss' or 'live your most powerful life' books and Youtube videos. The only ones getting rich and powerful are them. Live your life on your own terms, not defined by others or compared to others; that will be your best life. Fill it with as much love, laughter, and joy as you can. Die satisfied, die content, everybody is going to die, anyway. And the kicker per Marcus Aurelius: the remembered are soon forgotten as are the rememberers. So fame, achievement for others' approval or great wealth, comparison to others, all become pointless eventually when you release your final breath.

These thoughts kept Michael awake that morning before school and recurred the next few mornings as well. But each time, somehow, he felt more energetic and optimistic; there was much to look forward to still: other volunteer digs, in Greece, or Rome, or even Salem, Massachusetts. And always, with his beloved Stephanie at his side. And though he was not one to live his dreams through his children or grandchildren, and considered himself a mediocre father at best, he was looking forward to experiences like Christmases and Disneyland with the grandkids.

The morning of his mother's religious conference at USC, the ideas had played through his waking moments once again. He took the day off from school for the conference, so he was able to sleep in and make up for the hour and a half of sleep disruption. When he plodded into the kitchen for a cup of coffee, Stephanie stood sipping her smoothie. She glanced at her watch and smiled up at him with a soymilk and blueberry moustache.

"You weren't kidding about sleeping in," she said. "It's a little after ten."

He nodded and kissed her cheek. Her brows knitted with slight hurt and confusion.

"Too much blueberry for me right now," he said. He made an oval gesture around his mouth. He poured a cup of coffee. Stephanie snorted and wiped the smoothie from her mouth.

"Better?"

Michael pulled her toward him and laid a deep kiss on her.

"Much better," he said.

"I'll say. So what time is this shindig again?"

"I'm outta here by noon. That should get me to USC by 1:00ish. Starts at 1:30."

She fixed his hair mussed from sleep and kissed him again.

"It's back to work I go," she said. She made her way down the hall toward her office. Michael took a deep sip of coffee and enjoyed the comforting sound of his wife's flip-flops slapping the wooden hall floor.

The drive from Burbank to USC near downtown Los Angeles took only twenty-five minutes. By the time he had pulled into the parking structure and made his way down the arched-lined cloister of the gothic, brick building with its soaring steeple, it was nearing twelve forty-five. He noticed a couple of vans with techie types jumping in and out, loaded with various kinds of equipment. They passed through French double doors under a weathered brick archway with signs that read 'restricted' posted on each door. Michael noticed a fountain in the middle of a stone courtyard near the doors with a large inscription. He stepped close and read it: 'O stream of life run you slow or fast, all streams reach the sea at last.' He had no idea who coined the idea, but he had no quarrel with it. Michael decided to step back into the cloister and take a walk to kill some time.

When he got to the end of the cloister, he saw a large pick-up labeled 'USC Campus Security' and two burly men unloading what looked like an airport-style metal detector security gate. A strident female voice from around the other side of the truck made him pause.

"Gentlemen, I really see no need for this. Really, we are all people of God assembling today."

Harriet Dunphy, donned in her usual white, diaphanous robe and hair pilled under a white turban joined the men at the tailgate. She even sported her fancy white purse on her left arm. Michael just watched.

"Ma'am, the university has to protect you and your guests today. There just is no choice about this."

"You really think the Dalai Lama or Patriarch Bartholomew will be carrying concealed Magnums under their holy robes?"

"You need to take it up with the chief, Ma'am. Right now, we're setting this scanner up at the entrance."

The man politely pushed her aside and nodded toward the other man. The two began to hoist the security gate from the back of the truck. Harriet shook her head in frustration.

"I'll go have a word with that chief of yours." She stormed away.

Michael was glad they missed each other. There was usually not much they had to say and especially when she was in her manager-control frame of mind. As Michael made his way out of the cloister and on to the campus, he saw two news vans pulling in near the building. Campus security staff members were beginning to rope off a perimeter near the building and curious students began to pause and gawk. It suddenly occurred to him that not only was this going to be a big event as Harriet had said, but he had no ticket, no pass, no anything to prove he was attending. Stephanie was usually on top of those kinds of details in their lives, but he realized they had never talked about specifics. He rubbed the back of his neck and decided to turn back toward the building and the cloister.

"You need to stop right there, sir," a woman's voice said behind Michael.

He turned to see an African American woman and a skinny Latino young man in navy blue campus security uniforms. The woman had her hands rolled on her hips and Michael noticed an array of leather pouches ending at a gun holster on her right side.

"It's okay, it's okay. My mother invited me to this event."

The woman shook her head.

"You have an event ID or is your mama holding that for you?" she asked. The other campus security officer chuckled.

"This looks weird. I get it. My mother is Harriet Dunphy."

"And?" the Latino man chimed in.

"She's the host and organizer of this whole thing."

The two security officer glanced at each other. The woman's eyebrows knitted as she nodded.

"That woman all in white who just busted in on the chief as we were leaving? That's your mama?" she asked.

"Yup," Michael said with a hint of resignation.

"Hmmm," the woman said.

She and the other officer exchanged glances again. They stepped toward Michael.

"Since you don't have an event ID, why don't we head on over to the office for a minute? Your mama can vouch for you if she's finished hollering at the chief."

"Can't I just show you my driver's license? I'm Michael Dunphy."

"We believe you," the man said. "It's just this is a very high-profile event and security is really tight. The

Dalai Lama is supposed to be here, for crying out loud. I heard the Pope might show up."

"By satellite," Michael said.

The two officers escorted Michael to the main security office. In moments, they stepped through the glass doors. An officer sat behind a long desk and looked up. Michael could hear the murmuring of his mother's voice.

"What's up, Ellie? Hector?"

"Hey Dominic," the female officer said. "This guy doesn't have an event ID for that thing over at Mudd Hall. He says his mama's the organizer. I think she's the one in with the chief right now?"

Dominic shrugged.

"Yeah, if it's the lady in white, she's still in there. She's all crazy about the metal detector," he said.

"You're not going to run off or anything?" Hector asked Michael.

"Of course not."

"Dominic, can you please have the lady identify this guy?" Ellie said. "If everything's cool, then you can issue him an event ID."

"Yeah. Why don't you go ahead and take a seat," Dominic said.

Michael sat. Ellie and Hector nodded toward him and left. A few moments later, the door behind Dominic opened.

"Thank you, Chief. I will let the emissaries know that I will escort them past the security gate and into the library. If you wouldn't—"

Michael stood when his mother caught his eye. He nodded.

"Hi, Mom."

"I don't understand, Michael. Why are you here?"

"I don't have a pass—"

"An event ID," Dominic corrected him.

"Yeah. An event ID. So they brought me here."

"Chief Larson?" Harriet called.

260

A stocky African American man with a handsome face and warm grin stepped into the doorway. He glanced at Michael and then Dominic.

"Ms. Dunphy?" he said with a rumbling voice.

"This is my son, Michael. I invited him to the conference but completely forgot to arrange an event ID."

"We can take care of that in no time," Dominic said.

"Any reason he can't just join the emissaries and me?" she asked.

Chief Larson scanned Michael with his eyes. He glanced at Dominic, who shrugged.

"That will be fine, Ms. Dunphy. Mr. Dunphy, sorry for any trouble with my officers."

"No trouble at all. They were fine."

"We need to get a move on since the emissaries should be arriving any minute now," Harriet said. Dominic raised the counter gate and stepped over and took Michael's arm.

"Let's go, son."

When Harriet and Michael arrived back to Mudd Hall, the campus street was filled with Lincoln Towncars and Mercedes limos. Students had gathered in a large crowd just beyond the ropes that had been set up. Phone cameras were flashing as the Dalai Lama slid gracefully from the back seat of a Towncar. He paused, bowed his head toward the students, many of whom hollered with joy. Harriet clutched Michael's arm and pulled him toward the Dalai Lama. With a quick introduction and instruction to the Dalai Lama's assistant, she and Michael hustled over to a white Mercedes in time to greet Cardinal Torelli. His red satin and black robes fluttered lightly against the gleaming white car. Harriet introduced Michael to Torelli through his aide and translator.

"Your eminence, thank you for joining us all the way from Rome. This is my son, Michael."

"Hello, to you both. The Holy Father is pleased that you have arranged this momentous meeting," the translator said. "On his behalf, we bestow appreciation and blessing."

The greetings continued at the cars of Patriarch Bartholomew, the Grand Imam Sheik Akmad Al-Bayat, the Sunni Muslim leader, Mohammed Jawiri Al-Qawda, a Shiite leader, and Chief Rabbi Ismael Yosef. Sai Maa, Hong Chen, and leaders from the Los Angeles Sikh and Baha'I centers emerged from their cars, each smiling and waving to Harriet.

With each greeting, Harriet bowed and touched her right palm to her heart. Pleasantries were exchanged between the translators who accompanied the leaders. Michael awkwardly nodded and smiled, which was met only once with a curious glance by the Rabbi. Harriet rushed to the final limousine, pulling Michael along.

"This man has just an amazing charisma. You'll see."

As Harriet and Michael reached the car, the rear door swung open. Out stepped an athletic man with Brad Pitt's looks. His blue-green eyes flashed a sparkling smile toward Harriet.

"Welcome, Mr. Boyce. You will add so much to the conversation today. Thank you for taking the time to join us."

The man embraced Harriet and kissed her cheek. He smiled at Michael over Harriet's shoulder.

"Call me J.P. That's how we Baptists and folks from Georgia do things."

Michael was not only put off by J.P., who looked no older than his mid-thirties, but also by the strange coquettishness his mother displayed. It felt almost flirtatious and creeped Michael out a bit.

"Come along, J.P." Harriet said. She slid her arm through his and he raised it to escort her. Harriet led J.P. and Michael to the gathering of religious luminaries and their translators who now formed a small cluster on the patio of the building. A line of spectators including news people and others formed at the double doors that were opened to reveal the security gate each person was stepping through. Harriet addressed the group.

"As you can see, the university has concerns about security," Harriet said. The translators spoke quickly to the nods of the leaders.

"However, I was able to convince the security chief to allow me to escort you all around and past the gate. There is no need for concern."

The translators spoke and the leaders broke out into smiles and enthusiastic nods. Harriet raised her arms, palms up, then gently rotated her wrists and pointed toward the doors. Harriet led them past the line of people. Some pointed, others clapped softly, and a collective gasp of astonishment echoed on the patio.

A stern security officer held the right double door open to let Harriet and the group in and past the security gate. Michael was the last of the group and he looked back in surprise at the growing audience crowd. His mother had really accomplished something special and odd as it was to admit, he felt a pang of pride. 'Pride goeth before a fall,' he thought and chuckled quietly. 'Pride doesn't know my mother—she never falls.'

Voices echoed off the white plaster walls as the group of leaders made their way down the main hall. Their shoes made clicks and clomps against the porcelain tile floor. The aged, dark walnut doors of the library stood open with a security guard posted at each door. Michael noticed Ellie, the security guard who had escorted him before, standing at the left door. He smiled but she stared straight ahead. The group paused at the doors. Harriet addressed them:

"There will be a translation headset for each of you around the long table. If you wish to comment, your translator will come over the speaker system. Please locate your name card at the table and make yourselves comfortable. There are two ushers who can help as well."

Once the group crossed the threshold and began to distribute itself, Michael was able to see into the library. He had to look past rows of folding aluminum chairs arranged like pews with a center aisle to see the table Harriet had mentioned. The polished slab of dark wood seemed to stretch the length of the library, ending at a short dais. Behind the dais to the left was an eighty-inch flat screen television ready, Michael supposed, for the Pope to beam in. Rows of antique walnut bookcases fifteen feet tall lined the library. Four two-story stained-glass windows on a curved wall at the end of the gallery cast a cathedral glow to everything. He hadn't been in a university library in decades, but the same feeling came back to him again: like a cathedral of knowledge, the ideas of the millennia humbled him. It was one thing to have practical smarts, but it was another to challenge a quick mind by diving into the pool of collective and ever-expanding human thought. Whatever all this would lead to, Michael thought, his mother once again displayed her talent for pageantry by staging her act in this vaunt-worthy venue.

"Michael!" Harriet called out. She pointed at a folding chair in the front row of the right-hand section, at the aisle. "Reserved this one for you."

Michael nodded and made his way to the chair. Just as he sat, he looked back to see two news people with television cameras enter and begin to set up tripods at the back of the library on either side of the entrance doors. For the next several minutes, as more people streamed in to take chairs, he watched with amusement as the religious leaders around the table struggled with their headphones while their translators spoke in frazzled tones with tech staff. The hall began to pop and screech with sound tests and microphone feedback.

"Check. One-two-three. Check. Check..." he heard repeatedly over the sound system. More people filled up the chairs behind and around him, speaking softly as the library suggested quiet. Somewhere above, the air conditioning rumbled to life and a cool breeze laced with competing perfumes, colognes, and stale coffee tickled his nose.

At the point the room seemed to be crammed with people sitting and standing, with all the leaders now donning their headsets, the library doors closed with a thudding echo. The library's dimmed chandeliers blazed to full, golden glory as lights from the TV cameras in the rear added an LED penumbra to both sides of the gallery. The TV screen erupted with its blue light and paused on a still of the Vatican with a small photo of Pope Francis in the right corner. Moving swiftly like an angel atop the head of a comet, Harriet stepped up to the microphone on the small dais at the head of the table.

"Welcome distinguished leaders of the world's faiths, scholars, and guests. We meet today as a communion of the faithful, to consult on the goals of resolving the plights of hunger and poverty. Before we begin, may I ask that we all bow our heads and pray silently for a moment, for wisdom, guidance, and grace in this monumental task before us…"

Michael glanced around at the sea of bowed heads. Just like his days in church masses, he felt a slight guilty pleasure at looking around when his head should be bowed. He looked toward the back wall and noticed the news people and camera operators were looking and taking footage. He heard someone's stomach rumble with hunger and hoped the minute would be over soon since he was sure someone would fart.

"Thank you, my brothers and sisters in faith," Harriet said. "And now, the Holy Father Pope Francis addresses us first from Rome. After all, it is probably past his bedtime."

The audience chuckled. Harriet pointed toward the flat screen TV.

"I bless you all in this very important work for the children of God," the Pope said in English with his light voice and the rolling r's of his Spanish accent. "But I am going to speak from my heart so will use my Italian and translator. I hope that is okay."

The audience applauded. Though the TV image remained fixed and only Pope Francis's voice could be heard, Michael was charmed by the pontiff's easy, almost common voice.

"We ask ourselves today, how in a world of great achievements, technical and medical marvels, and great wealth can poverty and hunger still afflict so many…" his translator spoke with a thick Italian accent. "I turn to our Lord's words in guiding us to find answers: 'But when you give a banquet, invite the poor, the crippled, the lame, and the blind, and you will be blessed…' It is time we who have so much find a way to share with all those who have so little…"

The Pope continued for another ten minutes. Michael's sense of his address was that while it was the usual inspirational, he would expect, there was nothing concrete or practical about it at all. He realized it was going to be a long afternoon.

When the Pope finished and signed off, Harriet returned to the small dais. The flat screen TV snapped to a black screen, giving off a faint electrical discharge. Harriet glanced at it a moment.

"Perhaps that was the Holy Spirit joining us," she said.

Some in the audience chuckled.

"Hallelujah!" J.P. Boyce hollered. The other dignitaries around the table sat silent.

"Poverty and hunger, then," Harriet said. "Who has an idea for a strategy?"

The sikh leader raised his hand. Harriet acknowledged him. He stood and bowed his head, wrapped in a cornflower blue turban. He opened a folder and began to speak.

"Our ancient clerics tell us: '…the poor and rich are all brothers…this is Lord's immutable design…'" He spoke English with no perceptible accent. "I therefore suggest that as for my brother I put aside food for a meal, we form an international food bank like the central banks of Europe or Asia. We establish

266

one on each continent, and open 'food accounts' for every person who is poor…"

Heads around the table nodded. Some in the audience clapped and whistled.

"Yes!" Mohammed Al-Qawda said through his translator as he stood. He pointed toward the sikh and nodded. "And from our holy Qu' uran, this we know: '…and whatever wealth you spend on helping them, Allah will know of it…' It would be very possible to establish these banks in the same way we have international monetary management. This can be done."

Sai Maa raised her hand and stood. She smiled toward the others at the table and toward the audience, too. "Hello," she said in accented English. "It can also be found in our Upanishads as follows: '…like in a well, the more you fetch, the more it oozes water…the more you give, the more you receive…' By rising up together to make this food bank, we will bring health and hope to many. And some of them who are thus raised may then bring a cure for cancer, or the equation to unite the two branches of physics. For all of us, this we can do."

Michael sighed. Somehow, while this was seeming to come up with some solid ideas, it also felt like a holy scripture pissing contest. The Rabbi chimed in eventually about the Talmud mentioning that the vineyard shouldn't be picked clean so that the fallen fruit would be left for the poor and strangers, and the Taoist Hong Chen said something about the wise man who sees all others as part of himself being the best at guarding others. The ideas were all good, but would they really lead to action?

The conference paused for a break at three-thirty, then resumed. When Michael retook his seat after a short campus stroll, he saw a large dry-erase board standing behind the short dais. The dignitaries around the table chimed in randomly with an idea and Harriet would nod and jot it down. When the board had been filled with notes, Harriet gestured toward the audience to now participate. 'Mom,' he thought, 'You are good at all this.' A woman raised her hand.

"Hello and thank you all," she said with a soft French accent. "Once you devise this plan of action, how will you formulate the policy to get governments to carry it out?"

"I think we would present our plans to policymakers the world over," Cardinal Torelli said through his interpreter. "That would be the next step."

A bearded man with disheveled hair raised his hand.

"I am a professor of economics here at the university. I think the food bank plan is solid and can be done."

The audience erupted with applause.

"But wait," he went on. "Feeding people is one thing. There have been very few ideas on practical solutions to poverty."

This interchange brought a fresh round of discussion between the leaders. As the minutes wore on, more hands shot up and the economics professor eventually left his seat and joined the dignitaries. Growing more fatigued, Michael studied all the faces around the table. He compared them to his mother's for hints of similarities. Were they all zealots like her? And suddenly, almost like a seizure coming on, he was ready to 'stir it up' like he and Stephanie had talked about a few days back. He shot up his hand.

"Michael?" Harriet said. "We can talk after."

"Let him speak!" the Dalai Lama said.

"You don't understand. He's my atheist son."

"Let him speak!" Rabbi Yosef interjected.

Harriet nodded with resignation.

"Fine. Michael?"

Michael stood up. He rubbed the back of his neck then straightened his shirt.

"You're all here to do something important. Poverty and starvation need to be remedied; I get it. You have mentioned your sacred texts and found common ground. That's to the good. But what if you could also do something like stop all wars based on differences in faith? That would be huge, too. What happens when we're dead just can't be more important than how we will live and treat each other. How about leaving people alone to be themselves, trust that most people are struggling like you for the same good things and stay out of damn politics."

A few students in the audience applauded. A few people in the audience gasped in surprise at his words. The table of dignitaries looked more frozen than Leonardo's painting, 'The Last Supper'. Harriet's face tightened with anger.

"Ideas without proof and evidence are just that. Anybody could imagine anything but without proof and evidence ideas are just passing things. I had hallucinations last year and believed I could see molecules and particles, too. But I didn't—it was my epilepsy."

Michael felt a surge of energetic confidence. He continued:

"So it always comes down to faith, but faith means different things to each of you, to everybody. I have a suggestion. While you're all here, why don't you all come up with a basic code that all humans can live with and stop all this picky crap about what happens when we're dead? Love, you can all get behind that. The highest value any of us can offer and receive with our families and our friends. And then empathy and compassion for everybody else. Why not? And then let's not forget reason—learning, and testing. The conflict of ideas, and evidence to seek out truth and then refine it as new ideas emerge? And with all those things in play, all the other ethics like honesty, fidelity, integrity, and non-violence and any other rules and morals your books lay out will naturally follow. No magic man in the sky necessary. No one truth above all others. What's so damn complicated? You keep it complicated and we all stay tribal and kill each other."

The students applauded again. Someone from the back yelled "Sit down already". Michael waved his right arm toward the heckler. The rest of the room was silent.

"Each of your faiths has harmed as many nonbelievers as they have helped believers—the net result is that humans continue to suffer. All of you can't be right. Only one of you can be. Just one. And look where that has led us. Or I'm right and there's nothing out there but a decaying universe. Whether one of you is right or I am, we all come from the same source. So we really are one people. Why care so much about creation and death when there's so much hatred, oppression, and bloodshed you might be able to do something about right here and now? Please don't waste this opportunity. Until you, all of us, can get over this, it's a cross we all bear. A shadow over all of us."

"That's enough!" Harriet roared. "Sit down, Michael."

Michael had run out of steam anyway. He shook his head and sat.

"Please pardon his offensive remarks. He's my faithless son and will be escorted out if he opens his mouth again. Is there anyone else who wishes to address the topics at hand—poverty and hunger?"

The dignitaries all shook their heads. Harriet looked toward the audience.

"Is there anyone else who wishes to speak?"

After nearly four hours, and Michael's outburst, it seemed the whole library dripped with fatigue. Harriet glanced around the audience once more and at the dignitaries.

"Very well, then. I assembled all of you to start a war of faith over poverty and starvation. Each of you has spoken in your turn. The audience has given us their ideas. But there really is only one way, one Truth in all of this…"

Harriet stepped away from the podium and crossed around the side of the table of dignitaries. She paused and stood directly behind the Dalai Lama. Michael noticed her purse hanging from her left forearm just above her white glove. Harriet unclasped it. She reached into it and pulled out her Smith & Wesson twenty-two pistol. She placed the barrel against the Dalai Lama's right temple. The audience gasped. Harriet looked back toward the security officers at the doors.

"You need to stand down. All of you! I'm well versed in using this."

"Mother!"

"You spoke your piece, Michael. You can shut up now. My turn. The Blessed Virgin told me she will appear today. Right here and now. If we all pray to her. She insists everybody pray."

None of the dignitaries responded.

"Bow your heads and pray—NOW!"

The Sunni and Shiite muslims raised their eyes and looked straight at Harriet. They shook their heads, as did the sikh and Rabbi. The conference room was silent.

"Pray. Now!"

Harriet raised the pistol and let off a shot toward the ceiling. The gunfire echoed obscenely off the walls.

Michael jumped to his feet and leapt at his mother. The Dalai Lama dropped his head to the table. She let off a shot as Michael tackled her to the floor. The gun skittered across the tile floor. Security guards swarmed Harriet and Michael. In the tussle Michael sat up, clutching his bleeding shoulder.

"The Blessed Mother says this is the only way, the ONLY way…"

"Oh, mother. Just oh…"

Michael's head began to spin from the blood loss as the security officers restrained Harriet. In his last moment of consciousness, he felt Sai Maa's hands gently guide his head to the floor. Just before his eyes went dark, he noticed his mother's turban and a silver wig lying on the floor. Her head was mottled flesh. She was bald.

"Not that again," Michael said from his hospital bed at County USC the next day. The wall-mounted TV screen showed his photo with the caption 'Two Time Hero'. A slight itching ache stirred in his bandaged shoulder as it lay in a sling.

"It's not your best picture, that's for sure," Stephanie said. She sat in a tan visitor's chair. "And by the way, let's get outta here as soon as the doctor clears you to go. I'm a bit tired of visiting you in hospitals."

"You and me both. But I'm even more tired of this 'hero' crap."

He went to make air quotes around 'hero' but his injured shoulder made him wince. Stephanie smiled and shook her head.

"Midee, you're just never going to have your mind and body in the same place at the same time, are you?"

"I guess not."

"That's okay. I'm here to kiss your boo-boos and make them better."

"But seriously, I'm a freaking history teacher again. No Indiana Jones, and sure as hell no hero."

"Now that I don't want to hear anymore. You *are* a hero. I guess you'd say a 'quiet hero'. You have *always* been that for me, and the kids. I'm sure there are tons of students over the years who would say the same thing. So, and here comes that bad word, you're just going to have to *settle* for being a quiet hero."

Michael sighed and nodded.

"Right as usual. That's good enough for me."

'Harriet Dunphy will be arraigned on charges of kidnapping, extortion, and attempted manslaughter. The tee vee and Youtube religious influencer is being held for psychiatric observation until her hearing...'

Stephanie muted the television. Michael dropped his chin to his chest.

"I can't deal with *that* right now," he said. Stephanie nodded and shut off the television.

"Plenty of time to deal with all of that," she said. "Plus, after that impromptu speech I heard you gave before Harriet went bonkers, you need to sit down and work on your Evolutionary mind thingy."

"'Constructs.' Yup. Going to work on the development of love, compassion, and reason from a brain evolution standpoint. A published paper or maybe even a book."

"Oh, crap. I forgot to give you this."

Stephanie pulled a manila envelope from her purse and handed it to Michael. He glanced at the return address and his eyebrows furrowed.

"From Trinity?" he said.

Stephanie had no idea and shook her head. He tore open the envelope, pretty sure of what it contained: the metals materials report on the cross. Dr. McDonald, the materials specialist, had told him that before the robbers stole the cross, the Trinity lab tech had already filed enough shavings for analysis.

"Midee, what is it?"

"Hang on. I didn't think they were ever going to get this to me."

He slid out a stapled set of several pages with a note on gray stationery paper emblazoned with: 'Aidan McDonald, PhD. Trinity College of Chemistry'. He read it:

Michael:

I'm afraid you won't find this report as interesting as the story of the alleged cross of Judas you shared with us—people rarely like facts more than stories.

But be assured that the report shows the silver to actually be a type of precious metal found in the near and middle east that is of non-terrestrial, meteorological origin. It was often used in the coin of the realm in ancient Rome, mistaken for genuine silver, through the third century C.E. While we can't carbon date metals at this time, it is safe to say the cross, based on its design, was most likely created some time in the second century C.E.

It is oddly reactive to temperature change and would be especially responsive to a person's physiological temperature change in situations such as fear or anxiety. Cold hand, cold cross, for example.

273

Sorry for the non-romantic conclusion, but I am more astonished at uncovering elemental bombardment from exploded stars or in this case, meteors, than some magic charm from our ignorant past.

Read on and enjoy-HA!

Best wishes, always—

Aidan

"I knew it!" Michael exclaimed.

"What? What?"

"This *is* the metals materials report from the cross," he said. "It has no magic powers. It's not even old enough to reach back to the first century."

He removed the note from the report and began to read the first page:

Authors: Aidan McDonald, PhD

Quy-An Phong, PhD candidate

Phillip Hogan, PhD candidate

Performing Organization: Trinity College of Chemistry-Materials

Dublin, Ireland

Abstract

The purpose of this report is to determine the composition of a metal object of cross form and to investigate the alleged temperature reactive properties of the object. Shavings from the metal object of unknown origin were collected...

Stephanie tapped his arm. Michael paused and looked up.

"Oh, and Midee. Our next vacation?"

"Yeah?"

"Hawaii."

"Oh, they have been doing some interesting digging in the Pali cliffs."

"Midee, that would be a 'no'."

Acknowledgement

The speech by Terrence Albert Flynn in chapter 10 is adapted from the final speech of Blessed Terrence Albert O'Brien, delivered at the gallows before his execution on October 31, 1651.

From Hugh Fennin's "The Last Speech and Prayer of Blessed Terence Albert O'Brien, Bishopp of Emly, 1651," in Collectanea Hibernica, *No. 38 (1996).*